The Mistress of Murder Hill

The serial killings of Belle Gunness

by Sylvia Elizabeth Shepherd

The Mistress of Murder Hill

The serial killings of Belle Gunness

by Sylvia Elizabeth Shepherd

Historical photographs, LaPorte County Historical Society

ISBN: 0-75960-665-X

This book is printed on acid free paper.

1stBooks - rev. 4/30/01

For Helen Schultz Shepherd and S. Ross Shepherd, loved and missed, who first pointed out the Gunness property many years ago

CHAPTER ONE

It was in the predawn hours of a spring morning near a small town in northern Indiana that one of the most gruesome true stories of all time began to unfold. Before the months of prolonged horror were over, this town would receive a national, even international, reputation as the home of a Lady MacBeth, a moral monster, a fiend incarnate. It would be the scene of one of the most puzzling mysteries in the annals of crime. A newspaper of that day correctly predicted that what happened here would not be forgotten for a generation; and the people of LaPorte, Indiana, still remember generations later.

It was an unlikely location for what happened. Only 60 miles away, in Chicago, residents in this first decade of the 20th Century coped with typical big-city fears, and visitors were regularly warned to guard their money and their personal safety. Here in LaPorte all seemed safe in the quiet countryside of McClung Road, only a dozen miles from the Michigan border. The maple trees were coming to life for a new season, and nearby lakes were clear and serene. The only blight on the beauty was Fish Trap Lake, which was really just a swamp and appropriately next to what came to be called "Abbatoir Acres."

On a hill a mile north of LaPorte sat a two-story part brick and part frame farmhouse not unlike other farms of the day with its main house, barn, carriage shed, and chicken yard fenced with woven wire. This was the hub of a 48-acre farm owned by a widow who had arrived from Chicago in 1901. On this particular morning, April 28, 1908, just before daybreak, the farm's hired hand, Joseph Maxson, was asleep in a room above the kitchen at the back of the frame portion of the house. He had gone to bed about 8:30 after an evening of playing parlor games with others who lived in the house. It was 4 a.m. when he awoke to a crackling sound. He could see and smell smoke in his room. Jumping from his bed and looking out the window, he gasped at the sight--the entire brick side of the house was engulfed in flames. Quickly pulling on some clothes, he ran to a door leading into the brick part of the house. But the door was locked, as usual, and no amount of pounding could rouse anyone on the other side, so Maxson finally fled down the back stairs to save himself. "I tried to break the door down--tried to kick it down," he later explained. "I then hollered 'fire.' I did not succeed in getting it down or open." There was a strong wind, and Maxson gulped in the fresh air before deciding on another attack on the door. "I went back to my room at the head of the stairs. That was as far as I could get," he said. "I couldn't get into my room on account of the fire in my room at the time ... I went to the front door and tried to kick that in." The persistent Maxson hurled bricks at the windows and shouted but still received no response from anyone inside the burning building. Frustration mingled with desperation because he knew that the house could hold at least four people, Mrs. Belle Gunness and three children.

By now flames had attracted the Clifford household, just a half mile north. William Clifford was awakened by his mother and told about the fire. He excitedly put on his clothes and biked over to the Gunness property, where he saw Maxson circling the house and yelling. Together they broke a door pane, trying to enter a different part of the house. This idea was abandoned after a sudden flash of fire leaped through the broken panel, cutting off all entry. About now, down the road, William Humphrey was awakened by his sister-in-law. "I could see the whole roof afire. When I got there, the roof and the whole east side were afire," he said. Humphrey asked Maxson for a ladder, and one was retrieved from the woodshed. The men carried the ladder to the west side of the house. Humphrey climbed up, broke a window, and peered in. He described what he saw: "'The bed in the corner of the room--there was nothing on the bed but a mattress. I couldn't see no bodies, just a mattress on the bed, no body or sheets." Maxson theorized that this was the room being readied for the return of a young woman, Jennie

Olson, said to be attending school in California. The men moved the ladder to another window, and the sight there was described by Humphrey: "I went to the other window and saw no body in the other room ... The fire was coming through the floor again, and I saw a bed and mattress, and I cannot tell what was laying there. There was something." Whatever it was, Humphrey was sure it was not a body. Meanwhile, Clifford had gone to the house where Daniel Hutson lived and pounded on the door until Hutson woke up. Shoes untied and half dressed, Hutson rushed to the scene, only to find the southwest corner was the only part of the house not engulfed in flames. There was nothing more he could add to what had already been tried.

At about 5 a.m., Maxson did the only thing that seemed to be left. He hitched up a horse and went into LaPorte to get the sheriff. Later, he would say that he thought some sort of crime had been committed here. His summons brought Sheriff Albert Smutzer and Deputy Sheriff William Anstiss to the scene, along with a corps of firemen with hooks and ladders. At first, there was nothing to do but watch until the flames died down, but finally, the heat had subsided enough for the firemen to begin tearing down the walls so that diggers could safely start to excavate for any possible victims. Beginning at about 8 a.m., the crew did its best to poke and dig amid the blistering embers. Soon they had an audience of about 50 people who had heard the news and had biked, walked, or driven out to see the excitement.

In addition to the physical activity, there was quite a bit of talk. Probably, it was agreed, the fire had started on the rear east side near the outside cellar entrance. Maybe it was started by someone exiting that door. The idea of arson may never have surfaced without Sheriff Smutzer's prior knowledge of the trouble between Belle Gunness and her former hired hand, Ray Lamphere. Belle had asked the law repeatedly for help in keeping Lamphere away from her, and she had even gone so far as to try to get him declared insane. With the suspicion that he might have retaliated, the authorities were searching for

Lamphere even before the fired cooled. They found him just where he was supposed to be, working at his job as a hired hand on the farm of John Wheatbrook. He was taken into LaPorte without difficulty and charged with arson.

Meanwhile the digging had unearthed numerous articles such as bedding remnants and bedsteads. Almost ready to give up, the diggers reached the southeast corner of the large cellar, where they finally discovered that death had indeed visited McClung Road. In quick order, they unearthed the charred remains of two girls, a boy, and a woman.

Indiana law specified that any arson resulting in death would carry a charge of murder in the first degree. Lamphere, therefore, now faced a murder charge, to which he would plead not guilty. He was held without bond awaiting the May 11 convening of the grand jury to determine whether the evidence was sufficient to indict him. At this point, he had no attorney and had not asked for one. He was thought to be penniless and in need of a court-appointed defense attorney. Although LaPorte Attorney H. W. Worden had defended Lamphere in previous legal troubles, he was not immediately summoned by the defendant. Keeping Lamphere in isolation, Prosecutor Ralph N. Smith and Sheriff Smutzer attempted to coerce a confession by what was called "sweating," which today would be called "grilling", but the hired hand stuck to his admission of seeing the fire only from a distance, although his alibi changed in detail somewhat from one telling to another.

Meanwhile, Maxson was describing the family's activities on the evening before the fire. At 6:30 p.m. or a little after, he joined Belle, age 40 plus, Myrtle Adelphine Sorensen, age 11, Lucy Berglist Sorensen, age 9, and Philip Alexander Gunness, age 5, for supper. He recalled nothing unusual in the events of the evening, which ended for him when he went to his room to bed about 8:30 p.m. He later said, "Mrs. Gunness and her children were the only persons in the house at that time." The fire in the cook stove, which was used for supper, was out; and no fires were burning in any other stove in the house. Kerosene lamps illuminated the rooms, and Maxson blew his out before retiring. He believed that Belle also extinguished all lamps before going to bed because he never saw any lighted on the nights when he returned to the farmhouse after all others were in bed. The kerosene oil can had been filled in town a couple of days before and was kept in the hallway of the frame section of the house. Maxson considered himself a light sleeper and yet had heard no barking from Belle's dogs, which were chained that night as usual in the back of the house. "The shepherd dog would bark perhaps a couple of barks even when I would come in from a neighbor's house," Maxson explained. When asked, he said he believed that if Lamphere came on the property, the dogs would bark until they recognized him. "Of course, they were very well acquainted with him," he added.

The report of the postmortem on the bodies was expected to say that no evidence of violence was found, but some people thought Belle and the children were murdered before the house was torched. The head of the adult female body could not be found, giving some people cause to think she had been beheaded before the fire. However, the postmortem said the fire could have dislodged and consumed the head. During the autopsy, one of the other heads had broken away, demonstrating to those present the fragility of the remains. Some people even opted for suicide, but the only motive anyone could offer was that Lamphere had driven Belle crazy.

On April 30, two days after the fire, relatives of the dead and missing arrived on the scene. Belle's sister, Mrs. Nellie Larson, along with her son John arrived from Chicago, apparently to contest Belle's will, which gave her estate to Norwegian orphans in the event the three children died without heirs. Nellie spoke a little English but John had to serve as interpreter in Norwegian in most cases. On May 1, several days before the real nature of Belle Gunness would be revealed, John talked about his aunt: "My aunt Belle Gunness was a strange woman. When you first knew her she was very cordial. Then she would get offish ... It is perhaps 20 years since my father told Aunt Belle Gunness that he did not want her to come to the house. Since then, she and my mother have not seen very much of one another, and for 12 or 15 years my Aunt Belle had not been at our house. But my sisters have visited at her house." Also arriving was Mrs. Leo Olander of Chicago, sister of the Jennie Olson who was supposed to be at school in California but whom no one could find. Her quick arrival in LaPorte was prompted by the fear that one of the dead in the cellar might be Jennie. She had learned of the fire from a story in a Chicago newspaper.

On the third day after the fire, a series of incidents became known that proved to be the very tiny tip of a monstrous iceberg. These incidents concerned the activities of Belle and a man who had trouble getting a bank draft cashed. When the cash was finally handed over to this man, Belle paid off some of her debts and even deposited some money. Then Lamphere came to the sheriff and accused this stranger of being wanted for murder in Aberdeen, South Dakota. However, when Sheriff Smutzer checked with Aberdeen authorities, he found the man was not wanted for any crime there. Shortly after, the man was not seen again; and an inquiry came to a LaPorte bank from Aberdeen asking his whereabouts because the man had not returned home as expected. When the local bank representative questioned Belle about her former companion, her reply was said to have been, "Do they think I made away with him, too?"

The real drama was about to begin. The cast of characters would include hired hands, deceased husbands, would-be suitors, prominent citizens, and political rivals, with the starring role occupied by a woman whose charms were no less fatal just because they were hidden.

CHAPTER TWO

The inferno that destroyed the Gunness home had now escalated from an arson investigation to a murder case with four victims. It might have stayed there, except for a stubborn Norwegian farmer from Mansfield, South Dakota, who loved his brother and wanted to find him. Asle K. Helgelein's brother Andrew was a wheat farmer from Aberdeen. S. D. Andrew left home Jan. 2, 1908, saying he would be gone about a week. After the week had passed and nothing was heard from Andrew, his brother began to worry. Finally, in the first week of March, Asle wrote to Mrs. Minnie Cone in Minneapolis, to whom he believed Andrew had paid a visit. Mrs. Cone replied, "I am surprised to learn that Andrew is not home, for he told me he was going back in a few days. He came up to my house and was there about one hour."

Meanwhile, Asle found among Andrew's possessions some letters from a Mrs. Gunness in LaPorte, Indiana. They urged Andrew to sell his farm and stock and bring the money to LaPorte, where the two of them would have the finest home in northern Indiana. One of the letters to Andrew, dated Sept. 17, 1906, can be seen to this day in the LaPorte County Historical Museum, with other Gunness memorabilia. The translation reads: "Dear Friend: I went to the post office this morning and had the great pleasure of receiving one of your very welcome letters. Many thousand thanks for them all--I keep them all as I would a great treasure. You truly do not know how highly I prize them as I have not found anything so genuine Norwegian and real in all the 20 years I have been in America. I do not think a queen could be good enough for you and in my thoughts you stand highest above all high and I will not let anything stand in the way of my doing anything for you or so that we can meet each other. We shall be so happy when once you get here, then I will make a 'cream pudding' and many other good things. When we get all settled, we will have your dear sister Anna in Lebanon visit us. She means to do well by you, you can be sure of that and I know I will think as much of her as my own sister if not more. But, my dear, do not say anything about coming here. Then the surprise will be so much greater when she finds it out. Now sell all that you can get cash for, and if you have much left you can easily bring it with you whereas we will soon sell it here and get a good price for everything. Leave neither money or stock up there but make yourself practically free from Dakota so you will have nothing more to bother with up there. You have been there long enough and worked hard for many a day and now you must take it a little easier for the rest of your days and do not fear but that we will think so much of you. How lonesome it must seem for you to be up there all alone, but you must hurry and come to us as soon as you can. I long for you more each day that goes by. You must forgive for not writing before but we have been so busy picking fruit for market and then all of us big and little are kept busy as long as it lasts. There was an old man who became sick and died here last week and I had to help these people a little to straighten things so I have been very busy all the time but when you come it will be better, not so? It is so much pleasure to me to keep this secret to ourselves and to see how surprised everyone will be when they find it out. I have none of my relatives here now so I am practically alone. I have a sister who lives in Chicago. I also have a brother who lives in Norway. His son Ed was in America a while and studied with a landscape painter but he went home again. Oh, I can tell you so much about everything when you come. Well, I must now close for this time, waiting to hear from you soon and then I will write again immediately. A thousand hearty regards from your friend. Bella Gunness. P.S. As I think we are well enough acquainted, I signed my given name to this letter, now my dearest friend, once again, come soon." Belle enclosed a four-leaf clover, which is still in the museum-kept letter.

Asle Helgelein then wrote to the LaPorte postmaster, asking the whereabouts of a Mrs. Gunness. There was no reply, and the self-addressed envelope he had enclosed came back empty. A second request to the postmaster was answered with the information that such a woman did live near LaPorte. Asle wrote to Belle, asking for information about Andrew. In a reply postmarked March 9, 1908, Belle said Andrew had visited her for a little over a week in early January but had left to go to Chicago and then perhaps to Norway. She said he planned to return to her after the trip. Asle wrote to the LaPorte police and received an answer from Chief Clinton Cochrane, who said he thought a man who might be Andrew had been in LaPorte. This prompted another letter from Asle to Belle, who replied on April 11. Asle later described this letter:

"There was nothing new in this letter excepting that it said that a man named Lamphere, who worked for her, reported meeting a man who claimed to have lived in Mansfield, South Dakota, and said that Andrew Helgelein was in Mansfield and had been there for some time."

In the same letter, Belle complained Lamphere had been intercepting letters that Andrew Helgelein had written to her. She said her hired man (Maxson) had found in the barn door a piece of a letter from Andrew to her. This was discovered, she claimed, after Lamphere had been seen around the property.

Asle wrote again, asking for the name of the man who had seen his brother in South Dakota. Belle replied that it was "that crazy Lamphere." Belle also wrote that she could not furnish Asle a letter Andrew had written her from Chicago in which he announced intentions of going to New York and then to Norway. This letter, Belle wrote, was left in the kitchen while she went to milk the cows. When she returned, the letter was gone, a theft she attributed to Lamphere. Belle, however, did send Asle a piece of the letter that she said had been found in the barn.

Belle also reiterated that she did not know where Andrew was, but that she herself was trying to find him. Andrew, she wrote, left her farm on Jan. 16 or 17 to go to Michigan City, a distance of about 12 miles. He was driven to a train station by her 11-year-old daughter. She refused Asle's offer to send money for the search, saying she was so anxious about Andrew that she would spend her own money. However, she did suggest that Asle sell whatever Andrew had left and bring the money to her in May so that they could look for Andrew together.

Asle already knew that Andrew had sent money to LaPorte. At his urging, another brother, Henry, asked the First National Bank in Aberdeen if Andrew had drawn out any money. The bank verified that money had been sent for collection at the First National Bank in the city of LaPorte. A query to the LaPorte bank brought the information that Andrew was without doubt the man who picked up the money there. He was easily identified from the picture that Asle sent to the bank.

"I also asked them (the bank) to employ reliable parties to quickly investigate and if possible to learn what had become of my brother," Asle later stated. "I told them I would pay the bills."

The last letter from Belle to Asle, in which she invited him to visit her in May, was dated April 24. The verification from the bank was dated April 27, one day before the fire.

On May 1, Asle received more information from the LaPorte bank. It was a copy of a local newspaper, the LaPorte Herald, telling of the fire at the Gunness home and the four bodies found. That same day, Asle went to Aberdeen, where Andrew had his farm, to express his worry about his brother's safety to the sheriff and police chief there. Both men gave him letters to present to their counterparts in LaPorte.

Asle arrived in LaPorte on a Sunday night, May 3. The next morning he checked on something Belle had written him. She said Andrew gave her some money, and she in turn had signed over her mortgage to him. Asle found no record of this transaction. A visit to the sheriff got him a ride out to the Gunness ruins, where he got Joseph Maxson and Daniel Hutson to help him look around the place. The rest of that Monday, Asle spent looking through the debris in the cellar where the bodies had been found in an attempt to find something that might be linked to Andrew. On Tuesday morning he returned to the fire site and found Maxson and Hutson still working in the cellar. Neither knew anything more than what Belle had told Asle--Lamphere was jealous of "the man from the West" and "would like to get at him." Maxson told Asle that Belle was afraid Lamphere would kill her and the children.

What happened next was later explained this way by Asle:

"I walked all over the farm around the house, back to the cellar, asked some questions again, whether there were any holes in the ice on the lake in the winter, how deep the lake was, etc. I told the boys goodbye and I started down. When I came down into the road, I was not satisfied and I went back to the cellar and asked Maxson whether he knew of any hole or dirt having been dug up there about the place early in spring. He told me he filled up a hole in the garden in March. He did not remember the date. Mrs. Gunness had told him she had the hole dug to put rubbish into it. Mrs. Gunness helped, raking, picking up old cans, shoes, or rubbish, and the man Maxson, I think, wheeled it in a wheelbarrow to the hole and dumped it in. I got Maxson to show me the hole and all three of us started to dig."

In a short while, the men noticed a bad smell, which Maxson said could be from all the old tomato cans and fish dumped into the hole. Undaunted by the odor, the men continued to dig until, at about four feet deep, they hit something hard covered by a gunny sack. Lifting the sack, they saw a human neck and arm. Stunned and sickened, they decided Maxson would be the one to summon the sheriff. Asle remained behind, covering the spot with an old coat while Hutson cleared away the dirt around the hole. The persistent Asle had found his brother. Under the sheriff's direction, more digging revealed the arms, legs, and head, all of which had been cut neatly from the torso. But as these pieces emerged from the hole, they were mere harbingers on a twisting trail of horror and mystery that lay ahead.

As Helgelein's body was being examined, Maxson pointed out a second "soft spot" a few yards away. Sheriff Albert Smutzer told the men to dig at that spot. Two or three feet down, the diggers unearthed a skeleton that was almost totally fleshless and appeared to be that of a young girl. The thought now came to mind that perhaps Jennie Olson had not gone off to school after all. Under the skeleton was what looked like a rotted mattress. It was so decayed that it fell to pieces as it was lifted up. Below it, in the mud, were protruding human ribs. Here were more gunny sacks that disgorged the dismembered skeleton of a large man, whose only recognizable features were dark hair and a mustache. Steeling themselves, the diggers plunged still farther, until about a foot deeper, they found the skeletons of two children, probably about 12 years old. The flesh was totally decomposed and the bones had separated, making it impossible to know if they had been packed as the others. These bare remains of human lives were put under guard in one of the farm's outbuildings.

Andrew Helgelein's remains were identified by his brother. Photos from that time show him round-faced and clean shaven with short, close-cropped hair. Although Lamphere had been wrong about Andrew's criminal career as a murderer, a later check revealed that Andrew had served time for arson and larceny. It was ironic that he would tripped up by someone practicing the same kind of treachery. In addition to Asle's identification, the measurements taken at the time of Andrew's jailing coincided with those of the newly uncovered body. Helgelein was a big man, about 200 pounds, and so once was this corpse. An autopsy on the remains, which had been buried about three months, was performed by Dr. J.H. William Meyer. It found, in part, the following:

"The skin is largely discolored by putrefaction, the changes being in the face most of all, but is still firm. Left leg sawed off about four inches above the knee joint. Skin and flesh are smoothly cut. Right leg is sawed off above the knee, three inches. Flesh and skin cut smooth. Left arm, covered by knit cotton undershirt, has been disarticulated at the shoulder. In the back of the wrist joint are two deep cuts laying the joint open and exposing the carpal bones. The right joint of four fingers missing. The hand is closed. On opening the hand, it is found to grasp short brown curly hair. The hair is saved and turned over to the coroner. Asle Helgelein was present to identify the body. He is sure from the spacing of the teeth that it is his brother, Andrew Helgelein. All the teeth are present except the second right upper molar. All the teeth in good condition with several amalgam fillings. No beard. Hair on head medium long, straight brown; scalp incised in media line and pulled down, exposing the skull bones from the nasal to the occipital. All the bones are intact, without holes or fractures. From the finding, it is evident that this man died an unnatural death, but at whose hands or how it cannot be determined. The hair in the hand is likely from the head of his murderer; or the stomach may show what poison, if any, killed him."

Dr. Meyer's examination told him something else about Helgelein's death. The damage to severed fingers from the right hand and the strands of hair clenched in the fingers indicated to the doctor that Helgelein might have died struggling painfully with his murderer.

CHAPTER THREE

The Statue of Liberty was only half a pedestal high when Brynhild Paulsdatter Storset sailed into New York harbor as an immigrant. Already a young woman, she had been born Nov. 11, 1858, in Norway to Berit Olsdatter and her husband, Paul Pedersen Storset, a poor tenant farmer and stonemason. As a girl, Brynhild had worked at neighborhood farms around her home in Selbu, a small provincial town near Trondheim on the Norwegian west coast. When she later became infamous in the United States, the villagers she left behind had mixed memories of her. Some recalled her as hard-working. A local newspaper was reported as printing this reminiscence: "Here in Selbu she is remembered by many, and most they tell she was a very bad human being, capricious and extremely malicious. She had unpretty habits, always in the mood for dirty tricks, talked little and was a liar already as a child." But perhaps those memories of her past were tinged by the horrors of the present.

Trondheim, the ancient Viking capital, stands on the Trondheim fiord, 225 miles north of Oslo. People there, like those in other countries, received what were known as "American letters," glowing accounts from friends and relatives who had sailed from the land of their birth in search of better opportunities in America. They told how much easier it was to earn money in America and how much acreage was available to an industrious farmer. To Norwegians, who placed high value on being their own masters, the lure was enormous.

In September of 1881, the time of Brynhild's arrival in this country, about 26,000 immigrants from Norway lived here. Most of them settled outside the cities, with a higher percentage of Norwegians farming than any other national group. About 80 percent lived in Illinois, Iowa, Wisconsin, Minnesota, and the Dakotas. Many had been enticed by claims that were vastly exaggerated. While some immigrants did well, others found themselves in situations where the gap between the rich and the poor was much larger than back in the old country. This was especially true in the cities. The city of Chicago was Brynhild's destination, and her occupation was listed upon arrival as servant girl.

Chicago was the home of Brynhild's sister, Mrs. Nellie Larson, who lived in the 900 block of North Francisco Avenue. She invited Brynhild to come from Norway to her home and paid the expenses of getting her there. For some Chicago Norwegians, fresh from the farm, life was not often pleasant as they tried to fit into the city's social mixture. Many lived in tenements, where the absence of grass and trees brought them more than their share of mental problems and conditions drove some to suicide. Opportunities were particularly scarce for women, whose employment outside the home was limited to being maids, seamstresses, or tailors. Lurking on an even darker side of city life was the possibility of being trapped, through desperation, into prostitution. The danger of this was so great in urban areas that the labor authorities in St. Paul, Minnesota, warned young women and girls, "Do not go to the large cities to work unless you are compelled to." The difference between the expectations of American life and the realities may have played a part in what happened later to Brynhild. Living with her sister, she had a place to stay but her days were consumed in sewing and laundry work. In later years, relatives would look back at this newly arrived young woman and say there was "something wild" about her, a something very evident in her "mental makeup." She was not one, perhaps, so easily fitted into the mold of her fellow young immigrants. At any rate, Brynhild was soon to discard her name. She changed it to Bella and would later become known far and wide as Belle.

In Chicago, the wealthier Norwegians clustered in the Wicker Park district, which was northwest of the central downtown area. Those with lesser incomes were congregated around Milwaukee Avenue, which was often called Norwegian street. Somewhere in this mix, Belle met Mads Sorensen, and the facts here are sometimes conflicting. Mads has been called both a detective and a watchman, and their wedding year has been listed anywhere from 1883 to 1889. They operated a confectionery store at Grand Avenue and Elizabeth Street, whose existence became important only in the manner in which it ended. It burned in 1898, and insurance money was collected.

The Sorensens used the money to move farther west to Alma Street in Austin, where they boarded foster children, at least two of whom died. Belle's own childlessness, according to her sister Nellie, was a painful reality to the woman, and she even asked to adopt Nellie's oldest daughter Olga, who was four years old. Nellie later explained how her refusal launched an estrangement between the sisters because "from that day my sister would hardly speak to me."

In 1900, Mads Sorensen died suddenly. A death certificate citing "cerebral hemorrhage" as the cause of death was signed by Dr. J. B. Miller and Dr. Charles E. Jones. Mads' brother Oscar was sufficiently suspicious to come from Providence, Rhode Island, to have the body exhumed. The exhumation as far as it went found nothing suspect, and Oscar balked at the money required for an examination of the brain and stomach. The widow Sorensen was the recipient not only of Mads' life insurance but also some nasty comments in the neighborhood, with gossip circulating that she had murdered her husband with poison. Escaping from this suspicion, Belle visited a cousin on a farm near Fergus Falls, Minnesota, and inserted an advertisement in the Chicago Tribune offering her city property in trade for a farm.

The advertisement was seen by Arthur Williams, whose in-laws had tired of the three years spent living in a farmhouse on McClung Road outside LaPorte, Indiana. A trade was agreed to, using $6,000 as the value point, and Williams consented to Belle's request for a new barn on the property. History was about to be made in the northwest corner of Indiana.

The residence on McClung Road had an unhappy history. The brick farmhouse that Belle purchased was built in 1877, replacing a cabin erected there in 1857. In 1888, it was purchased by Grosvenor Goss, a farmer, one of whose family members committed suicide there by hanging. In 1890, it became the property of C. M. Eddy, a street car conductor from Chicago. His wife died on the farm, and Eddy returned to Chicago where he, too, committed suicide. In 1892, the property was purchased by Mattie Altic, who ran it as a brothel. Her success attracted similar establishments, and McClung Road gained an unsavory reputation. Altic died suddenly in the house of what may have been either a heart attack or hemorrhage, having earned the distinction as mistress of "no better known establishment of the kind in northern Indiana." In 1894, the place was purchased by Thomas Doyle, who sold it in 1898 to Williams, who saw Belle's ad in the Tribune.

The city of LaPorte was an unlikely spot for a house said to have "an ill-smelling reputation." Since the days when it was only a path in the wilderness, LaPorte drew those who needed rest before continuing their journey. Situated just where forest met prairie, it was a natural route between east and west. The French gave it the name LaPorte, meaning "the door." Even when it was only a path, it was a well-worn path. Indians, trappers, explorers, and settlers found serenity beside the nine nearby lakes. One of those lakes was the sparkling, pear-shaped Clear Lake, and it was right there that Belle chose to relocate. At the time of the Gunness case, a newspaper in nearby Hammond, Indiana, called the city "one of the most beautiful places in one of the grandest commonwealths in the greatest country in the world." The writer wondered almost with incredulity that such a locale could have housed such a "hellish harpy" and "vampire as the Gunness creature."

Belle bought the house with 48 acres in November of 1901, and she remarried the following April. Her new husband was Peter Gunness, who had courted her for two months. Their household consisted of Belle and Peter; two girls, Lucy and Myrtle Sorensen, and Jennie Olson. Although Belle referred to Myrtle and Lucy as her own, their birth certificates listed only a father and carried no mother's name. Jennie Olson was staying with Belle because her mother had died. Later little Philip arrived, but no birth certificate for him was ever found.

Only eight months into the marriage, Peter Gunness was killed by a blow to his head. Belle explained that her husband had been sitting near the kitchen stove when a sausage grinder that had been drying upon a shelf fell on his head. Not everyone believed this explanation, so a hearing into the death was held. The coroner admitted he was baffled by the circumstances surrounding the death, but an open verdict ended the whole affair. Belle was once again a widow.

CHAPTER FOUR

Now, eight years after Gunness' death, the story that began as arson, then turned to revenge, had suddenly burst open on a massive scale as multiple murder for who knew what reasons. The discovery of five new bodies, obviously murdered and not all at the same time, smelled of an evil on a level with the most infamous crimes in history. Immediately there were comparisons to Henry Holmes of Chicago, called "The Monster of Sixty-Third Street" and Kate Bender of Kansas, both of whom were notorious murderers in the latter half of the 19th Century.

A local newspaper called the developing repulsion and apprehension "the greatest murder mystery that had ever engaged the authorities of any city in the world." LaPorte, it stated, had been "shaken to its depth" by the ongoing revelations of murder, adding that "the world stands aghast" at the discoveries. It did not take long before Belle's past caught up to her. Both of her two husbands had died under suspicious circumstances. The burial records show that Mads Sorensen died July 30, 1900. At the request of relatives, his body was exhumed Aug. 30 and a postmortem was conducted. The intestines were not examined because that procedure would have added $300 to the cost. Now, in hindsight, the enlarged heart that was found could have been caused, it was said, by arsenic or strychnine. Records also showed the death of two Sorensen children, Caroline, age five months, in 1896, and Alex, listed as an infant, in 1898. Cause of death in both cases was listed as colitis, or inflamation of the large intestine, which was now viewed as a condition that could have been induced by poison. It was believed both children were adopted. Belle collected $8,500, the amount on Mads' life insurance policy.

After the death of husband number two, Belle testified at an inquest that her husband had been sitting beside the kitchen stove and reaching over to pick up his shoe. Peter Gunness jarred the stove, causing a sausage grinder and a stone jar of hot water to fall on his head. Belle said the blow stunned him, sending him to rest on a couch with vaseline applied to the wound. Several hours later, Belle said he called to her and she found him losing consciousness. He died before a physician could be summoned. On Dec. 16, 1902, H.H. Martin conducted a postmortem on the body of Peter Gunness. The following day, he wrote: "There was no evidence of scalds or burns on the entire body or marks of bruises, contusions, or lacerations, only as herein stated. The nose was lacerated and broken showing evidence of severe blow or the result of falling upon a board. There was a laceration through the scalp and external layer of skull about an inch long, situated just above and to left of the occipital protuberance. Upon removing the pericranium, there showed a fracture and depression of the inner plate--the skull at a point corresponding to the external laceration. There was also marked intercranial hemorrhage. Death was due to shock and pressure caused by fracture and said hemorrhage."

Martin was puzzled by the fact that Gunness did not lose consciousness immediately after the blow. At the inquest, Belle was asked if Gunness was a good man and if they got along well. Her answer was: "He was a very nice man. I wouldn't have married him if I had not thought he was nice, because I didn't only want a nice man for myself, but a nice father for my children. I never heard him say a word out of the way so long as he was here." Much later in her testimony, she once again was asked if she and Gunness had always lived happily with each other. "As far as I know," was her reply. "Was he good to your children?" came another question. "Yes, good to me and he was good to the children." When she was asked, "Have you suspected or have you been afraid that somebody might have come in there and killed him, hit him with that sausage grinder?" Her reply, which can easily be believed when considering what was to come: "I have never been afraid at all." But, just as in the Sorensen case, suspicions were pushed aside and the coroner's verdict left Belle in the clear.

Now, eight years later, a peek behind the scenes at the inquest on Gunness was furnished by L. H. Oberreich, a lawyer who was stenographer to Dr. Bo Bowell, the coroner investigating the death:

"Her story of how she placed a crock of hot brine on the shelf of the kitchen stove and of how Peter knocked it over on himself, when he went to place his shoes behind the stove, seemed a strange accident to cause death. The falling of the auger of the sausage grinder at the same time was another peculiar thing. How the crock of brine struck Gunness on the back of the head, fracturing the skull, and how the sausage mill auger fell and struck him on the nose, fracturing it, simultaneously, we couldn't understand. There was only one thing to do, however, and that was to take the word of the woman for it. She was the only person present with him when the alleged accident occurred."

Oberreich said there were also two things in Belle's favor. First, she seemed "greatly grieved" over Peter's death. Second, and more important to the investigation, was testimony taken from neighbors by the coroner on his way to interview Belle. In every instance, without exception, the neighbors said the couple were "as happy as children." Belle was not Gunness' first wife. He had arrived in the United States from Christiana (Oslo), Norway, in 1885. From pictures he appears to have been a handsome man, blond and blue-eyed, with regular features and neatly trimmed mustache and goatee. He lived for awhile with two uncles near Janesville, Wisconsin, before going to Minneapolis, where he married Sophia Murch in 1892. The couple had two children, one of whom died in infancy and another who now became the object of a custody battle. Gunness' daughter Svenveld had gone to live with her granduncles in Janesville after her mother died. When Gunness died, however, Belle appeared in Janesville and took Svenveld back with her to the LaPorte farm. This did not meet with the approval of Gunness' brother Gust in Minneapolis, who believed his brother had been murdered. He demanded the custody of his brother's child and a portion of the $3,500 life insurance for her. When Belle refused both demands, Gust abducted the child and took her back to Janesville. After a suspicious stranger was seen around the child's new home, Svenveld was taken at night to the home of a friend and later hidden on a farm near Edgerton, north of Janesville. Her relatives were preparing to renew their fight for Gunness' insurance money when LaPorte suddenly became the nation's murder center. Svenveld's relatives were now saying that they saved her life by plucking her from Belle's clutches, where she would likely have been murdered to stop her claim on her father's estate.

Svenveld escaped, but authorities in LaPorte now had nine who did not, four of whom died in the cellar and five found in garbage pits. The work of digging resumed on May 6, and this day would bring additional shocks and increasing dread, as four more bodies were unearthed, bringing the total number of dead to 13. Three bodies were taken from a grave on the south side of the farmyard at the edge of a slope leading toward Fish Trap Lake. Tangled wire had been twisted into the wire fence there, but the bulk of the wire covered the grave. Attention was drawn to this spot after a boy kicked up a human rib that had caught in the fence. The excavation yielded three dismembered skeletons that had been wrapped in gunny sacks. One skull was missing, and the quicklime that had been placed the bodies made it impossible to determine age and sex of the skeletons. The search then moved to a brick archway hat had recently been added to the rear of the house. Although removing that archway produced no more bodies, another "soft" spot was detected in the chickenyard. There diggers unearthed an old vault that contained another human torso that had been wrapped in gunny sacks. Here, too, quicklime had done its job of disguising the identity and like all the others, the body had been dismembered.

By now, the collection of bits and pieces of bodies had grown to the point that a charnel house had to be set up. The little red carriage shed was selected for that purpose, and its contents were described by Dr. J. H.William Meyer, formerly employed at Cook County Hospital in Chicago and now placed in charge of postmortem examinations:

"It is horrible. I am at a loss to express an opinion of the whole case. I believe nothing like it ever was encountered before. No jury of the foremost of the country could say how long ago and just how these different people were killed. In the first place, the action of the ashes and quicklime which is apparent in every body except Helgelein's has been so severe that no estimate of the year of death can be made. Three months of soaking in such a solution as that seeping down upon those bodies would do nature's work of 10 years. In Helgelein's case we are puzzled by the condition of the organs. They are in such a condition as we find in a man who had been dead only two or three days. We are convinced that this is of significance. It may be the result of a poison that acted as a preservative.

"The next startling thing is the manner in which the bodies have been taken to pieces. In every case the legs have been cut off at about the same distance above the knee. The flesh appears to have been cut with a keen knife, and then the bone sawed squarely off. More important than this is the method of the disarticulation of the ball and socket joints of the shoulders. This cannot be done by an amateur with an ordinary instrument. Every one of these operations was clean cut. It was done by a strong hand with nothing less sharp than a surgeon's knife. The capsule is severed in a curve, as it would have been done in a clinic. Our considerations have been informal thus far, but before we are through with this, we will have definite conclusions that should be of importance."

The LaPorte County coroner, Dr. Charles S. Mack, said inquests on the bodies would not begin until the investigation was completed. "We have no juries here," he said, "and while I have taken numerous depositions in these cases and had four physicians consider the cases of the bodies taken from the house after the fire, no cause of death has been assigned and none will be until we know how we stand in the entire matter. More thorough postmortems than have been possible so far will be made under the direction of Dr. Meyer upon all the bodies, and we will wait for the results of them before getting down to real business. One important possibility is anticipated in the autopsies upon the bodies supposed to be those of Mrs. Gunness and her children. The four are said to have eaten the same food the night before their death, and the contents of their stomachs naturally would be the same after a certain period had passed. By this examination we can tell whether the body is that of Mrs. Gunness." This, it turned out, was the epitome of wishful thinking.

CHAPTER FIVE

By definition, a mystery is something unexplained, unknown, or kept secret. All those elements festered inside the puzzle of McClung Road. There was the mystery of who set the fire? Was it the fire or something else that killed the four in the cellar? How many people had Belle killed? Did she have an accomplice? The greatest mystery of all: Was Belle herself really dead?

Coroner Mack, an optimist who believed "we can settle this," did admit to one small problem: "The only chance there is anything wrong with the whole affair being that a corpse was placed with the children by their mother, who fled after setting fire to the house." This "chance" was worrying quite a few people. Several things argued against the cellar adult being Belle. The dead woman's size was much smaller than Belle, who had a hefty torso. Of the four bodies found in the cellar, only the adult's was missing a head. Everything in Belle's known character pointed to another of her schemes. To think of Belle as a victim was incredible.

There were two camps of opposing opinion. Here, in a spectacular murder case, much of the opposition was absurdly divided along political lines. Republicans thought she was dead; Democrats believed she escaped. The Republicans included the sheriff and the prosecuting attorney and one local newspaper. The Democrats included the mayor, the police chief, and another local newspaper. The mayor belonged to the same law firm that was defending Lamphere. The sheriff, as will be seen later, may have had his reasons for wanting Lamphere to pay for Belle's death. Aside from all this, and the fact that it was an election year, there were plenty of pros and cons to keep the average person guessing.

Consider the dead body's size: Belle was about 5 foot 7 and weighted around 200 pounds. The dead body, though stocky, was estimated by a couple of doctors to belong to a woman 5 foot 3 and 150 pounds. Dr. Meyer, who wasn't bothered by this discrepancy, commented: "Ask a housewife how much fat roast beef will shrink when it is cooked in a hot oven. All cooks to whom I have propounded this question agreed that at least one-third of the weight will disappear in the evaporating fat, and some of them say that the shrinkage amounts to one-half."

Next, the missing head: It had not been, and never would be, found. The heads of the three children were where they should have been. Would the larger, adult woman's head have melted in the intense heat leaving the smaller children's heads intact? To this, those who believed Belle dead said that a digger's shovel went into the ground at the spot where Belle's head had lain, thereby destroying it. Besides, her rings were found, along with the buckle of the money belt she frequently wore and the key to her safety deposit box. If the body were not Belle's, where did she get the substitute? In reply, those who thought Belle alive said she was seen driving a strange woman to the farm on the Saturday before the fire, and this woman was never seen again.

Then there was the curious position of the piano. Its remnants were found atop the bodies in the cellar. Yet the piano was housed on the first floor. The bodies, therefore, must have always been in the cellar. It appeared the fire could not have caught them sleeping in bed. There were many other tantalizing questions with elusive answers. Did Belle commit suicide after torching the farmhouse? It hardly seemed her style. She was patient and dogged in going after what she wanted. Her letters to Helgelein coaxing him to come to LaPorte show her to be clever, devious, and manipulative. She could lie glibly. The murders she committed to get what she wanted demonstrated her coldbloodedness and total lack of conscience. If she and the children had been trapped in the fire, why didn't the noise and smoke rouse them the way they had Maxson? Or why didn't Maxson hear their cries? He had worked for Belle only a couple of months, and they had no record of animosity. If they had been murdered before the fire was set, why hadn't Maxson heard any noise in connection with that? If she had killed the four, set the fire, and then escaped, how did she get away without being helped or seen? All her horses were in the barn on the morning after the fire. Even if she walked away, someone would have seen her boarding a train.

"You cannot make me believe that she is dead," Police Chief Clinton Cochrane said. "There are so many circumstances against it that I feel sure she is miles away from here, alive and well, and perhaps planning to continue her crimes."

Prosecutor Ralph N. Smith was equally sure that the body was Belle's. He thought Belle and Lamphere, possibly partners in murder, had a falling out, and Lamphere set fire to the house to kill the family. "If anybody wants Mrs. Gunness," he was fond of saying, "I can produce her in five minutes. All that is left of her is in the morgue."

The LaPorte Herald, the local newspaper that believed Belle was dead, had this to say: "The score of trained newspaper writers who are in the city from all the big cities are almost agreed that their investigations failed to give them grounds for the stand that the woman is not dead. These men have investigated scores, yes hundreds of cases in the criminal line. Their judgment is worthy of consideration; in fact, they are paid for being able to correctly theorize in cases of this kind. It is contended by them that Mrs. Gunness, had she fixed up a corpse after killing the children, would not have thought to place Philip, the little boy, on the breast of the corpse and to entwine the arms of the corpse around him."

One of those newspaper men was William Blodgett of the Indianapolis News, who had been covering the story since its inception and sent this to his newspaper: "Mrs. Belle Paulson Gunness is dead and nothing in her life so became her like the leaving of it. That is the belief of the majority of the people of the city, of Sheriff Smutzer and his deputies, of Detective Smith, of the Pinkerton men, of Prosecuting Attorney Smith, of a number of doctors and surgeons, all of whom have thrown prejudice aside and have given this case careful investigation and thorough consideration. Even the attorneys for Lamphere, the man accused of murder and arson, are not strong in the thought that she is living. They think her dead, but by her own hand. Mrs. Gunness is kept alive by a few yellow newspapers who see in her living the possibilities of a better story than if she was lying on the slab in the morgue. One or two physicians, too, intimate that they doubt the headless body in the morgue was once that of the arch murderess. But everything points to the fact that Sheriff Smutzer was right when he said long ago that Belle Gunness was not living." Almost a half century later, an author writing about the case would come up with her own version of why Smutzer was so sure of this.

Belle's activities the day before the fire do not seem those of someone getting ready to flee. Still, her complaints against Lamphere might have been lodged just to set him up as the fall guy in her latest escapade. At any rate, Maxson was left at home to work while Belle went into town that Monday. The children, for some unknown reason, stayed home from school that day. In LaPorte, Belle was busy, perhaps because she saved all her chores for one day. Whatever the reason, she made many stops. She went to the grocery store of John S. Minich, where she purchased coffee, sugar, and two gallons of kerosene in a five gallon can. Later, George Wrase, the head clerk in the store, said that Lamphere was in the store at the same time. "Ray Lamphere did not come in the store as though his object was to make a purchase," Wrase stated. "He walked in slowly and, after gazing around, during which he looked at Mrs. Gunness, who was in the store, and rather leered at her, he asked for a plug of tobacco. Mrs. Gunness did not seemed pleased to see him. There was no conversation between them."

Several days prior, Lamphere had been acquitted of one of Belle's trespassing charges. Belle was letting everyone know that she was afraid of him. So, this day she went to her attorney,

M.E. Leliter, once more grumbled about Lamphere and made out her will, which she placed in a safety deposit box in the bank. At 10 minutes to 4 p.m., she also deposited $720 in the bank. This was the only money she had in any local bank.

After her chores in town, Belle arrived back home about 5:30 p.m. She prepared a supper of bread and butter, dried beef, salmon, beefsteak and potatoes. Maxson later said they all ate well. After dinner, they played two games, Red Riding Hood and the Fox until 8:30, when Maxson went to bed. If it wasn't Belle in the cellar, then, unknown to Maxson, someone else was in the house that night. That someone had to be recently murdered because the cellar body, while badly burned, had not been dead long enough to show signs of decomposition.

CHAPTER SIX

Lamphere's accusers believed jealousy was the motive for the arson and deaths of four people. The defendant admitted, "We got along all right before that (Helgelein's arrival), and she used to come to my room at night; but after Helgelein came, she had no use for me." Lamphere also said Belle had suggested he get insurance from a fraternal organization and marry her. However, he dragged his feet on the insurance, a procrastination that probably saved his life.

Belle met Lamphere in August of 1907, and he worked for her for six months. From the first, they were lovers; and he remained infatuated with her even when she banished him from the house in favor of Helgelein. When Helgelein disappeared, Lamphere tried to return to Belle's bed, only to find that she was no longer receptive to his advances. Even his place as hired hand was taken on Feb. 10 by Maxson. His persistence led her to have him arrested March 12 for annoyance and trespassing. In a trial before Justice of the Peace S. E. Grover, he was found guilty and fined $1 and costs. The fine was paid by Mrs. Elizabeth Smith, the black woman who would later be his alibi for the night of the fire.

According to Belle, the pestering continued, so she filed an affidavit charging Lamphere with insanity on March 28. This statement is still in existence and details her reasons for thinking him insane. "He told me things that I knew were not true and unreasonable," she claimed. "He comes to my house every night, at all times of night, and looks in the windows, commits misdemeanors." She also said Lamphere "gets intoxicated." The statement lists the qualities that she thought Lamphere had, namely, he was silent, quiet, seclusive, dull, profane, filthy, intemperate, sleepless, and criminal. He was not noisy, cheerful, violent, or hysterical. From the blank space in the questionnaire, it seems she could not make up her mind whether he was homicidal. The medical profession did not agree with Belle. Dr. Bo Bowell, Lamphere's doctor for the prior five years, declared he had "never treated him for any mental disturbance" but that Lamphere "has been and is a hard drinker." Bowell concluded, "'I do not consider him insane."

Having failed in this attempt, Belle filed another complaint March 31 that charged Lamphere with trespass. Again he was found guilty, his $1 fine being paid this time by John Wheatbrook, his employer. She appealed for help a third time, in April, and asked that her tormentor be placed under a peace bond. This time her testimony about the specific times of Lamphere's appearances on her property were disputed when two farmers, Wheatbrook and W. W. Proud, gave him alibis. The trial took place the Saturday before the fire, and Lamphere was acquitted. The following Monday, the day before the fire, was the occasion for Belle's trip to town and her visit to her attorney, who described her as "in an hysterical mood" and demanding he make out her will because of her fear of Lamphere. Should Belle and the children not survive, the estate went to the Norwegian Children's Association in Chicago.

In hindsight, the question immediately arises of whether Belle was telling the truth about Lamphere's harassment. Maxson later said he had seen Lamphere on the property once in March, but that hardly would qualify as harassment. Was she cleverly setting up Lamphere to take the fall for the arson and murders? If so, what did Lamphere think as charge after false charge was made by Belle against him? Was he mostly in an alcoholic stupor or had the long-term use of alcohol affected his brain? He certainly was not the neatly groomed type that Belle usually took up with. He was 38 years old, short, with a slight build. In photographs, he is seen with a drooping, unkept mustache, bowler hat and baggy pants or looking wild-eyed with a Bible in his lap. He had no money, but perhaps Belle figured to use him in some other way.

It was this background that sent Sheriff Albert Smutzer immediately on Lamphere's trail the day of the fire. Lamphere was located on the Wheatbrook farm and brought into town, where he was placed in secluded confinement in the jail. Visitation was allowed only to Prosecutor Ralph N. Smith and Pastor E. A. Schell of the First Methodist Church in LaPorte. His lawyer, H. W. Worden, was allowed to see him only after threatening to file habeas corpus papers.

Pastor Schell, recently elected president of Iowa Wesleyan University and a prominent churchman, confirmed that Lamphere was jealous of Helgelein. "But there are a great many citizens of LaPorte who feel that he is not guilty," he said. "He is not a vicious man--just a farmer's son who had picked up a little knowledge of the carpenter's trade and, of course, cannot be expected to rate high mentally. But there is little in his past life to lead one to believe that he would be guilty of the crime of firing a house containing four people. He is a toper, and his relations with women are open to criticism; but he is not a bad man."

After a week in jail, newspaper reporters were allowed to talk to the defendant. Unaware of what the digging on the farm had produced, Lamphere appeared stunned when told by reporters about the bodies. He reportedly "gasped" and then commented, "That woman--I knew that she was bad but that's awful." As reporters described what was going on at the farm, he insisted he knew nothing about the bodies. Finally, he mentioned his misgivings about the fate of Helgelein: "I always suspected that she killed Helgelein, and now I am sure of it. My suspicions were aroused soon after Helgelein came to the house. Once she wanted me to buy 'Rough on Rats' for her, and another time she wanted chloroform. I would not get them for her. As for the others, I don't know anything beyond what I suspect. Things that I know look different to me now, and it may be that things I noticed were more serious than I thought they were. The girl must be Jennie Olson. I never believed she was in

California. I never heard of any letters coming from her." When prodded for more information on "things he had noticed", Lamphere explained: "About a year ago, there was a man with a black mustache who came to the farm, and Mrs. Gunness told me he was a friend of Jennie's. I think she said he was her sweetheart. He had a big trunk with him, and a long while after he went away the trunk was sent back to the house, and used to stand upstairs. I saw some clothes in it that the man used to wear ... Who the children were I don't know; I guess one was a baby brought to the house by a man and a women in a carriage. When they went away, they did not have the baby. I remember Mrs. Gunness said something about it--that she thought they murdered it. She went into town and told the sheriff about it, but he did not pay any attention to it." In connection with this story, Police Chief Cochrane did visit the Gunness farm and investigated a hole in the woods that, while freshly dug, was empty.

Sheriff Smutzer prevented Lamphere from talking about the Helgelein case, but the defendant did manage to deny that he had any part in helping dispose of the 200-pound body. "She used to tell me not to talk to Helgelein," he explained. "And one time when she found us together in the sitting room, she drove me out of the house." Lamphere was reported to have been seen in February wearing an overcoat similar to the one owned by Helgelein. While it may have been similar, it was later determined that it never belonged to the dead man. A revolver said to be the dead man's was seen in the defendant's possession during his visit to a barber shop while the South Dakota man was visiting Belle. At the time, Lamphere was said to have commented, "I may have to use it before long." Later, when Belle charged him with trespass, he told police that Belle wished he would forget something but he would not reveal what that something was.

Lamphere's possible involvement in Helgelein's death concerned his alibi for the night of January 14, believed to be Helgelein's last. In one explanation, Lamphere said Belle sent him that day to Michigan City to trade horses. He was to meet a certain man in a livery stable there. If that man did not show up, he was to stay in Michigan City and not return to LaPorte until the next afternoon. He did go to Michigan City but disobeyed the other instructions and returned to LaPorte when no trader appeared at the stable. He went to the Gunness house and then returned to Michigan City, where still no trader appeared. Returning to the farm, he was told by Belle that the trader must have changed his mind. Lamphere said when he left the farm that night, Helgelein was there. When Lamphere returned, Helgelein was gone; and Lamphere said he never saw him again. In another version of the story, Lamphere said a man and a woman from town asked that he go to Michigan City to pick up her cousin at the train. He was told to stay all night if necessary to wait for this person. Just before receiving these orders, Lamphere said his conversation with Helgelein in the house was interrupted by Belle, who took him aside and once more told him to leave Helgelein alone. "I want to get some money from that man'" Lamphere quoted Belle. "He don't need to give it to me unless he wants to, but if you talk to him, you will spoil the game." Even in this version, no one showed up in Michigan City and Lamphere returned to the Gunness house the next day about noon. Another consistent detail: Lamphere's assertion that he never saw Helgelein again.

The new hired hand, Maxson, said that since he had come to work at the farm in February, he had seen nothing suspicious. "I don't believe I ever saw what you could call a visitor come to see her," he said. "There were a few men who came to buy stock, but that was all. She didn't seem to have any friends. She used to watch me at my work once in awhile, but didn't speak to me often except to give me orders. She used to do her own housework and stayed in the house most of the time. She seemed fond of her children and only got cross with them once in awhile. I don't believe she swore or drank. She didn't go to LaPorte often, was always home in the evening, and went to bed early. While I worked for her, she did not make any trips to Chicago or anywhere else. She didn't get much mail, and I never saw any boxes delivered here."

When asked about her hysterical appearance at the attorney's office with charges of harassment against Lamphere, Maxson said he had seen the defendant at the farm on only one occasion, on the lawn and not near the house. "On the day she signed her will, she just told me to hitch up one of the horses, as she had some business to attend to," Maxson said. "I asked her if it was important and she said it was. That she had to be there at 3 o'clock. She acted just as usual; and when she came back before dinner, I saw no signs of tears or anything like that. She did not say anything at supper about her visit to town."

CHAPTER SEVEN

On May 6, the day the body count rose to 13, the digging was interrupted by the arrival of Antone Olson and Mrs. George Olander, the father and sister of Jennie Olson, and Asle Helgelein, whose persistence had led to the discovery of the graves. Coroner Mack asked them to make positive identification of their loved ones, if possible. Helgelein was able to identify his brother Andrew by the corpse's teeth, high cheek bones, pointed chin, and forehead scar. Olson and Mrs. Olander refused to look at the remains spread out on a blanket in the charnel house. However, they insisted that Jennie was one of the victims, based on the distinctive marks on one body described by Coroner Mack and Dr. J. H. William Meyer, who was in charge of the postmortem examinations.

"I can't help feeling it is my sister," said Mrs. Olander, "and I don't think it is necessary that we must suffer that terrible sight. We have not heard from Jennie for two years. Until then we used to get letters every once in awhile, and then they stopped."

These three were not the only visitors to murder hill that day. In the early hours of the day, a small band of spectators gathered to watch the digging. Shortly after noon, however, the gathered crowd was said to be "hundreds of persons." Even so, those assembled were but a small group compared to the throngs that would soon be lured to the infamous barnyard.

The victims' relatives were not the only ones concerned with the tragedy. Belle's Chicago relatives, too, were now thrust into notoriety. Belle's sister, Mrs. John Larson of North Francisco Avenue, refused to believe that the body was not Belle's. Of course, if she were right, Belle's estate would be approved for disbursement. Mrs. Larson was contesting Belle's will, which left her estate to Norwegian orphans. After she and her son Rudolph visited a LaPorte attorney, Mrs. Larson explained, "We didn't want any of the money for ourselves, but Mrs. Gunness has a crippled sister and an aged brother in Norway who now are unable to support themselves. It was for their sake we wanted to contest the will."

The Norwegian Lutheran Children's Home was loathe to accept Belle's money anyway. Home Superintendent Caroline Williams explained: "Personally, I do not believe the directors will accept the money. Of course, I have no authority to speak for them, but the revelations at LaPorte have been so dreadful that to accept the money now would be like taking blood money. If it should be found that the money was the price of human life, I am sure the home would not take it. As for any undue influence being brought to bear on Mrs. Gunness to get her to will the money to the orphanage, that is all foolishness. We never heard of the woman until notified of her death and the legacy. She never, so far as we know, visited the home, nor had she any connection whatever with our work. We want to keep out of the case. It is too horrible to even think about."

Other than the inheritance issue, Mrs. Larson, too, was quick to distance herself from her infamous sister. "I haven't seen her since shortly after her first husband, Mr. Sorensen, died," she said, explaining how her refusal to let Belle adopt her oldest daughter had estranged the two sisters. "She hasn't been in my home in 20 years." Still, she hired a funeral director to receive the bodies of the four found in the cellar upon their release from LaPorte authorities. In her will, Belle asked to be buried in Forest Home Cemetery, a burial place west of Chicago where Mads Sorensen was interred.

Trying to make sense of the horror, Mrs. Larson made these comments about her sister: "When she first came from the old country, we noticed there was something strange about her. She seemed to be wild and flighty in her speech. Often she would mutter to herself. When we asked her what she said, she only laughed. My husband disliked her from the start, and that also did much to keep us apart. I don't known what to think of all this. It is terrible. I saw my sister shortly after her husband's death and she told me he died of heart disease. Some of the neighbors said Mrs. Sorensen had given her husband poison and murdered him, and I heard there was talk of exhuming the body. But my husband and I never mixed in the affair and I know little about it." In attempting to figure out what aspects of Belle's personality would include mass murder, Mrs. Larson offered: "All she loved was money; and we didn't have much to do with each other because she thought she was better than I was, because she had more money, a better house and clothes." But just where Belle got her money, she didn't know.

One of Belle's nieces, Mrs. Edward Howard of West Superior Street in Chicago, added: "There was something strange about my aunt, and people didn't understand her. If she did these things, she must have been crazy." She said she had not seen the body supposed to be Belle because she "couldn't bear to look at it." Her brother, who had seen less of the living Belle, did look but could not identify her. Mrs. Howard stated, "So far as her immediate relatives are concerned, Mrs. Gunness has been identified by none of them."

Mrs. Larson said another characteristic of her sister was her fondness for children. Both she and Mrs. Howard were questioned about a previously unknown fourth grave at the Sorensen plot in Forest Home Cemetery. While Mrs. Larson believed it might be a certain child that Belle had taken in many years ago, Mrs. Howard refuted that by saying she had seen this child, now grown up, recently. There was a young girl remembered only as "Lucy" who disappeared suddenly from the Sorensen home at Elizabeth Street and Grand Avenue in Chicago. Some people now thought she may have been Belle's first victim. Visitors to the Sorensen home recalled a little girl who greeted them as they entered the house. After about a year, she was gone; and no one seemed to get a definite explanation about where she went. To those who thought she went back to her parents and those who believed she might have gone to a sanitarium, Belle confirmed nothing. Her brief stay with Belle was thought to be in 1893, a long 15 years before Belle's villainy was discovered.

On May 7 the rainy weather prevented further digging, but the investigation continued. LaPorte authorities called in the Pinkerton National Detective Agency, which had a reputation for success, to help in solving the case. Meanwhile, another victim had been identified. Here, too, Belle had left a trail of the lies she had used to capture and then eliminate Ole Budsberg, the body with the black mustache.

Budsberg had farmed for many years just outside Iola, Wisconsin. In March of 1907, he told his sons, Mat and Oscar, that he was going to the Gunness farm to see if he wanted to manage it. No mention was made of how he learned of Belle. A week later, he returned to Iola and announced that the farm was a good one and he was going to return and stay there. Budsberg sold his farm to Mat, the oldest son, and took $1,000 to LaPorte with him on April 5, 1907. When the sons did not hear from him, they asked the LaPorte Savings Bank for information because they had learned their father had secured a mortgage from that bank. The bank dispatched a cashier to talk to Belle, who said Budsberg had gone to Chicago and then to Oregon to buy a farm. A little more detail was given by Belle in response to a query from the Farmers' State Bank in Wisconsin. Belle said Budsberg was robbed of $2,000 in Chicago and returned to LaPorte and told her about the robbery. She said she begged him to return to his family. She claimed he decided to go to Oregon to remake the money he had lost. Belle said she accompanied him to the railroad station and saw him leave.

While the sons were waiting and wondering, they received a call from LaPorte requesting they come to that city. They took Benjamin Chapin, an Iola hardware dealer, with them. James Buck of the LaPorte Savings Bank, with whom they had corresponded, met them at the station. After a stop at the courthouse, they were taken to the farm and the charnel house. Entering the little shed, they faced the skull and bones of what was thought to be their father. They peered dry-eyed at the mustached skull, looked at each other, and left the shed. Without a word, they walked out into the fresh air and away from the onlookers watching their every gesture. Then, after the curious had left the shed, the brothers returned for another look. "It is his face," said Mat, refusing to comment further. Even after reaching their rooms at the Teegarten Hotel, Mat's only comment was, "I feel sure it is my father."

Later in his deposition for Coroner Mack, James Buck would tell what little was known in LaPorte of Budsberg: "I first saw Ole Budsberg March 23, 1907. He came into our bank that day with Mrs. Gunness. He wanted us to send a mortgage note for $1,000 to Iola, Wisconsin, for collection. We sent it and collected it. The next time I saw him, which was the last time I saw him alive, was April 16, 1907. That day, too, he came into the bank accompanied by Mrs. Gunness. We paid him the thousand dollars, two five hundred dollar packages. His looks impressed themselves upon me that day more than the first time I saw him. Still, I am not certain that I would now recognize him so as to pick him out if he were with several other men. Last fall our bank received from a bank in Iola, Wisconsin, a letter of inquiry as to whether we had seen anything of Mr. Budsberg lately. That letter was dated October 14, 1907. Shortly after the receipt of this letter, I, at the request of the cashier of our bank, went to Mrs. Gunness and inquired if Mr. Budsberg was there. She said he wasn't. I asked her when she saw him last. She said that she did not know; that she did not keep track of dates; that the last time she saw him he left her house to catch the 2 o'clock train; and that he said he said he was going to Oregon to see about buying some land or something like that. I asked what day it was he left, and she said she did not keep track of dates. I did not go into the house. Our conversation was at the door. Her statement that he had left in time to catch the 2 o'clock train was in reply to my inquiry as to the time he had left, whether in the day time or in the night. I reported my visit to the LaPorte

Savings Bank and they wrote of it back to the bank in Iola. When the fire at the Gunness place was reported in the papers, the cashier of our bank sent copies of these papers to the bank in Iola, Wisconsin."

Mat Budsberg, in his deposition gave his recollections: "The last time I saw my father was at our home near Iola on April 5, 1907. He was a subscriber for a Norwegian paper called Scandinavian, published in Chicago, and the Decorah, Iowa, Posten. He left home on April 5 to come to LaPorte to run a farm for Mrs. Gunness. I do not know how he had heard of Mrs. Gunness. Before leaving, he told his brothers that he was going away to be married. When he left home, he had with him, according to what the cashier of the bank told us, about $800 in cash and a draft for $1,000. This was his second trip to LaPorte, for he had been in LaPorte a week late in March. When he left the second time, I understood he intended to remain in LaPorte. He bought some seed potatoes in Iola and sent them to LaPorte. After leaving Iola, he never wrote me or any of us, although he had promised to write as soon as he got settled.

"When he had been away for a week and we had not heard anything, we began to think something was wrong. I and my brothers wrote to him. My brother wrote two letters and sent some insurance papers for him to sign. My letter was returned from the dead letter office in Washington. I do not know what became of my brother Lewis' letters. About the same time, a letter came from Mrs. Gunness, addressed to my father. We opened it. In it, she said she wanted to send him some letters and papers that had come for him after he had left her house, and she wanted to know whether he was at home to receive them if she sent them there. She said, too, she hoped he was not offended by her not marrying him. She said she never thought he would ask her because she had not encouraged him any. She said she hoped if he was going West, he would find some land as a homestead; but if she were in his place, she would go to the old country to visit. The letter was written in Norwegian. Then we thought he had gone out West and we did not look for him any more. April 15, 1907, he had borrowed $100 at the Farmers' National Bank in Iola for six months. When the note was due, the bank tried to hunt him up. The bank wrote down to LaPorte to Mrs. Gunness and she wrote back that father had been robbed in Chicago of most of his money and some clothes and that he had told her he would go out West and try to make up what he had been robbed of before any of the relatives should learn of it. She said that he had left at her house a trunk and a few clothes and would send for them as soon as he got settled down. We still had no suspicion of his having been harmed by Mrs. Gunness."

Once again, the extent of Belle's duplicity and cunning was revealed in the way she enticed Budsberg into her net and the way she concealed his murder.

CHAPTER EIGHT

Dozens of newspaper reporters, editors, and artists converged on LaPorte to cover the sensational developments. "No story in years has attracted the widespread attention that has the Gunness case," boasted a local newspaper, "and in every city, town, and hamlet there is a craving that must be satisfied by the newspapers."

All the Chicago newspapers had several people in LaPorte, a few even commuting back and forth each day. The wire services, Associated Press and United Press, were present, along with reporters from as far away as New York City. Many had arrived the day of the fire, expecting to stay only a few days. Now they found themselves in the midst of a major ongoing story with no chance to return home for more clothes or other essentials. Their home away from home was the Teegarten Hotel, within easy reach of Western Union and the Postal Telegraph offices.

One of the Chicago Tribune's reporters called himself Ralph Waldo Emerson, but was neither the famous essayist and poet, who died in 1882 nor his son Waldo who died in 1842 of scarlet fever. He told a story about asking a Tribune artist back in Chicago to send him some more clothes. When his request was answered, he opened the canvas bag to discover a Prince Albert coat, one soiled collar, one shaving mug, one shaving stick, and one dull razor. A Chicago American reporter, A. E. Pegler, told a similar tale. In the absence of his wife, his 9-year-old daughter sent him a suitcase containing one old cap, 42 handkerchiefs, one bottle of cough medicine, one box of pills, and 18 neckties that had been thrown away.

A local newspaper, the LaPorte Herald, was regularly printing from 500 to 800 extra copies each day. Not only were visitors buying the papers, LaPorteans also were snapping up extra copies to send away to friends and relatives. The Herald reported that the big-city boys were sending out from 75,000 to 100,000 words of news every day either through Western Union, the Postal Telegraph, or long-distance telephones, services that often had extra people working sometimes late into the night in order to expedite the press copy.

The worldwide publicity given to the murder farm brought innumerable inquiries from people whose loved ones were missing. In the small town of LaPorte, curiosity centered around the fate of Belle's former hired hands. Olaf Limbo, in Belle's employ seven years before, had suddenly "gone to Norway to witness the coronation of the king." Or had he? Another worker, Amel Green, was supposed to be in the West somewhere. But was he? In Chicago, because of Belle's connection to that city and the city's proximity to the farm, many people wondered if Belle were responsible for the absence of friends and family. Investigators were looking at a few of those cases that seemed promising. Max Worchowski of West 14th Street thought his 16-year-old sister Esther might be one victim. She had disappeared from her Chicago home on Waller Street on October 16 after answering an advertisement to go to Indiana. A month later, a friend said he saw her, but now no one could remember the name of the town. Also missing was Herman Konitzer, who lived on North Halsted Street and who disappeared in January of 1906 after receiving a letter from a widow in LaPorte. Mrs. B. F. Carling of Calumet Avenue went to LaPorte to see if her husband was one of the victims.

Wisconsin, which seemed to be a fertile field for Belle's activities, yielded its share of possibilities. Frank Riedinger was missing from Delafield. He left town early in 1907 for some place in Indiana as a result of a matrimonial advertisement. Friends and relatives of Anna Tillman, a native of Kenosha, thought she might be a victim. She had disappeared two years ago from LaPorte after saying her health was poor and she was accepting an invitation to go to the country.

Other inquiries came from near and far. William Fries of Richland Center, Wisconsin, wrote expressing fear of the fate of his friend Frank Brodright, who had lived in Medina, North Dakota. "I have been trying to find a friend of mine who was last heard from in Chicago in February, 1907," his letter explained. "Since reading the terrible tragedy in LaPorte, I cannot help believing that he might have been one of the victims. He was about 40 years old and crippled in both feet, the right foot, I think, being turned more than the left. This fact ought to make the identification possible. He was a bachelor and might have answered one of Mrs. Gunness' matrimonial advertisements."

A Mrs. H. Whitzler of Toledo arrived in LaPorte to find out if her missing daughter, who had attended Valparaiso College in 1902, was a victim. A wealthy family from New York wondered if a former coachman had been murdered by Belle. From Duquesne, Pennsylvania, came a query about John Burtner, who left his home in November of 1907, not disclosing his destination to relatives but having previously mentioned marrying a woman "out in Indiana." His daughter, back in McKeesport, furnished a description: 52 years old but appearing younger, light gray hair, 165 pounds, 5 feet 10 inches tall, shoe size 8½ .

A real estate agent in Sandusky, Ohio, asked about his wife's uncle, Patrick Griggin, a railroad man who was known to have corresponded with a woman in Indiana. He had left home wearing diamonds and carrying money. Later, the Sandusky postmaster had received a query from a woman who signed herself "Mabel Pierce" who wanted to know if Griggin was a man of his word and what he was worth. As with most of the others, no link could be made between what was known of him and what was left of the bodies. In his case, he was ruled out because he wore upper and lower dentures.

Fueling the seekers of lost loves were also the newspaper stories such as the one coming out of Oklahoma where Emil and Fred Greening, who had worked on the Gunness farm in the summer of 1907, were quoted. They said a dozen men visited Belle's home and disappeared. Commenting on the anxiety created by such statements, the Chicago Tribune devoted an editorial to "The Army of the Missing", which stated in part:

"For every body that is found in lake, in vacant lot, on the railroad track, in 'murder yard', or where ever the flotsam and jetsam of life finds lodgment, there is a procession of anxious sufferers who seek relief from the torment of uncertainty which attends the friends of the 'lost' and 'missing' ... The identity of some of the mutilated bodies taken from the barnyard on the Indiana farm may never be disclosed. The sickening tales of the investigation in a case like this are spread throughout the country. But for every body found in such a time of excitement, there are many more whose fate never will be known. Just how many no one can tell. But the constant search for the 'missing' indicates the size of the army of those who have drifted away from home and friends."

High up on the "torment of uncertainty" was the continuing question of whether the woman's body in the burned house was Belle's. Mrs. Olander, who had finally identified her sister Jennie's body by her teeth, also examined the headless corpse found in the cellar. Her first impression was that the body was not large enough to be Belle's, but she later said she was not sure of this. More than a week after the fire, searchers had not yet uncovered any melted gold that had crowned Belle's teeth. I. P. Norton, a dentist, had informed investigators that he could identify Belle's teeth if they could find them. At this stage of the investigation, Coroner Mack stated his position: "I never have permitted the body of the woman at the morgue to be described as that of Mrs. Gunness in the official record. I shall have to have more evidence before I am satisfied that it is hers."

Rain continued to fall on May 8, the fourth day since the digging discovery in the farmyard. Postponed by rain the day before, it was decided that the work must go on today rain or shine. The neighbor Daniel Hutson and Sheriff Smutzer began at the north end of the small fenced enclosure. The men launched into the mixture of clay and rubbish, shoving away bits of glass, old shoes, and cans. At about two feet into the pit, a familiar and ominous sight appeared--ashes and quicklime. Moving gingerly with their shovels, they carefully probed farther. Soon, a human thigh bone was uncovered, followed by so many bones that at first the onlookers thought they had two bodies. The presence of only one skull but a possible extra femur led to a minor debate on the spot. Coroner Mack first said there were two bodies, but he was contradicted by Sheriff Smutzer, who had been a funeral director for 12 years, and who insisted only one body had been uncovered. Smutzer took a pitchfork and arranged the bones in proper skeletal form, stopping only when Mack agreed that he had seen enough to agree with the sheriff. The remains had been surrounded by a box, but this had rotted away. Pieces of flesh hung to the bones, which gave evidence of being dismembered before being placed in a gunny sack.

Following the technique that had turned up additional bodies two days before, the men dug trenches around the new grave. They stopped only when the hardness of the clay showed that it had lain undisturbed for years. No additional bodies were discovered. The newest victim in the yard was believed to be a woman because items found nearby seemed to be a woman's pointed shoes, the metal frame of a purse, and metal from a truss. The condition of the remains indicated that this body was probably one of the first to be buried.

By now, all the so-called "soft spots" had been examined. Some transplanted lilac bushes became suspect, but they yielded no surprises. The hunt then moved back behind the farm's outhouse where an old filled-in well was also found empty.

A local newspaper carried the news of the latest find and reflected the general feeling of all who had been following the story: "LaPorte's murder horror grows. Every hour seems to add some fresh chapter to the most revolting, most sensational and most astounding criminal case in the history of the world. No blood and thunder story ever written by the most wild-eyed dime-novel author surpasses in bloody details this story of the woman blue beard, this high priestess of murder."

CHAPTER NINE

Jennie and Belle had lived together almost 18 years. For both, teeth would be pivotal in determining their deaths. The teeth that played a role in the identification of Jennie were the two upper front ones. Her sister had begged off viewing the body because she did not think she could bear the sight. She felt she could identify her sister's teeth because they were so like her own and included a cavity on the left side of an upper front tooth. When Coroner Mack supplied the teeth, Mrs. Olander made the identification. The autopsy brought forth this information: "Head is that of a female about 16 or 17 years. The age is determined by the wisdom teeth which have perforated the bone, but in life had likely not come through the gum. Long blonde hair is on the scalp. Several of the teeth have large cavities not filled ... All gums and soft spots are in advanced state of putrefaction ... The trunk is in an advanced state of disintegration, so that it is impossible to be sure that the trunk and head belong together. The sex is not possible to determine by outward examination. On opening up of the abdomen, it is possible to find the uterus. The organ is of natural size and easily distinguishable from the rest of the putrified mass. Nothing more could be learned by further examination, except that the arms had been taken out of the shoulder joint socket, and the legs sawed off at the lower third of the femur. From the examination, it is evident that this person died an unnatural death, but how and by whom cannot be determined by this examination."

Mrs. Olander was able to describe Jennie's association with Belle and to shed some additional light on Belle's personality. She had, after all, been a guest in Belle's home, which was more than most anyone else could claim. Jennie would have been 18 on the day that her body was discovered, and she was the little sister of Mrs. Olander, who was 23. "Jennie was only eight months old when my mother died," explained Mrs.Olander. "My father had known Mr. Sorensen for years; and when he married Belle, the young couple asked to be allowed to care for Jennie. Papa gave his consent but never relinquished claim to her." Jennie's sisters sometimes visited with her both in their own home and at the Sorensen home in Austin. This visiting continued until Belle, with Jennie, moved to Indiana. Two or three years later and about five years before her death, Jennie left Indiana for a month's visit at her father's house on Evans Avenue in Chicago. Although she seemed happy during her visit, she did not want to stay, preferring to return to Indiana and Belle. She told her sisters she liked Mrs. Gunness and wanted to remain living with her.

The next meeting of the sisters took place in LaPorte, shortly after Peter Gunness' tragic demise at the edge of the meat grinder. Although Belle did not notify Jennie's family of the death, they read about it in a Chicago newspaper. Mrs. Olander remembered this meeting: "I came out to LaPorte at that time and stayed the day, arriving in the morning and going back in the evening. I did not want to broach the subject of Mr. Gunness' death and waited, thinking she would speak, but she did not. It was perhaps half an hour after I entered the house that I spoke of Mr. Gunness' death. When I asked if it was Mr. Gunness who died, she said, 'Yes.' She asked how I learned of it. I told her I saw mention of it in the Chicago paper. She said, 'My, was it in the Chicago papers?' She asked me what it stated. I told her they seemed to think it was mysterious--that the papers spoke of it as a mysterious finding, that a sausage grinder had hit him. She laughed and made light of that. She said, 'Oh, no, there was nothing mysterious about it. This is the way it happened. He went to LaPorte in the morning to purchase a sausage grinder and saw one on the shelf that he wanted. He reached up to get it, it slipped and fell on his head and killed and they brought him home dead.'"

The last time Jennie's relatives saw her was two years before the fire. Her two sisters had been staying in nearby Kingsbury and were driven to the Gunness farm for a visit. They stayed less than an hour, listening to Jennie play the piano and visiting with the children, Myrtle, Lucy, and Philip. Mrs. Olander later explained, "I had no talk with Jennie alone on that visit. She just sat in with all of us. I asked Mrs Gunness if she wouldn't let Jennie come to visit us at some time and also let me hear from Jennie by mail. She said she would. That is the last time I saw Jennie or Mrs. Gunness or heard from either of them. I wrote several letter but got no answer to any of them. Mrs. Gunness never seemed anxious to have Jennie on friendly terms with us. We thought it was jealousy on Mrs. Gunness' part and fear that Jennie would get to liking staying with us. I thought Mrs. Gunness was a good, kindly woman. I always thought so until her home burned."

Jennie's sister had heard through a friend that Jennie was being sent to school in Fergus Falls, Minnesota. When she heard about the fire, she thought Jennie was safely away from home. A telegram from Sheriff Smutzer asked her to come to LaPorte because one of the bodies was believed to be that of her sister.

Jennie had another identifier, John Weidner, a LaPorte carriage house worker who had visited her at the Gunness farm. In a later deposition, he told of his friendship with Jennie: "I made Jennie's acquaintance two years ago. We were good friends. We never could have much conversation that was not heard by Mrs. Gunness. I have been in Mrs. Gunness' house. Jennie would play the piano, and we would talk, but Mrs. Gunness was always present." The last time he saw Jennie alive was about 10 days before the Christmas of 1906. She told him she was going to Los Angeles to school and would like him to visit her the following Sunday to say goodbye. "I went. I hired a cutter. When I got to Mrs. Gunness', I rapped and asked for Jennie. Mrs. Gunness had a kind of grin on her face and said, 'Why, Jennie has gone to Los Angeles.' After telling Weidner that Jennie had left the previous Wednesday, she invited him into the house. "I went in and sat down and she introduced me to a fellow who she said was her brother. It seemed as if the fellow couldn't talk English--anyway he didn't say much, and I couldn't understand him. I came home and picked up a LaPorte Herald in which it said Jennie Olson had gone with some professor to Los Angeles, California. After that when I asked her for Jennie's address, she always put me off in some way."

"About the middle of October, 1907," Weidner continued, "I met Mrs. Gunness, who said Jennie was going to stay in California, and that she had just sent Jennie $100. It was then I wrote Jennie, mailing the letter to Los Angeles, but the letter came back. When I told Mrs. Gunness this, she said Jennie was away from Los Angeles on vacation--perhaps in San Francisco. The way Mrs. Gunness watched Jennie and me, I thought Jennie knew something about the death of Mr. Gunness, something which Mrs. Gunness did not want her to tell." A similar story was told by Emil Greening of Oklahoma City, who had considered himself Jennie's suitor when he and his brother worked for Belle. "Jennie told me a good deal about herself when we were alone," he explained. "Then her mother decided to send her away to California with a professor, who was reported to have come after her, but whom I never saw. Jennie came to me and declared that she would never go. In the morning I did not see Jennie, and her mother told me that she was still asleep and did not want to be disturbed. I was sent on an errand late in the afternoon, and when I got back, I was told that Jennie had gone. I wrote to her, but I gave the two letters to Mrs. Gunness. I never received any answer, and finally I got so tired working around the place without Jennie that I left. I don't believe there ever was a professor, for I slept in the room next to Jennie's and I didn't hear any man's voice. Mrs. Gunness later told me that Jennie had left at 4 o'clock that same morning, but no one saw her leave and no one about the place ever saw the professor."

Greening said men from all over the country visited Belle. "A different man came nearly every week, and they always stayed at the house. She introduced them as her cousins and they came from Kansas, South Dakota, Wisconsin, and many from Chicago. Several were never seen to leave the place. Most of the men that came brought their trunks with them, but they rarely took the trunks away. We never knew when to expect these fellows, but they almost always had money. Mrs. Gunness was always careful to make the children stay away from her 'cousins,' who rarely tried to show them any affection.

"I never knew of Mrs. Gunness bestowing her affections upon any of her hired hands except Ray Lamphere," Greening explained. "So many men came and I saw so little of them that I can't remember many of them, but I distinctly remember Mr. Moo, who came from Chicago the day before Christmas, 1906. He was with Mrs. Gunness almost constantly. When he left, his trunks stayed behind and no one saw him go. It was several days before Mrs. Gunness admitted he was gone.

"Shortly afterwards Mrs. Gunness sent me to Michigan City (12 miles away) to get a horse that she said Moo had promised to give her. I took a day to make the trip. When I got to Michigan City, something was wrong and I was told to come back for the horse later, but when I returned to the farm, another 'cousin' who was there when I left was gone. In about two weeks, I was again sent to Michigan City and still there was no horse, but when I got back another 'cousin' was missing, and no one around the place had seen him leave.

"Moo's trunk was in the Gunness home on July 11, 1907, when I left the place. His wasn't the only one. There were about 15 other trunks and one room was packed full of all kinds of men's clothing. Mrs. Gunness said that the cousins had left their clothes and she wasn't certain that they would be back for them. In the light of what has happened recently, I can see that many bloody and mysterious things were done right under my nose."

Greening later said he thought Belle may have murdered three victims a month while he was there, although he knew no specifics. "While I was there, Mrs. Gunness had us dig up a large number of huge stumps on the farm, and when we refilled the hole, a spot was left. This would have been a good place for burying victims, and the officers should search these old stump holes." It seemed that Greening's mother, too, had an opinion. This she derived from a visit to the farm, where she observed Belle wearing a leather sack about the size of a man's hat around her waist. "Do you know there is over $5,000 in that sack," Belle reportedly told Mrs. Greening. Also during the visit, Mrs. Greening wandered toward the cellar door, only to be stopped by Belle, who said, "Don't do that. I never let anybody go into my cellar. That's private property." A conversation between the two, said in jest at the time but now appearing macabre, concerned the nearby pond. Mrs. Greening jokingly suggested that Belle might kill her, row her by boat into the pond, and throw her overboard. Belle's response was to turn "as white as a sheet" and fall back against a wall, only regaining her composure after several minutes. For that reason, Mrs. Greening believed there were bodies in the pond.

Perhaps the most poignant epitaph for Jennie came from the rural mailman on the McClung Road route. D. J. Hunter recalled the young girl this way: "I used to see her often. Late in the afternoon I would meet her driving home the cows. She was barefoot in the dusty road and wore a faded, torn dress that came only half way to her ankles, though she was a grown up girl. She had wispy hair and big blue eyes. She was shy and serious. I felt sorry for her and I always made it a point to speak to her. She would say 'hello' and her eyes would brighten. She seemed pleased to have any one take notice of her. At other times, I would see her working out in the garden. She had to work hard, poor girl, but once or twice just before time to drive home the cows, I would see her sitting, reading by the fence along the road, and I often wondered what book it was she read."

CHAPTER TEN

While the digging went on in LaPorte, the Chicago authorities pondered the possibility that Belle had left a grizzly trail of victims while living in Austin. This fear was prominent enough to require the personal supervision of Assistant Police Chief Herman Schuettler. As he looked at the developments in Indiana, Schuettler became convinced that Belle had murdered Mads Sorensen, her first husband, in 1900. He based his conviction on two elements of the Sorensen death: Belle's delay in getting medical attention for Mads and what seemed more pretense of grief than substance. When the summoned doctors arrived, Mads was already dead, and Belle's brief hysterical outburst now appeared like melodramatic acting. He did not, however, believe she had been on a killing spree while living in Austin.

"I don't believe she killed anybody else in Chicago," he stated. "She hardly could have committed such atrocious crimes as are attributed to her in LaPorte while her husband was living, for from all accounts, he was an honest man. There is no evidence that she endeavored to attract men into her net during the time that she resided in Austin. There is no evidence either that she conceived the idea at that time of answering matrimonial advertisements from persons who had tempting bank accounts, although we are still looking for evidence of that nature. She left Austin because, as the neighbors confirm, the children continually were taunting her two children with the accusation that their mother had murdered their father. It is known that such taunts were made, and what more natural under the circumstances that the woman should wish to remove from the scene of the crime?"

Cook County Coroner Peter Hoffman was at first a little less vocal in his opinions. "We are ready to do anything in our power to aid the Indiana authorities," he explained. "But I do not think anything will be gained by opening that grave (Sorensen's) again. It was opened once, and the conclusion reached that the man did not die as reported and that he was the victim of foul play. It looks as if the woman murdered him for the insurance. If this were the only case against her, I would order the grave opened. We might find some trace of poison in the dust that remains now. But there is so much evidence at hand in LaPorte that I will not go further into this nine-year-old death unless I am requested to do so by the LaPorte authorities."

Hoffman also reported these details from the undertaker who had embalmed Sorensen: "I used only two kinds of embalming fluid at the time of his death. One of them was the hexatone fluid, but whether it had any arsenic in it or not, I do not know. The other was the Oregon fluid, a formaldehyde preparation. I am almost certain that I used the Oregon in embalming Sorensen's body, for I used it nine times out of 10, especially on large persons, and Sorensen was a large man. I recall distinctly at the postmortem that the body contained blood, and only the formaldehyde solution could have preserved it in such shape." From this information, indicating no probable arsenic used in embalming, Hoffman concluded that any arsenic now found, even these years later, could point to poison.

The coroner also became a staunch supporter of those who believed Belle was still alive. It seemed that the current owners of the Alma Street property in Austin were going to see some digging on their property because Hoffman requested through police channels that the grounds and cellar be excavated. On May 9, he told reporters: "I am giving you a straight tip. Until 10 o'clock this morning, I was of the opinion that the woman's criminal career did not begin until she moved to LaPorte, but what I have since heard convinces me that there will be a Chicago angle to the story. We know that some persons who were supposed to have started back to Norway never got any further than Chicago, and it seems likely from what comes to me privately that some of them visited Mrs. Sorensen at her Alma

Street house. My information does not come from gossiping women or people who are inspired by malice. It comes from bona fide sources--people interested in relatives missing for years. They are not Chicagoans but strangers from all over the country and naturally their cases were not reported to the police until now. Of course, we may not dig after all, but until they furnish proof that Mrs. Gunness is dead or the other clews we have prove fruitless, I will insist on turning the ground."

This was a very difficult time for the owners of Belle's former home. The Nellis brothers were plumbers who had left Wisconsin to buy the Alma Street property in November of 1907, long after Belle had left the house. Now they were hearing about murder and mayhem in and about their new investment, and they were angry. They argued that the sensationalism was ruining the value of their property, and they threatened legal action to prevent any digging. To add to their aggravation, some newspaper reporters even announced that they themselves might start the digging.

Lt. Matthew Zimmer, commanding officer at the Austin police station, had the arduous task of convincing the Nellis' to allow the digging. One of the brothers, J. Nellis, was coaxed into admitting that he ought to know if there was "anything wrong" with his property. Later, he said no digging would be allowed unless police had some evidence that there was a body buried on the premises. "There is no demand either by me or by my neighbors that an investigation of that sort be made here," he said. "Neither are the residents of Austin excited, as they have been represented to be. As soon as there is any indication that something can be gained by turning this lot upside down, we will be glad to assist in turning it up."

On May 10, it was decided not to dig up the Austin property. With only rumors to support the digging, both the police and the coroner decided that a court order could not be obtained in the face of a threatened injunction against the search by the Nellis'. Not unless Belle was proved still alive or her victims proved traceable to Alma Street would the excavation necessity outweigh the damage that would be done to the Nellis property values. At the same time, it was decided not to exhume Mads Sorensen again, although no reason for this was officially stated. Still, all this did not prevent crowds from gathering outside the Nellis house, and the owners asked Lt. Zimmer for protection against any independent digging on the property. A police officer was stationed at the house just as, 60 miles away, some of the men of LaPorte were being paid to guard what was left on McClung Road.

Naturally, the two doctors who attended the dead Mads were trotted out to give their explanations of what happened in 1900. Each was inclined to blame the other for listing the cause of death as enlargement of the heart. Dr. J. B. Miller now thought the autopsy had not been thorough enough but said he deferred to Dr. Charles E. Jones' seniority in pronouncing death due to natural causes. Belle had told them that Mads complained of a headache and she had given him something procured from a druggist. When questioned at this later date, Miller said, "I told her then that perhaps the druggist made a mistake and gave her morphine instead of quinine, and I asked her for the paper to examine it, but she said she threw it away. I didn't have the experience then, but that circumstance looks pretty bad to me now. I now believe that he was poisoned and think a thorough search of the premises should be made. I had boarded with the woman for a time and suspected that she might have conducted a baby farm." Jones recalled the episode of the druggist's medicine, but added, "The circumstances of Sorensen's death were peculiar, but Miller was the family physician and I was guided largely by his opinion. Sorensen was a night watchman and had just come home from work. We found him dead on the top of the bed with all his clothes on. There was no evidence of a struggle, and he looked just as natural as in life. The relatives afterward complained of suspicious circumstances, but I lost track of the case."

If anyone had much doubt about Belle's guilt, he or she would have to explain away how Sorensen came to die so conveniently on the one day his wife could collect on two insurance policies. Only on this day did a $2,000 policy, which Sorensen was not renewing, and a new $3,000 policy overlap. One day sooner would have brought Belle only $2,000. One day later, she would have received only $3,000. As it turned out, she got $5,000.

Even without the knowledge of those insurance policies, some of the neighbors sensed a red flag in Mads' death. Mrs. H. Carsten of Alma Street offered this recollection: "Two hours before Sorensen's death, he was on the front porch and seemed to be in the best of health. After his death, the house was damaged by fire that started in the house next door. Mrs. Sorensen moved temporarily to Sophia Street, which place was also damaged by fire during her occupancy. Then she moved back into her house in Alma Street." A soon-to-die Sorensen's activities on the porch were also contained in some comments by a friend of Jennie Olson: "She (Belle) was dreadfully cruel to Jennie when they lived in Alma Street. The girl could not move from one room to another without getting Mrs. Sorensen's permission, and whenever she came out on the porch to talk with us, her mother came out and sat beside her, listening to every word we said and rebuking Jennie and dragging her back in the house if either of us happened to express any ideas or opinions that she did not like. The only day I remember of that she granted Jennie any freedom was the day she murdered her husband. I say murdered, because I believe she did kill him. I called for Jennie and asked if she could go with us to get apples. We were surprised when Mrs. Sorensen said Jennie could go. When we were out in front of the house, Mr. Sorensen was sitting on the porch. He had the two children in his arms and was trotting them up and down on his knees. He was as happy as could be, and I remember thinking afterward that he must be in good health and not the least bit sick. That was at 10 o'clock in the morning. We went to Ridgeland to gather apples. We got back at 5 o'clock in the afternoon. Sorensen was dead then. He had died at noon, and preparations were being made for the funeral. I remember that Dr. J.B. Miller entered the house and asked about the death. Dr. Miller used to room at the Sorensen home. Mrs. Sorensen told Dr. Miller that her husband had complained of a fearful headache and that she gave him a powder."

Whatever Belle did in Austin, that location never had the possibilities for murder that rural LaPorte had. In LaPorte, she had no nosy neighbors, acres of room, and the lure of a successful farm. There is every evidence that she was pleased with her move. As she wrote to one friend, "It is beautiful here in LaPorte, and if you visit me, you will never want to go away again."

CHAPTER ELEVEN

Matrimonial advertisements, which have reemerged in Europe since the break-up of the Soviet Union, are rare in the United States. But the 1990s have seen the blossoming here of what are known as "singles ads", which appear in the classified sections of many newspapers. While they seldom mention marriage, they are often paid for by people who have matrimony in mind. Modern ad-buyers do not openly appear as mercenary as those in earlier generations. For example, this advertisement, which came right to the point, dates back to a Boston newspaper in 1759: "To the ladies: Any young lady between the age of 18 and 23 of a middling stature, brown hair, regular features and a lively brisk eye; of good morals and not tinctured with anything that may sully so distinguishable a form possessed of 300 or 400 pounds entirely her own disposal and where there will be no necessity of going through the tiresome talk of addressing parents or guardians for their consent; such a one by leaving a line directed for A.W. at the British Coffee House in King Street appointing where an interview may be had will meet with a person who flatters himself he shall not be thought disagreeable by any lady answering the above description. Profound secrecy will be observ'd. No trifling answers will be regarded."

More than a century later, during Belle's era, immigrants who had left family and friends behind sometimes found themselves without opportunity to meet potential partners. Hence the appearance of what were called "lonely hearts" ads. In Belle's case, she sought out her own ethnic group, Scandinavians. This was evident in the men she attracted. The Norwegian daily newspaper in Chicago at that time, the Skandinaven, did carry such ads. The following three ads, reprinted at the time of the Gunness case, illustrate what was being printed:

"A bachelor, 28 years old, owner of farm in Canada, wishes to correspond with an honest woman of attractive appearance. Letters enclosing photographs will be answered first.

"A widower, 45 years old, wishes to become acquainted with a young woman or widow, between 25 and 40 years old, of Norwegian birth or descent. Good references required and will be given. Can give such a woman a good home, as I am in good financial circumstances. Write to this paper for my address.

"A farmer, 26 years old, living in North Dakota, wishes to correspond and become acquainted with a Scandinavian girl or widow. I am not a fortune hunter."

The editor of Skandinaven, Nicolay Grevstad, found an ad, written in Norwegian, and inserted by Belle on March 21, which read, "Wanted--A woman who owns a beautifully located and valuable farm in first class condition, wants a good and reliable man as partner in the same. Some little cash is required for which will be furnished first class security. Address C.H., Skandinaven office."

Grevstad said such ads were printed all the time in other newspapers and that there was no way to know any secret motive behind these appeals. "We do not print matrimonial bureau ads," he claimed. "We do print matrimonial ads from readers of the paper who are known to us to be reliable. There are many young Norwegian farmers in the Northwest who, after becoming well-to-do, want to marry but who have not had time to become acquainted with women. Such men advertise for wives occasionally and we believe that is perfectly legitimate." Any investigation of what Belle claimed in her ads would have found the facts to be true. She was a widow living in Indiana on a farm that she owned. She was what she said she was. Her hidden agenda was beyond belief.

The Chicago Tribune, which did not carry such ads, criticized the practice. Its front page for May 8, 1908, carried a large cartoon on the topic by John T. McCutcheon, later a Pulitzer Prize cartoonist, which depicted men, valises in hands, rushing into a black spider web labeled "Matrimonial Bureau." The cartoon carried a text taken from the famous Judge Kenesaw Mountain Landis' charge to a jury in a matrimonial case: "A newspaper man who takes the money for these advertisements knows that for a paltry 75 cents he is becoming the agent of crime. But I saw here during the trial and I saw the people who had been defrauded, and some of them were congenital inferiors. The witnesses for the most part formed a procession of mental derelicts who had been victimized by this scheme, and the question is, shall the laws be enforced for the future protection of this class of people as well as for the presidents of banks and the leaders of the bar?" Landis, who was at the time the U.S. District Judge for the Northern Illlinois District, would go on to become a respected commissioner of baseball credited with restoring the reputation of the game after the 1919 White Sox scandal.

The Tribune took another swipe at the ads on its editorial page the same day. It claimed that the ads were instruments of "serious criminal enterprise" that needed to be exposed to the public and that the LaPorte murder mystery would now give the public a good look at this danger. "Wherever in America people can read, the story of LaPorte will make its way," the editorial stated. "The remote mining camps in Alaska and the lumber camps in the northern wilderness, the lonesomest farms, ranches of the Far West, the plantations of the South, and the most ignorant districts of the great cities will each in their due time be full of the wonder and grewsome (sic) fascination of this mystery. The name of LaPorte will fix itself in the memory of at least a generation."

The office of the U.S. District Attorney in Chicago became interested in the problem, and Assistant District Attorney Seward Shirer took charge of investigating the "cupid maters." After gathering evidence, with the help of the postoffice, on more than 20 mating bureaus, Shirer announced on May 7:

"We have conclusive evidence to prove certain so-called matrimonial agencies have sent young girls to disorderly places in the red light district. The revelations in LaPorte have been such that we almost believe different alleged 'matcher up' bureaus have sent men and women to such murder establishments as the one thought to have been run by Mrs. Gunness in LaPorte. This probably was done in order to rob them of the few cents they may have had in their pockets. I believe the managers of the bureaus will go to any depth in order to wring a few pennies from these poor persons who answer their alluring advertisements. The persons who answer these advertisements are an unintellectual set and could be murdered and put out of the way without much danger of exposure. While I do not mean to say all matrimonial agencies do this class of work--murder on wholesale style--I insist all are illegal, and there is no telling how far each manager will go in his desire to secure all the money he can."

The postman on Belle's route knew she was a prolific correspondent: "I would deliver from one to four at her house with her papers every morning," he claimed. "And she would go to the postoffice always once and often two and even three times the same day to ask for letters that came after the morning delivery. Before the rural route was put out that road, she nearly always called at the office twice and usually three times a day. The few days that I had not letters for her, she would seem provoked. She would frown when there was only one. But if nothing annoyed her, she was friendly. The first morning after her mailbox was put up she came down to meet me. The ground was covered with snow and she wanted me to get out and hand the letters to her at the gate. She was very angry when I didn't. But in a few days she asked me to see her new barn. I was rushed, but to please her, I let her show me through it. She told me the names of her horses and asked me to come again and bring my wife."

An example of the bait that Belle threw out to men was contained in a letter she wrote in Norwegian to a man who answered one of her ads: "Dear Sir: As I some time ago received from you a letter in answer to my advertisement in the Scandinaven, I will with pleasure answer the same. The reason I waited for some time is that there have been other answers in the same advertisement. As many as 50 have been received, and it has been impossible to answer all. I have picked out the most respectable, and I have decided that yours is such. First I will tell you that I am a Norwegian and have been in this country for 20 years. I live in Indiana, about 59 miles from Chicago and one mile north of LaPorte. I am the sole owner of a nice home, pretty location. There are 75 acres of land, also all kinds of crops, improved land, apples, plums, and currants. I am on a boulevard road and have a 12-room house, practically new, a windmill, and all modern improvements, situated in a beautiful suburb of Chicago, worth about $15,000. All this is pretty near paid for. It is in my own name. I am alone with three small children, from 5 to 11 years old. The smallest is a little boy. The two largest are girls, all frisky and well. I lost my husband by accident five years ago and have since tried to get along as well as I could with what help I could hire. I am getting tired of this and I have found that it is not well to trust others with so much. It is too much for me to look after things, and things are not as I want them anyway. My idea then is to take a partner to whom I can trust everything and as we have no acquaintance ourselves I have decided that every applicant I have considered favorably must make a satisfactory deposit of cash or security. I think that is the best way for parties to keep away grafters who are always looking for such opportunities, as I have had experience with them, as I can prove. Now if you think that you are able to some way put up $1,000 cash, we can talk matters over personally. If you cannot, is it worthwhile to consider? I would not care for you as a hired man, as I am tired of that and need a little rest in my home and near my children. I will close for this time. With friendly regards, Mrs. P. B. Gunness."

This letter was sent to Carl Peterson of Waupaca,Wisconsin, a fireman in a veterans' home. Peterson, it turned out, did not have the money Belle was looking for. His letter, expressing regret for his financial lack but offering himself as "respectable and worthy in every way," arrived in LaPorte after the fire. Peterson, therefore, became one of a number of people congratulating themselves on having escaped interment in Belle's private graveyard.

Another escapee was Peter Frederickson of Janesville, Wisconsin, who answered a matrimonial ad placed by Belle shortly after the death of her first husband, Sorensen. Belle visited Frederickson and learned that he had $1,000 in life insurance and a home worth $1,500 free and clear of mortgage. She told him Janesville was too small and encouraged him to join her in Chicago. Frederickson, who died later from natural causes, was warned off Belle by Peter Gunness' mother. Ignoring the warning, Frederickson planned a wedding supper until learning his friends refused to attend. At this point, he did break off the association with Belle, thereby no doubt saving his life. Why Peter Gunness then dared to go where Frederickson feared to tread is unknown.

Mrs. John Olsen came forth with a story about her close call 21 years ago when she was only three years old:. "My mother was not able to take care of me, and as Mrs. Gunness, then Mrs. Sorensen, had no children, arrangements were made for me to make my home with her. I lived with her for three years and was cruelly treated. It was her practice to take newborn babies, receiving $1,000 each for their care and keeping them until she could rid herself of them conveniently. She never had a child of her own in her life." Mrs. Olsen, the former Emma Anderson, now lived on North Campbell Avenue in Chicago and offered her opinion that Belle was alive and headed back to Norway.

Another close call was related by a young girl who, with another girlfriend, almost went to visit Jennie Olson the week she was murdered. This story was told by Harriet Danielson, who lived in Chicago on Chicago Avenue:

"I think it was about Sept. 19, 1906, that Jennie wrote to me from LaPorte. I tried to find the letter for the detective today, but somehow it has been mislaid. I remember perfectly what she said. She told me what a beautiful home they had down there, how much money she had, and what a delightful time we could have together. She said her mother urged me to come, too. This was the last letter she wrote to me. Before that, she sent me at least three other letters begging me to come and visit her as long as I liked. It was just an accident that I did not go. A friend of mine did not want me to; there was some pretext or excuse for me not to go at the time, and so I wrote Jennie saying I could not visit her at that time. I got no reply. I afterward wrote again and then again. I never heard of her again. Nobody else ever did, and I believed the last line she ever penned was in the letter to me. Had I gone down there, I am firmly convinced the woman would have murdered me."

Escapes do not come much closer than the one achieved by George Anderson of Tarkio, Missouri. Belle's letters lured him to the farm, but he neglected to bring enough money to meet Belle's requirements. She told him that, before they could wed, she would like him to pay off her mortgage. Before he could return home to collect more cash, he was spared becoming a McClung Road corpse by being a light sleeper. One night while sleeping in the farmhouse, he awoke to see Belle standing over him with a flickering candle. Startled, Anderson yelled out and Belle ran from the room. Anderson quickly dressed and just as quickly left the farm and walked as far as the train station, back to Missouri to ponder what it all meant until the newspapers brought the stories of Belle's true activities and the realization of a brush with death.

CHAPTER TWELVE

What kind of woman takes candle in hand, creeps silently through the darkness down into a cellar, unlocks a basement room, stares at a table holding a dead or unconscious human being, and then bends over the table wielding a surgeon's knife to cut away arms, legs, head? What is missing in a person who can drop bloody body parts into a vat of quicklime and then stuff them into gunny sacks? What is added to someone who can drag gore-filled sacks into the black night and plant them like rose bushes in the backyard?

Belle was a contradiction even in physical description. "She impressed me as a big, rough Norwegian woman, but I noted that she was shrewd," said Arthur Williams, who traded his farm in LaPorte for Belle's Austin property. She was "a coarse, fat, heavy-featured woman 48 years of age, with a big head covered with a mop of mud-colored hair, small eyes, huge hands and arms, and a gross body with difficulty supported on feet qrotesquely small," stated the New York Times a week after the fire. H. W. Worden, the attorney for Ray Lamphere, described her this way: "Mrs. Gunness was rather masculine in appearance. She was about 5 feet 10 inches tall and weighed between 210 and 225 pounds. Her hands and feet were large. She had a peculiar disposition."

Photographs, however, do not depict her as particularly coarse or masculine-looking; and at least one acquaintance saw her physical shape less imposing. Dr. J. G. Campbell, who served at the Methodist church attended by Myrtle, Lucy, and Philip, denied that she was as large a woman as the newspapers were saying. His estimate of her weight was about 150 pounds, and he thought her attractive in appearance and quiet in disposition.

One thing was sure. The woman had acquired an impressive number of possessions. In addition to the 48 acres, she owned a house insured for $1,500 and household goods insured for $800. Her farm housed sows, a boar, stoats, heifers, calves, a bull, chickens, horses, a foal, and a Shetland pony. Equipment included wagons, a cultivator, planter, harrow, binder, plow, harnesses and saddles, saws, ladders, wheelbarrow, buggy, pony cart, bales of wire, and all sorts of buckets and rope. So, even if her appearance was merely average, her wealth as an unattached female was appealing and exceptional for that time. A few other possessions, though, told of other interests: Among the ruins of the house were found a partially burned book on hypnosis and a few pages from a book on anatomy.

The house ruins also gave up a scrap of a letter in Belle's handwriting. The only distinguishable words were: "I seem changed since that time. Despair and terror are with me in the last few weeks. I cannot understand why."

She could not understand why. With bodies buried around her, a human butcher shop in the basement, and the blood of babies on her hands, she could not understand why. "People would sometimes say that she was insane," was the post-fire comment of Miss Cora Larson, who lived next door to Belle in Austin. "Mrs. Gunness, or Mrs. Sorensen, as she was called then, was a mighty peculiar woman. Whenever she talked to you, she would close her eyes. The children of the neighborhood always thought there was something uncanny about her and refused to go near her if they could help it." A slightly different memory belonged to Dr. Charles Jones, one of the doctors called in after Sorensen's death. Jones wondered if Belle was a religious fanatic who self-hypnotized herself into crime. "I remember her well as a religious fanatic type," he said. "The sudden wealth, comparatively speaking, that came to her at her husband's death, I believe, may have had for her an irresistible suggestion of the ease with which money might be obtained."

"I never heard anybody say anything good about her," Miss Larson explained. "She was so sweet to everybody that it was sickening. She fawned over people and seemed to want to love them to death. That was the way she acted toward strangers. But at home everybody in the house was afraid of her. She had nothing to do with the neighbors and had no real friends. Her husband was afraid of her, I know. She used to go out late at night and would be gone for hours at a time. Nobody ever knew where she was. She was peculiar in her actions about her home. She would go wandering about the yard, acting without purpose and moony and preoccupied. She was mean to Jennie. Nobody in the neighborhood thought she was mother of the children who were at the house. She had plenty of money most of the time. Folks said she got children to take care of from almost every direction. People didn't like her at all."

The LaPorte Herald thought Belle "betrays the most marvelous characteristics ever known in a criminal" in her letters to Andrew Helgelein: "At times she devotes a page to appreciation of the quality of sincerity in human conduct. She descants of honesty as a virtue to be cultivated, rhapsodizes on love and friendship, preaches religion and records her detestation of falsehood. With the blood of many human beings on her hands, she posed in her letters as a model of humility. She was the lone, unprotected widow with a comfortable little fortune who must needs seek protection from among the hardy men of her own race.

"She was the clinging vine in her letters to Andrew Helgelein. She needed him. She sent him four-leafed clovers and her heart's love. She subtly roused his jealousy with tales of the perfidious Lamphere. She sent him pressed roses and wrote tearfully of the Norwegian Christmas. She drew pen portraits of herself and Andrew snugly ensconced by the big red blazing stove in her back parlor next to the slaughter chamber, where she cut up all her victims. In the meantime, she murdered, cut up, and buried her niece, Jennie Olson. She writes of heaven and eternal bliss, the reward of well-spent lives, meanwhile sharpening her dissecting knives preparatory to contemplated butcheries of human beings. The letters cover nearly two years.

They run the gamut of emotion and veiled cupidity. They are the most extraordinary documents in the light of this woman's known crimes that ever were printed."

Although the above information about Belle's relationship to Jennie is not correct, nor is the generally accepted location of the slaughter chamber near the parlor, the letters to Andrew are truly masterpieces of manipulation. A selection of them can be read in an addendum toward the end of this book, but a few excerpts tell worlds about the woman's deviousness. "I long to know you better," she coos to Andrew while repeatedly urging him to come to her. She entices him with the warmth of her feelings for him, the size of her farm, their mutual dislike of Swedes, and even with food: "We will have some good Norwegian coffee, waffles, and I will always make you a nice 'cream pudding' and many other good things." She is most adamant about secrecy: "... do not tell a word to anybody up there before you go ... do not let anyone know anything of what we write about ... Remember the advice I gave you in regard to your money. Do not tell anything even to your dearest. They could soon tell it to someone else, and it sems as if one cannot fully trust anyone nowadays ... Let it be ... a little secret between us two and no one else, not so?"

A Pinkerton man assigned to the case gave this analysis of Belle's thinking: "She killed her first husband, Mads Sorensen, in Austin, because she was tired of him, and she killed her second husband, Peter S. Gunness, at the farm here for the same reason. The first murder had taught her how easy it was to rid herself of persons whom she did not desire to have about her--by murdering them. It has been my experience that there is much of the tiger in the human heart, and the taste of blood in those first two murders awoke in Mrs. Gunness a desire for more and aroused a ferocity which might have lain dormant all her life if she had been happily married in the first place. As she lay there, sleepless, in the bedroom on the second floor of the murder mansion thinking over the manner in which her plans for the death of Gunness had worked out to the letter, the brute in her arose to the surface."

The Pinkerton detective called her "a woman absolutely without fear" whose nature "delighted in intrigue and the exercise of cunning." He accused her of developing a blood lust, a "mania," which required that she "hacked and hewed until the insanity within her was temporarily gratified." It was this sick drive, he contended, that prevented her from just burying the bodies whole. Had she done so, any discovery of human remains might have been laid at the doorstep of former farm owner Dr. B. R. Carr, who had a family cemetery there. When her "murder lust" combined with "her greed for money", the detective found her obsessively drawn to the need to advertise for more victims.

Dr. C. P. Bancroft of Concord, New Hampshire, president of the Medico-Psychological Association, believed Belle was doomed from birth: "She was undoubtedly a degenerate. The argument is that if a person's body is irregular or unsymmetrical, the chances are the brain will be formed badly. Mrs. Gunness had a peculiarly shaped head, a very large frame, and small feet, and her eyes were irregular. These malformations would indicate a similar malformation of mind. This malformation may express itself in various ways. A thorough examination of Mrs. Bella Gunness during life might have given more opportunity to base conclusions on. But from a cursory examination, I judge that Mrs. Gunness was a degenerate."

The idea that physical appearance reveals a corresponding mental state was the latest theory in the study of the mind. The originator of this doctrine would also be heard from eventually, all the way from Italy. But it was a Frenchman who was most often mentioned when trying to pin a label on Belle. He was Gilles de Laval, Baron de Retz, marshal of France and a patron of the arts, who was born in 1396 and was considered brilliant until rumors of his depravity finally led to his arrest in 1440, after which he was convicted of kidnapping, torturing, and murdering more than 100 children. He confessed to using their blood and hearts in satanic rites, and he was executed. He became the prototype of the villain in the 1697 story by Charles Perrault, who had his central character murder six wives and hide their bodies in a locked room. A seventh wife, Fatima, escaped and even outlived her evil husband. The story was called "Barbe Bleue," the notorious Bluebeard.

CHAPTER THIRTEEN

Because Belle's photograph appeared in newspapers across the country, it was inevitable that people thought they saw her. One of those occurrences caused New York police so much embarrassment that trying to avoid a repeat somewhere else could have allowed the real Belle to escape because authorities were now reluctant to detain any Belle lookalikes.

This serious mistake occurred May 9 after the conductor on the New York Central Railway's Atlantic Express traveling in New York was told by some traveling men that they were sure a fellow passenger was Mrs. Gunness. The conductor telegraphed ahead to Syracuse, New York, police. The train came in to Syracuse at 1 a.m. and two detectives boarded and went to the woman's berth, where she was sleeping. She was abruptly awakened and told to dress. Because the train would not wait, the detectives rode with her to the next station, Utica, New York, where they all got off. The shock of the nighttime arrest and the fright from learning the police believed her to be Belle Gunness combined to make the woman at first speechless. Finally, regaining her composure, she identified herself as Mrs. L.A. Heerin of Chicago, whose husband had died in that city January 1. In mourning, she had gone East to stay with a brother at Cooperstown, Pennsylvania. She was now on a trip with her mother to visit her sister in New York. She had certain papers with her that supported her claim.

When Mrs. Heerin and her mother, Mrs. Lucy Burton, reached their New York destination, they went to the home of their sister and daughter, Mrs. Charles P. Rockefeller on West 40th Street. Now recovered from being pulled from a sleeping car in the middle of the night, they began to mull over possible legal action against the railroad and the police in Syracuse and Utica. "There was not the slightest excuse for taking me into custody," Mrs. Heerin argued. "I do not answed the description of Mrs. Gunness in any particular. (Both, however, were described as stout and Mrs. Heerin had one gold tooth, where Belle had several.) I shall never forget the terrible sensation that came over me when I saw the heads of two men poked into my berth. I thought at first the train had been held up by robbers. When the officers showed their badges and said I would have to go with them, I was still more alarmed. Of course, I felt sure there must be some mistake, but when I heard I was suspected of being Mrs. Gunness, I felt as if I should die of horror."

While the New York police were in trouble, the Chicago police were continually following up Belle "sightings." One such occurred at Buchbinder's restaurant on Van Buren Street, where "Belle" and a man left hurriedly after seeing a newspaper story about the LaPorte murders. At 9 a.m. a man and a woman entered Buchbinder's after alighting from a Rock Island train. A waitress, May Wagner, took their orders for two steaks and handed them a newspaper with articles about the murders and a picture of Belle. The man looked at the paper, threw it down, and both left in a hurry. The waitress and several other employees thought the woman resembled the photograph in the newspaper. "Belle" was also seen at Heibel's restaurant at Jackson Boulevard and Halsted Street and on 41st Street and West Madison Street. An interesting, but untraceable, claim was that a Chicago funeral director named Hall or Ball, who was a personal friend of LaPorte Sheriff Smutzer, was seen on Cottage Grove Avenue with a woman who was either Belle or her twin. Smutzer could have had such a friend because he had been in the funeral business himself for many years before becoming sheriff.

The sheriff meanwhile was getting letter after letter in connection with the case. One came from Josef Hearst, a cart driver, who claimed to have driven a suspicious couple on the afternoon the day after the fire. He said he drove them from the Depot of the Lake Erie and Western Railway station to the Grand Rapids and Indiana Railway station, where they purchased tickets for Berne, Indiana. "I have been reading in the papers of the murders in your town," he wrote. "I am a drayman, and last Wednesday a man came to us and wanted us to haul a sick woman from the Erie depot to the Grand Rapids and Indiana station. He acted sneaky about it. He was about 6 feet tall, light complexion, dark hair, dark mustache, weighed about 180 pounds. He had a woman on a stretcher. It was a large woman, weighing about 225 pounds. The man said they were from South Dakota, but did not say where they were going. They went out on the Grand Rapids and Indiana road, and I learned they went to Berne, Indiana. From the way they acted, I think the woman was Mrs. Gunness trying to make her getaway. I don't think she was really sick but pretending. Her face was all wrapped up in cloths."

A couple of days later, the Pittsburg police were looking for Belle after she was reported seen on the Pennsylvania railroad. Conductor C. D. Burlingham said the woman boarded at Alliance, Ohio, and so convinced was he that she was Belle that he wired ahead to the police at East Liverpool, Ohio. An officer saw the woman but refused to arrest her after the recent mistake made by railroad personnel and police in New York. The train went on and got into Pittsburg at 6:40 a.m., with Burlingham assigning his brakeman to follow the woman. But she got on a streetcar, whose number was not noticed, and disappeared.

Still another train sighting came from Texas. A woman answering Belle's description traveled in a pullman from St. Louis to Fort Worth, with ticket of original departure from New Albany, Indiana. Both the conductor and the Fort Worth station agent believed she was Belle although she spent most of her time in her berth and was thought to be taking morphine. They believed Belle was heading for Mexico.

While sightings continued across the country, theories and strange stories abounded in LaPorte. Wesley Fogle, the appointed executor of the Gunness estate, thought Ray Lamphere was innocent but that another man aided Belle in the murders. "I don't pretend to try to tell who he is," he said, "but I believe she had a falling out with her partner in crime and he set fire to the house." Fogle spoke of a recent Sunday when Belle tried desperately to find Lamphere. To Fogle, it was apparent that Belle was not afraid of Lamphere. Another LaPortean, John Lower, told of Belle's appearance in his hardware store the previous summer with a man who looked like a farmer and was introduced as Belle's husband. Although Lower could not remember exactly what the man looked like, he did remember Belle's strange comment about her living in LaPorte and her husband living in Minnesota. Still others clung to the idea that the doctor who once lived on the property had a perfectly legitimate graveyard there. The corpses of Jennie Olson and Andrew Helgelein, however, were too recently deceased to support that idea.

Another story came from Alexander Winkrantz, a farmer, who went to the Gunness farm shortly before the fire to see a horse he was thinking about buying. Belle tried to persuade him to stay the night, but he fortunately refused. Still another tale told by Miss Carrie Garwood, who taught Myrtle and Lucy in the Quaker school near the farm. "On the morning of April 27 (the day before the fire), I noticed that the two little girls of Mrs. Gunness came into the schoolroom crying," she said. "Their cheeks were swollen from weeping and they seemed in great distress. I called Myrtle to me and asked her if she was in trouble. She replied that she and her sister had been given a terrible beating by their mother that morning. It was the first time I had ever seen the children behaving so and I was surprised. I pursued the questioning and Myrtle told me that she and her sister had started to play toward the cellar of the Gunness house. Mrs. Gunness rushed after them before they had reached the bottom of the stairway and dragging them back had given both a terrible beating. I asked the children if they had been forbidden to go down into the cellar and they said they had but that they forgot the injunction. In the light of recent developments, it seems to me that the action of the woman may have had a terrible significance."

Then an old-time LaPortean spoke up saying that she did not believe the little boy found in the cellar, named Philip, was Belle's son. It was her contention that the boy was born after Peter Gunness' death. "One night a woman came from somewhere," the oldtimer said. "When she came, Mrs. Gunness did not have any baby, but when the woman went away, Mrs. Gunness exhibited a baby and claimed to be the mother of it. In my opinion, it was not the child of Mrs. Gunness." This tale-bearer claimed to be a close observer of the Gunness household, saying, "The Gunness children were wonderfully well-behaved children considering the coarse, masculine woman who had charge of them. They went to the Methodist Sunday School every Sunday with a little cart and pony." Speaking of the children, someone suggested that one of their dogs, a collie named Prince, might be used to determine if the body of Belle had really been recovered. The dog was still on the farm being cared for by Joseph Maxson, who agreed that the dog's reaction when it saw the body might prove something one way or the other. Before the theory could be tested, though, the dog disappeared.

Even those people who had no theories had their curiosity. Livery owners were booked to capacity, forming a sort of horse-drawn bus line from the center of LaPorte to the farm.

LaPorte is the seat of LaPorte County. Because the murders took place outside the city, the county was placed in charge of the investigation. The county commissioners were William P. Miller, Charles Baumgartner, and John Terry, who agreed that offering a reward might help solve the mysteries surrounding the case. They wanted to offer as much as $5,000 but were limited by law to no more than $500.

An attempt to clear up the identities of the dead was made by tracing the watches found on the property. Women's watches and men's timepieces were traced all the way to the retail outlets, but no one could tell to whom they were sold. One possible identification came from a neigbor, Swan Nicholson, who mentioned that two of Belle's farm hands had disappeared. One was Olaf Lindbom, who arrived to help out Belle after Gunness died. Nicholson's story, which later gained credibility, was this: "He was a young fellow about 30 years old, fresh from Norway, seemed to be liked by Mrs. Gunness. I don't think he answered any of her matrimonial advertisements, but she was so kind to him that I guess he finally got to thinking he would marry her. He began to look upon himself almost as the real owner of the place, but soon there came some sort of separation between them, and right after that, Lindbom went out of sight. I asked her where he was, and she said, 'Oh, you know, he is a good Norwegian and went to the old country to see the king crowned.' Another man got his job, but he only stayed about three months, and then he disappeared. That was in August three years ago."

CHAPTER FOURTEEN

In an effort to lay to rest any doubts about Belle's death, a man experienced in the mining operation of sifting and washing for gold was installed in the yard to sort through the debris for any gold that might have come from Belle's teeth. Louis Schultz set up his "cradle" and went to work. In a further attempt to compare the body in the cellar with with the size of a live Belle, detectives learned that Belle wore a size 9 shoe, and they were asking stores about her corset measurements.

One question was answered. In answer to a query, the head of the Lutheran college at Fergus Falls, Minnesota, said Jennie Olson had never attended the school. The college had never had any sort of communication from either Jennie or Belle.

More, too, was learned about the Helgelein case. Joshua Dorner, a farmer near the Gunness property, said in a deposition that a stranger approached him at about 10 a.m. one morning the past January and asked directions to the Gunness farm. The man, of medium height but heavy set, wore an expensive overcoat. He said his plans were to return from the farm that evening to Michigan City, where he had just arrived by streetcar. Dorner said the man resembled Andrew Helgelein. Definite identification of Helgelein's presence in LaPorte came from Frank Mack, cashier at the First National Bank, who said Belle appeared at the bank January 6 with a man she identified as Helgelein. The man had bank certificates totaling $2,800, which he wanted to cash. Mack refused even after Belle said she would endorse them. Mack said he was told the money was needed for a real estate deal and that the couple would take as little as $1,500 if he would agree to advance that amount. To a plainly upset Belle, Mack explained that it would take four or five days to get vertification of funds from the bank in Aberdeen, South Dakota. When this was achieved, the couple returned to the bank January 14, and Belle insisted on cash rather than the cashier's check that Mack offered them. At the time, Helgelein mentioned that he had been sick and that Belle had been caring for him. Mack said he never saw Helgelein alive again. But he had received two letters from Asle Helgelein, inquiring about his brother's whereabouts. Following up on this inquiry, Mack asked Belle about Andrew. She said he had gone to Chicago, from where he was planning to visit New York and probably return to Norway for a visit. Mack looked at the body in the morgue and decided the contour of the face and head matched that of the missing man. Shortly after Helgelein's arrival, Belle paid a $700 lien for an addition on the farmhouse. The lien was held by Harry Ritcher, who sold building materials. Ritcher said Belle had also purchased small amounts of lime from him during the past year.

Another of Belle's letters to Helgelein, this one dated December 16, 1907, was translated: "My dear Andrew: I am lonesome. I need help. I need a good strong man to help me. We have been true to each other. I put my confidence in you. I would depend on you more than any king in the world. How happy we will be when I see you. Come as soon as you can. Sell everything you can. Don't put your trust in the banks; that always makes trouble. Bring your money on your body. Sew it on your clothes. We must have some little secrets together. Don't tell anybody. Buy a good revolver to protect yourself with and when you come, we will have the prettiest and happiest country home in northern Indiana. I pray to God that He may bless us and my troubles may be over. My dear faithfullest friend on earth. Mrs. P.S. Gunness."

Meanwhile, the bodies from the cellar were examined by four doctors. Dr. Meyer and Dr. Wilcox were joined in the investigation by Dr.J. L. Gray and Dr. H. H. Long. Meyer, who was reportedly disgusted by the rumors of the condition of the bodies released his findings:

"1.Adult, head missing, neck burned and charred to seven cervical vertebra, left arm burned off to upper third, right arm burned off at shoulder and found separate and badly burned; piece of hand remaining was so badly burned that to detect evidences of 'manicuring' was out of the question; right leg off at knee and missing; left foot burned off at ankle and missing; all flesh gone below knee on left leg; right side of chest and abdomen burned deeply and bones showing; fat on abdomen two inches thick; stomach empty (stomachs of other bodies also empty); back of chest burned away as far as hips; the front of the woman and front of the boy, who was clasped in the woman's arms, were not burned like the backs, because the boy was lying face downward on the breast of the woman; back part of legs of woman were burned worse than the front.

"2. Boy, legs burned off at knee and missing; frontal bone burned through; posterior three-fourths being intact; no fracture or penetrating wounds of skull; worst burns in back; spinal column exposed all the way down and bones burned; both arms were burned off at the shoulders and missing.

"3. Girl, lower jaw burned across; right arm burned off at shoulder and left arm at wrist, both missing; part of intestines and stomach consumed.

"4. Girl, mostly burned in front; frontal bone burned through and separated from body; bones separated from flesh at touch; both feet off at ankle and right arm at shoulder, both missing; remnants of skull show no signs of fracture."

Dr. Gray made these additional observations on the body of the woman: "With the body but disconnected was an adult right arm burned and shrunken and fingers contracted on the palm. Clutched in the hand was a piece of burned cloth ... An adult hand and about one-third of forearm of the left side was with the body and on the third finger was found a gold ring with a small diamond set with engraving 'P.S. to J.S. Aug.22 - 94' and a gold band ring engraved on the inside 'P.G. to J.S. 3-5-95' ... The heart was found to be in distole, hard, and all four cavities filled with blood clots. The lungs appeared normal except cooked ... The body was free of decomposition." Dr. Long had these additional comments on the body supposed to be Lucy's: "No part of remnants of body showed wounds of any character as far as could be determined ... On third finger was found a plated ring containing three small sets, the two outer red stones and the middle a pearl or representation of pearl. From the condition of the body cause of death could not be determined nor was identification possible."

The startling part of Dr. Long's analysis came from his comments about the adult female body: "The bones of the woman that was found in the fire are not those of a large muscular bony person, which was Mrs. Gunness. Then there are certain marks of refinement apparent in this corpse even though it is badly burned. Mrs. Gunness was a coarse woman. I would also take it that this person in life was younger than Mrs. Gunness, who was 49 years old ... Then we found the one hand that was not burned to appear smaller than that of Mrs. Gunness, while the fingernails appeared to have been manicured. This was not the case with Mrs. Gunness' fingernails, I am told."

As badly burned as those bodies were, they had more substance than those unearthed in the yard. So authorities were struggling to identify those remains in a variety of ways. Letters became a chief indicator of identities. For example, E. J. Theilson, 45, a wealthy retired stock dealer from Minneapolis, was a suspected victim. Missing for about a year, Theilson was similar in appearance to the man seen with Belle by James Lower, the harness dealer. But the primary reason for suspecting that Belle murdered Theilson was explained by J. A. Warren, a Minneapolis detective who was in LaPorte to investigate any Gunness-Theilson connection: "I think he answered the same advertisement in the Minneapolis Times of August 8, 1906, that brought Helgelein to the widow's home. We know he corresponded with her for some time and that the acquaintance began in this way. That is shown by his statements to his relatives and letters he received from her. There are a number of them written in affectionate language."

Other possible victims were connected either by proximity to the farm or a link to a matrimonial agency. Edward Canary, 19, who disappeared July 6, 1906, from a farm near Belle at Pine Lake, had been living with his mother, Mrs. J. M. Canary. She said her son was working for a farmer on Pine Lake Avenue near McClung Road. Angered by something, he left without picking up his pay and had not been seen or heard from since. She did not know if he had been acquainted with Belle. While Canary was certainly working close enough to Belle, there were other circumstances to be considered before blaming Belle for this one. The young man was considered "very peculiar" and was often in trouble, including suspected arson in a cottage fire. He was believed to be alive by his cousin, L.T. Regan, principal at Sherman School, who thought the young man was probably missing for other reasons. A matrimonial ad connection was made in the case of Wakefield Barry, 50, who disappeared two years before the fire from West Monterey, Pennsylvania. An ex-detective from that town wrote that a woman very like Belle had visited Barry after answering an ad. After this woman left, Barry remained in town a few days and then disappeared.

Missing women were also brought to the attention of investigators. One of the more likely possibilities was Mrs. Anna Tilleman Groeger of Kenosha, Wisconsin. She disappeared after writing relatives that she was going to rest on a farm near LaPorte.

By now, the sheer scope of the mystery, involving the number of bodies and the fate of Mrs. Gunness, was mind boggling. People tried to compare it to something that had already taken place. Inevitably, the comparison between Belle and Kate Bender arose. Newspapers received many letters suggesting the two women were one and the same.

The Bender family arrived in America from Germany in 1871 and opened a small store near Independence, Kansas. Father, mother, son, and daughter murdered people during seances in which the daughter, named Kate, was the medium.

Seated in a dark room expecting to communicate with the spirit world, the victim was hit from behind a curtain with a hammer. Just to make sure he or she was dead, the throat was slit. Stripped of its valuables, the body was buried at night. Discovery, just as in the Gunness case, came about through the efforts of a victim's brother. It occurred on May 4, 1873, when Dr. William H. York's brother traced him as far as the Bender's store and there spotted something that had belonged to his brother. Before action could be taken against them, however, the Benders disappeared. Ironically, the fate of Kate was learned only during the summer of searching for Belle. The publicity of the Gunness case coincided with the illness of a man whose guilty conscience finally became intolerable and led to a confession. As shocking and gruesome as the deed of the Benders were, they were surpassed by Belle in both number of victims and nationwide horror.

As Sunday, May 10, approached, authorities in LaPorte anticipated an onslaught of curious visitors to the farm. This prospect was based on the unprecedented activity in the small town even during the week. The livery service was stretched to the limit, and people were sleeping on cots in the hallways of hotels. The LaPorte Herald made these predictions for Sunday: "From every nearby city, town, and hamlet comes word that hundreds of morbid curiosity seekers are preparing to make an excursion to LaPorte to view the scenes of the world's greatest criminal case and to discuss the story of the new Lucretia Borgia. The atrocities of the Gunness murders will be rehashed and retold, new theories will be advanced and each man will try to convince his neighbor that he has the only true ... explanation." Arrangements, therefore, were made to place guards in the ruins of the house itself but to leave the rest of the farm open to visitors. No one, though, foresaw what would take place on McClung Road that Sunday

CHAPTER FIFTEEN

It was "believed to be without parallel in the United States," according to the Chicago Tribune reporter who was present at the Gunness farm on Sunday, May 10. It was "an organized feast of the morbid and curious." Some 15,000 people converged on LaPorte by any means of transportation they could find. The well-to-do came in their made-to-order automobiles. Whole families arrived by interurban car. Even more came by train. The entrepreneurs were ready for them.

It was like some grand holiday outing, with postcards, ice cream and candy sold to the thousands of laughing strollers. Under the nearby fruit trees, picnic lunches were spread on blankets on the ground. One vendor, hawking pictures of Andrew Helgelein's remains, sold out his supply; but there were plenty of other pertinent postcards available, including those depicting other bodies. People stood in line to be hoisted up to the window of the little red carriage house that served as a temporary morgue. Several times during the day, the authorities opened the carriage house door so that the curious could file by and peer in. The sheriff and his deputies guarded the cellar ruins to keep them from being carried away by the bagfull because those who could not afford to buy a souvenir took home a brick or some other piece of debris from the property.

To some observers, those evidently paid to be there, the scene was appalling. "It is a queer phase of human nature and wholly out of harmony with a well-balanced mind," wrote an editorial writer for the Toledo (Ohio) Blade. "One would think there was enough unavoidable tragedy in everyone's existence to keep him from seeking the hideous and unsightly. And yet it may be the fact that each has his cross to bear that leads him to come in contact with the world's wretchedness as a sort of palliative to his own. But it is a pity there is not some way to check the impulse for it is dangerous and unhealthy." The

Hammond (Indiana) Times editorialist took a similar position, saying, "The whole scramble of those 15,000 Americans to the one spot, which one would think would be carefully avoided, is a galling incontrovertible admission that the race is still but a little removed from a stage of actual savagery." The writer also took note that there was not class distinction in the crowd: "Not only the hoi polloi, not only lower classes which are viewed with contempt by those in higher station, not only the ignorant and the crude, were represented in that orgie (sic) of the horror scene at LaPorte. There were well-dressed men and women from the large cities who went in the automobiles to the scene of those murders and then fought with the man from the street for the opportunity to catch a glimpse of the dismembered and foul-smelling bodies of Mrs. Gunness' victims."

The New York Times called the event "an organized exploitation of the farm," summing up the occasion this way: "The Gunness farm today rang with the laughter of children, the jargon of postcard sellers, and streetmen, and the loud disruptions of souvenir hunters." The Times thought "at least" 15,000 people showed up.

The sightseers came from towns nearby in Indiana and as far away as Indianapolis. Chicago was well represented by wealthy visitors in expensive clothes. The elderly were there, some on crutches. Country couples and hired hands were abundant. Sheriff Smutzer was heard to remark disgustedly, "I never saw folks having a better time." There was one casualty. A LaPortean, Mrs. Benjamin Zanel, broke her arm when a carriage overturned. As it turned out, a profit was made by more than the obvious salesmen. Busy hands were also picking pockets. John Kuhn, Henry Ulrich, and Adam Zumbaugh from Plymouth, Indiana, were relieved of their wallets for a combined loss of $16.50. A. L. Miller of South Bend, Indiana, had his pocket picked of $90 in bills. Cynics thought that, considering the size of the crowd, it was surprising that so few incidents like this occurred.

Some of the visitors had questions on their minds, and the sheriff and his deputies answered what they could and asked a few of their own. Two brothers named Lindboe were looking for a brother who left Chicago three years ago to work for Belle. They looked at the corpses but could not identify their brother, which was not surprising considering the state of the remains. Information of some interest, though, came from Frank Lapham, who had lived on a farm adjoining Belle's until two years ago. He recalled that a wooden box with a foul stench had been dumped by someone at Belle's place into Fish Trap Lake. A search for this box was put on the list of things to do.

More digging was also on the list. One area of suspicion was the barn that had been moved back about six feet three years before. Also under consideration by Lamphere's defense was a search through nearby Pine Lake Cemetery for any disturbed graves that might have yielded bodies taken and placed in the house for discovery after the fire.

Belle's relatives, of course, wanted her declared dead so that they could contest the will. A Chicago nephew, John Larson, said he was now certain Belle had died in the fire: "My aunt was bad enough, and we are not trying to shield her, but I think they are accusing her of a little too much. I went to LaPorte with my sister, Bertha, and my mother for the purpose of identifying the corpse. On the way, we met an old friend who knew my aunt well; and as soon as she said there was a big scar across the chest of the corpse, we concluded there was no doubt about the identification. We all knew of that scar, and so did the people whose children she nursed. I think that fellow Lamphere is more to blame than my aunt, and I believe that he alone can explain how Mrs. Gunness and the children met death."

The fate of a man remembered by neighbors as Lindblom turned out to be the brother of the Lindboes. Although Thorwald Lindboe could not recognize his brother Olaf from the remains in the carriage house, Belle's neighbors recognized a photo of Olaf as a companion of Belle's about four years ago. Thorwald and

Ole, both of Chicago, knew their brother went to work as a farm hand near LaPorte after answering an advertisement in a Scandinavian newspaper. They said he was lured by a promise of high pay and then kept there by the promise of marrying into ownership of the farm.

Unlike some others enticed to the farm, Lindboe was thought to have only about $300 and a gold watch. But he was only 32, handsome, a dancer and musician, and a knowledgeable farm hand. Belle's neighbors, Mr. and Mrs. Swam Nicholsen said Belle and Olaf were inseparable for a time and often visited the Nicholsens. Their relationship seemed headed toward marriage. Therefore, the Nicholsens were surprised in July of 1904 to hear from Belle that Lindboe had left angrily after she refused to marry him. Another neighbor was told by Belle that Olaf wrote to her, saying he was going to Norway.

After his LaPorte visit, Thorwald Lindboe made the following statement: "While Olaf was with her, she circulated in the neighborhood a story that he had received a letter from our father in Norway saying that he was delighted to learn that his son was to marry a fine a woman as Mrs. Gunness. Of course, that was a lie. How my poor brother met his death no one but that woman ever will be able to tell. He is probably the first victim of the 10 whose bodies were discovered. I have written today to our father of his death."

The manner of death, referred to by Thorwald, was now thought to be a dose of chloral, a drug used to induce sleep. Belle's purchase of chloral had been verified by various vendors. Investigators believed the dismemberments took place in the basement, and a surgeon's knife was found in the ruins.

A question that remained was whether Belle had an accomplice. Lamphere was, of course, the prime suspect for that role, at least in the death of Andrew Helgelein. Against legal counsel, Lamphere had been talking to the Rev. E. A. Schell, pastor of the First Methodist Church in LaPorte. Pastor Schell was a regular visitor in Lamphere's cell, sometimes spending hours there in conversation. While the minister persisted in his privileged information position, the comments he did make formed a sketchy story. Pieced together, the story was made public May 11 and contained the following information. Belle approached Lamphere in June of 1907 and asked him to perform some handyman work for her on the farm. Agreeing, he first began fixing a floor in the farmhouse. The very night he began working there, he also became Belle's sexual companion. Very soon, he moved from a room in an outbuilding to a bedroom in the house. Belle proposed marriage but only on the condition that it occur quickly and after Lamphere purchase life insurance on himself. Lamphere was not alarmed by the insurance requirement, accepting Belle's explanation that any future children would need this insurance protection. When he dragged his feet about getting the insurance, he was banished back to the outbuilding. Soon after that, one day as he was building a fire in the sitting room stove, he was astonished to see a man come down the stairs. This man was Andrew Helgelein, and he had taken Lamphere's place in Belle's house.

Jealous, Lamphere spied on the couple and heard Belle expressing a wish to get rid of him. He told a friend in LaPorte about his fear that Belle might kill him. But when the friend advised him to leave the farm, Lamphere ignored the advice but asked that his body be autopsied in case of his sudden death. On January 14, 1908, he learned that Helgelein had drawn $2,000 from the bank. Belle ordered Lamphere to go to Michigan City and to stay there all night. Instead, he returned to the farm about 10 p.m. and saw the couple walking in the farm yard with a lantern. While they were outside, he crept into the basement and bored a hole in the sitting room floor so that he could listen to their conversation when they came inside. That done, it suddenly occurred to him that their barnyard stroll might be for the purpose of selecting his gravesite. He became so frightened that he left the farm and spent the night in LaPorte.

The prosecution was not buying this version of events. Its announced intention was to tie Lamphere into the Helgelein murder, even if only to link him to the burial. If that were proved true, the prosecution thought the defendant might be involved in other murders on the farm. He was definitely to be tried for arson because he admitted seeing the fire, albeit from a distance. The fire was now said to have been accelerated with a five gallon can of kerosene poured at the house's southeast corner and outside the basement door. The murder charge against Lamphere was to be based on the law that provided murder in the first degree charges against anyone committing arson that resulted in death, regardless of whether the death was intended. So, for the prosecution at this time, only the Helgelein aspect of its case was uncharted.

On Monday, the day after the deluge of tourists, a couple of new items of interest arose and a couple of old topics resurfaced. The ruins yielded up a revolver, which was thought to belong to Belle and which had all its chambers fired. The empty chambers, however, were attributed to the intense heat of the fire. Less agreement was reached on the topic of whether hair was found clasped in Andrew Helgelein's dead hand. Dr. Meyer said the hair was seen by him only upon the second examination of the body. His report to Coroner Mack stated that the hair probably came from the murderer. But he admitted he was "puzzled" by the hair, not knowing if it belonged to a man or a woman or if it were even human. It was "kinky brown" hair", which some people said matched Lamphere's hair and others thought resembled the kind of hair found on the forehead of a woman. Belle's brown hair had a slight red cast to it. Meyer believed even a microscopic examination of the hair would yield nothing.

Then there was the rumor about a ring found on Belle's hand. Prosecutor Smith professed to know nothing about it. Coroner Mack said the ring was found in the ashes, the only ring being found on a hand was the one discovered on one of the girls. The rumor was laid to rest when both Sheriff Smutzer and the undertaker, who said a ring would have left a mark, denied knowledge of any ring.

Resurfacing was a story about a possible source of the stench from the nearby lake. The story teller was Frank Lapham, the onetime neighbor of Belle. He said Belle told him she had allowed a man to bury a dog on her property for the payment of $5. Once again, Belle proved she could think on her feet, coming up with an answer to any threat.

The mining operation was set to begin the next day, Tuesday, May 12. The investigators were hoping the intense heat of the fire would not have destroyed Belle's bridgework, but the first day's sluicing operation produced only parts of watches. In a separate search, three rings were found in a burned clump of debris thought to include human hands. One was a plain gold band, but the other two were jeweled and carried inscriptions: "P.S. to J.S. 5-3, 1905" and "P.G. to J.S. Aug. 23, '04." Although no one could identify them, the rings were presumed to belong to Belle.

Evidence had now accumulated to allow identification of two more of Belle's victims. One was John Moo of Elbow Lake, Wisconsin, who drew $1,100 from the First National Bank in LaPorte on December 26, 1906, while living on Belle's farm. He then disappeared. The details of what was known of Moo were contained in a letter written by Henry Sampson, an Elbow Lake bank cashier: "On Dec. 20, 1906, this bank issued two drafts on New York, payable to John O. Moo, one for $1,000 and the other for $100. We also wrote you (the LaPorte bank) a letter of identification of which we enclose a copy. Mr. Moo's relatives here have not heard from him since he left, and we now believe he was a victim of Mrs. Belle Gunness. His relatives here did not know his destination, nor had he informed them of the nature of his business. He told them he was going a short distance from Chicago. We exhibited to them this morning the cancelled drafts and our copy of the letter of identification, and there seems to be little doubt that he was one of the unfortunate victims of this woman. Mr. Moo was 40 years old, a bachelor, about 5 feet and 10 inches in height, and would weigh probably about 160 to 175 pounds. He carried, among other things, a large silver watch, which likely could be identified here if found."

The other was Henry Gurhat from Scandinavia, Wisconsin, not far from where victim Ole Budsberg lived in Iola. Henry's brother Martin first communicated with authorities in LaPorte in a letter to Sheriff Smutzer: "According to a report in the newspaper, all indications are that my brother was a victim of Mrs. Gunness. I inclose herewith a photograph of my brother, Henry Gurhat, which I ask you kindly to have Mr. Christofferson (a neighbor of Belle's) see, that he may say whether it represents the Mr.Gurhat with whom he claims to have been acquainted at Mrs. Gunness' place. Henry Gurhat left Scandinavia, Wisconsin, May 12, 1905, for LaPorte, Ind., when he hired out to a widow to look after the work on a truck farm. I later learned that the name of the woman was Mrs. Gunness and that Henry got the appointment there through some of Mrs. Gunness' relatives in North Dakota. We received a few letters from him. The last was written July 4, 1905. Since then we have not heard from him, and in December we wrote to Mrs. Gunness inquiring if she knew anything about where Mr. Gurhat was. In reply to this, she said that he had left her place in August, going to Chicago with some horse traders. Mr. Gurhat may be identified by three false teeth in the upper part of his plate."

Later, when Martin Gurhat arrived in LaPorte, he told this story: "My brother was duped into going to LaPorte by a man who posed as a brother of Mrs. Gunness. He found my brother working in a store in Wisconsin and was sought out by the accomplice who so graphically pictured the delights of the Gunness country place that my brother fell a victim to his blandishments and came to LaPorte. He wrote me soon after arriving at the Gunness home how pleased he was with the place and the woman with whom he was living. His last letter was July 4th, when he told of a ride in the country with Mrs. Gunness."

It was now believed that Gurhat died on July 4th. Neighbors remembered seeing him on that day but never again. To some, Belle claimed that Gurhat left his trunk and fur coat and gone off toward the east in the direction of Rolling Prairie. Some time later, Belle was seen wearing the coat.

A third victim, although nameless, was described in a deposition by Frank Coffeen, a bricklayer. He often saw Belle scratching in the ground of the chicken yard where the bodies were later found. Coffeen saw a man working on the barn's foundation in May or June of 1907. About 5 feet 8 or 9 inches tall, he weighed from 150 to 160 pounds. His gray beard was trimmed to a point, and he carried a satchel and wore a soft hat. Coffeen heard this man and Belle talking about money and investments.

Christofferson, the neighbor asked to identify the photograph of Gurhat, said he had known both Lindboe and Gurhat and also a third man who was from Ohio. When this man disappeared at oat cutting time, Belle turned up with his horse and buggy, for which she claimed to have paid $60. "I knew all three of these men," explained Christofferson. "I was at the farm when Gurhat came. He had a very heavy trunk, and I helped him to carry it to his room over the kitchen. ... There were two other men who came from a distance and spent some time at Mrs. Gunness' place. One of these was from Geneva, Wisconsin, and the other was from somewhere in South Dakota ... The South Dakota man had just sold a lot of cattle in Chicago, Mrs. Gunness told myself and wife. She brought both men to our home and introduced them, but I have forgotten their names."

Christofferson recalled that after Gurhat had disappeared, Belle said he had left his trunk and fur coat behind. "I have seen her wearing the coat often," he said. "I thought this was very funny at the time." That sort of brazen behavior seemed a trademark of the murderess. She had Gurhat write his brother requesting seed potatoes but specifying that they must be sent in gunny sacks, thereby providing his own shroud.

CHAPTER SIXTEEN

Lamphere had an impressive defense team. Worden's law partner was Lemuel Darrow, who at this time was mid-point in a long tenure as mayor of LaPorte. He was a former chairman of the Democratic Central Commitee in Indiana. In "LaPorte Today," a book published in 1904, four years before the fire, Darrow was described as "unquestionably today one of the best known mayors in Indiana" and as having "done more for LaPorte than any other single official." He served as mayor from his first election in 1898 until 1914 and was then reelected mayor in 1934, one year before his death. Worden himself would go on to election as judge in 1934 and 1940. Associated with them in 1908 was Ellsworth E. Weir, a native LaPortean with a reputation as a brilliant attorney, who was also active in Democratic politics and had been defeated for the judgeship of the 32d Judicial Circuit in 1898 by Judge John C. Richter, who would hear the Gunness case. These principals were all already prominent local men and would become even more so in the decades ahead.

The prosecutor was from the other side of the political spectrum. A Republican, Ralph N. Smith, would also stay in LaPorte for many years after the Gunness case and would be elected judge of the Appellate Court in 1933, three years before his death. One who did not remain was Coroner Mack, who renounced politics and dead bodies and took up religion. Immediately after the case, he became a minister in the Swedenborgian religion with a church assignment in Toledo, Ohio.

As it happened, 1908 was a presidential election year. At the top of the tickets, William Howard Taft and William Jennings Bryan were vying for the presidency. Toward the bottom were names like Ralph N. Smith, who wanted another term as prosecutor, and Deputy Sheriff Anstiss, who wanted retiring

Sheriff Smutzer's job. Each, however, was on a different ticket and knew the Gunness case could affect his political future. The Democrats were defending Lamphere and saying that Belle was still alive. The Republians were staking their reputations on the conviction of Lamphere. To add to the devisiveness, one local newspaper was Republican and the other was Democratic.

So, right from the start, there was more involved here than justice. Also from the beginning, the battle between the two sides was apparent. Unless aware of this division, one would wonder at the obstruction techniques and verbal posturing of the main characters in the drama. On the very day of the fire, Smutzer locked up Lamphere and would not let Worden talk to his client. Only after threatening to bring habeas corpus proceedings to claim unlawful arrest was Worden permitted to talk to Lamphere. Worden had to threaten the same action fewer than two weeks later. On that occasion Lamphere had asked that his trunk be brought to him for a change of clothes. But the prosecution already had the trunk, rumored to contain letters from Belle to Lamphere after he had left her employ. There were no letters, but Lamphere said he would make a statement after talking to Worden. When Worden responded to his client's request, the sheriff and his deputies were not at the jail. No one else would assume the responsibility of letting Worden in. Holding the threat of habeas corpus aloft, he finally gained access to his client the next morning.

So, although Darrow and Worden were influential, the opposition held the investigative tools in its grasp. Darrow and Worden were not out at the farm digging, but the sheriff's people were.

The verbal posturing can also be explained by understanding how the political lines were drawn. Anstiss, candidate for sheriff, said he could prove that Lamphere lied when he said he stayed over night in Michigan City on January 14. And Prosecutor Smith stated, "The proving of the death of Mrs. Gunness is one of the least troubles that I have. I have plenty of evidence to show that the big body which was found in the ruins of the Gunness home of the morning of the fire was that of the woman herself. That we will be able to prove without the shadow of a double, and that will be the first thing that will be shown. It is immaterial to the case what the coroner's conclusions may be. This talk that Mrs. Gunness escaped is very easy to understand if the people who are yelling the loudest that she was not burned to death will trace the matter to its source, they will understand fully the underlying motive. If Lamphere's friends can cast a shadow of a doubt on the identity of the corpse, they believe they will be able to get him off."

So, the political ramifications of the case permeated the course of the investigation. It influenced the intended use of the money appropriated for the investigation, and the way the news was presented in the local newspapers. Ultimately, it determined even the starting time of the trial.

The political overtones were evident from the beginning, if one was to look for them. Evidence of this is the following newspaper story written by William Blodgett, reporter with the Indianapolis News, the first week in May:

"One would naturally suppose that such a grewsome (sic) murder mystery as the Gunness affair at LaPorte would be free from even the semblance of politics.

"The idea of mixing politics up with dead people's bones is out of the ordinary, even in these piping times of politics in Indiana, yet the whole affair is permeated with politics, and I have no doubt that because of the political complications the investigation of the crime has been a measure delayed.

"LaPorte is the county seat, and there is at the county seat as smooth a set of political workers and managers as can be found anywhere in the state. And LaPorte tries to furnish all the officeholders of the county. That is the reason that the county of LaPorte, which is generally Democratic, once in a while goes Republican.

"There is considerable rivalry between Michigan City and the county seat in a business way, but that rivalry is nothing compared with the way they dislike each other politically.

"In the investigation of the mysterious murders at the Gunness farm, there are several political features. The county coroner, Dr. Mack, is a Democrat. The prosecution attorney, R. N. Smith, is also a Democrat, and is standing for re-election. He conducts a bureau of silence and wags his head in a mysterious way, but has nothing to do with the coroner. Sheriff Smutzer is a Republican and a prospective candidate for county clerk.

"And, for the sheriff, let it be said that he has spent a great part of his time since this murder case came up trying to unravel it. He removed the bodies; he is the chief police officer of the county; but the coroner's office will have nothing to do with him, and the coroner has not yet even taken the sheriff's testimony.

"'Bill Anstiss, the chief deputy sheriff, is a candidate for sheriff and is missing no opportunity to have a little credit charged up to him in the unraveling of this crime. Of course, he is on good terms with Sheriff Smutzer and works under his directions, but Bill is doing a little detective work along the lines of investigation, and it was he who tried to obtain a confession from Lamphere. It is agreed by every one that Bill will make a pretty good sheriff, and at this time it looks as if he will get the nomination without opposition.

"Roy Marr, another deputy sheriff who has really performed the best detective work of any in the lot, is a prospective candidate for the office when Bill Anstiss gets through with it, and anyhow he expects to be Bill's deputy. As in the case of Mr. Smutzer, neither Anstiss nor Marr has been called into the coroner's office to give their testimony.

"Darrow and Worden are the attorneys for the prisoner Lamphere. Darrow is the mayor of LaPorte and Worden was formerly city attorney. Consequently, the police department is Democratic, or at least the officers of the police force are, and the city police department has not been taken in with the sheriff's office--the sheriff and his deputies are working independently of the police department and the police department is not working at all. Once in a while Chief of Police Cochrane gets into the limelight through the medium of a letter he receives, but that is about all.

"The sheriff's office makes the assertion that the police are really gathering evidence to clear Lamphere at the order of Mayor DArrow, who is one of the attorneys for the defense. This is promptly denied by both the mayor and the police department, who declare that they are willing to assist the sheriff, but the sheriff will not accept their services.

"Mayor Darrow, deploring the absence of harmony in the way the investigation is going on, gives it out cold that the proper way to do is to have some head to the matter--let the investigation be made by every one under the direction of a responsible head--and he believes that responsible head ought to be Coroner Mack, the Democrat, while the Republicans in the sheriff's office say 'nay, nay'.

"And this is not all of it. LaPorte has two daily papers, and these papers are far and away above the average as newspapers in towns the size of LaPorte. When this mystery was first sprung there was a division of sentiment as to whether Mrs. Gunness was alive or dead. The Argus-Bulletin is the Democratic paper and is very friendly to Darrow and Worden: in fact, it is generally believed that the attorneys for the defense of Lamphere are stockholders in the Argus-Bulletin and that the paper assumes the position that the body found in the ruins was not the body of Mrs. Gunness.

"The Republican paper is the Herald, and the Herald from the start has insisted that the bodies taken from the basement of the house were those of Mrs. Gunness and her three children. The Herald and the Argus-Bulletin thus took opposite views of the situation.

"The county commissioners, at the instigation of Sheriff Smutzer, employed the Pinkerton agency to unravel this mystery, and the Republicans think it was the proper thing to do. Darrow and Worden, Democrats, have in interviews and statements attacked the methods of the Pinkertons and by so doing have reflected on the sheriff's office. And the sheriff's office, in words with a sulphur blue edge on them, has hinted that it will tell a few things if it is forced to do so, and the Democrats declare that if the sheriff's office knows anything to tell, it should have made its spiel a long time ago.

"The county council will meet at LaPorte, and the Republicans backing the sheriff and his assistants are insisting that there be a big appropriation made to carry on this work. The Democrats backing Darrow and Worden, attorneys for Lamphere, do not oppose a reasonable appropriation but say there is no need of turning over a lot of money to the Pinkertons, that LaPorte police can do the work, and money should be placed in the hands of the police and not the Pinkertons.

"The Pinkertons have C. J. Smith at LaPorte--one of the best and shrewdest men in that agency. He worked in the Schafer case at Bedford but for the man Reed who was his superior in that investigation, he might have brought about some results. He has the help of the sheriff's office and the Republican end of the political controversy, but the coroner's office and Mr. Smith are not on the best of terms.

"Detective Fish is also at LaPorte and is doing a little quiet 'sleuthing'. The story the sheriff's office got from Fish was that he had been sent to LaPorte to ascertain if there was a Chicago end to the mystery, and the sheriff's office took him into full confidence. Now the sheriff's office declares it has discovered that Mr. Fish was not on the job in behalf of the Chicago police department but is working in the interest of Darrow and Worden: at least the sheriff says that detective Fish is in constant consultation with the Democratic attorneys for the defense.

"There never has been much doubt that one of the bodies found buried on the Gunness farm was that of Andrew Helgelein. His brother identified the body, and the Herald declared the identification complete. Even the Democratic attorneys for the defense did not make much of a dispute on that question, but the friends of the mayor thought it would be wise to be sure, so a Bertillon expert from the Michigan City prison went to LaPorte at the request of the Democratic coronor's office to make a further investigation that there might be no doubt as to the identity of the body.

"Because of the differences between some of the politicians, there promises to be factions even in this murder case. The Republicans are trying to get all the credit for uncovering the crimes, and the Democrats wish some of it themselves.

"In the meantime, no one knows what the politics of Mrs. Gunness was. All her male victims were aliens, and it made no difference what their politics was, and her children could not vote even if they had any political preferences.

"Seriously, the affair gives great promise of being a political disgrace."

CHAPTER SEVENTEEN

Among the many people who played a role in the Gunness mystery, none proved more critical than Louis Schultz and Dr. I. P. Norton. Between the two, they would deliver up the detail that would finally sway the fence-sitting Coroner Mack to declare Belle dead.

On May 11, Schultz, the imported gold miner, began sluicing the debris in the burned-out cellar in his search for Belle's bridgework. As he began, he promised: "I will take my time and go over every particle of the wreckage. If the teeth are there, I will find them. And if it was Mrs. Gunness who perished in the flames, the teeth are there."

Agreeing with this optimism was Dr. Norton, who was Belle's dentist: "Mrs. Gunness had some dental work done with me a year ago. She made two visits and paid me $40 for my work. There was a plate of false teeth in her upper jaw. The four incisors in her lower jaw were missing. I put gold crowns on the lower bicuspids and bridge in the four porcelain teeth between them. I wanted to put in a plate, but Mrs. Gunness insisted on a bridge. The crowns were of 22 karat gold. The four porcelain teeth were re-enforced by a back of 22 karat gold. The porcelain of the false teeth could not have been fusible except under heat of 2,200 degrees Fahrenheit. The gold caps would not have fused in heat less than 1,800 degrees Fahrenheit. Such degrees of heat would not have existed in the burning of the Gunness home. It would have been produced only by a blow pipe. There is but one deduction. If it was Mrs. Gunness whose body was found in the ruins, her teeth are intact among the debris. The fire was not hot enough to melt the gold or incinerate the porcelain." By week's end, however, it was not Belle's bridgework that caused Norton to make a positive identification. It was a jawbone, which he positively declared to be Belle's, based on his knowledge of her mouth.

LaPorte Police Chief Cochrane remained unconvinced: "I was at the house when the body of the woman and those of the three children were found in a corner of the cellar. I looked carefully under the woman's body to find some trace of the missing head. There was nothing there to suggest a skull. There was not a sign of gold or porcelain or any other kind of teeth. I am convinced Mrs. Gunness escaped after leaving the body of some murdered and decapitated woman in her burning home to be mistaken for her own."

A similar opinion came from the Rev. E. A. Schell, the Methodist minister who had been visiting with Lamphere in his cell. Paster Schell broke his silence on the case twice that week. On Tuesday, he issued a brief statement: "Lamphere's statements as made on different days were conflicting ... What he said is inviolably sacred as the secrets of the confessional should be. No confidence he gave will be disclosed unless he shall first open his heart to the prosecuting attorney, as I advised him to do. If, on the advice of Attorney Worden, he refuses a full confession, I shall be surprised." The statement came from Schell while he was in Baltimore on business, and efforts to pry more information from him proved almost useless. Right at the end of his meeting with reporters, after he had been badgered for additional comments, he was finally asked straight out whether Lamphere had anything to do with Belle's death. His audience was startled when he blurted out, "I do not think the woman is dead." Later, the pastor evidently felt the need to repeat his claim of privileged communication in his conversations with Lamphere and to clarify his statement about Belle. He said his belief that she was still alive was not based on any knowledge but was merely his personal opinion. His opinion of Belle, the woman, also was offered: "Mrs. Gunness ... was an attractive woman in her way. She dressed richly, and even, you might say, in good taste, but her manner of talking and her speech itself--her vagaries of grammar--betrayed a low origin. She could best be described as 'Mrs. Newrich'"

The grand jury had already been chosen, and members were August Anderson, a farmer; N. D. McCormick, an ex-sheriff; Fred Zahrn, ex-county treasurer; Joseph Fraser, retired grocer; Henry Keithline, a farmer; and August Baeske, a farmer. Some 50 witnesses were being lined up to testify. Although the jury's proceedings were to be secret, some of what witnesses were going to say was being learned. First, many of the key witnesses had already spoken to reporters who had relayed this information to the public. Second, the others, who had been less exposed to the limelight, were now approached for information on their connection to the mystery. Prostitutes with whom Lamphere had dealings were being summoned to repeat his conversations with them, as were his drinking partners at Roule's tavern. Peter Colson, a former Gunness hired hand who lived to tell about it, was to testify about a conversation with Lamphere in which the defendant boasted, "I can go and get money from her (Belle) any time I want to. She gets down on her knees to me any time I say so. Whenever I want money I say so, and it comes. She knows that I know something, and all I have to do is to hint about it, and she gives me money." Another witness, John Rye, planned to tell of his trip to Michigan City with Lamphere on the day of Andrew Helgelein's disappearance. Rye and Lamphere took a horse-pulled cutter, which Lamphere unexpectedly decided to leave in a Michigan City livery barn. That meant the two men had to return to LaPorte by interurban car. Rye described Lamphere that night as restless, morose, and silent on the trip over and even more so on the trip back. At about two miles from LaPorte, Lamphere decided to get off the car, saying, "I must be at the old lady's tonight." When Rye last saw him that night, Lamphere was heading over a hill for the three-block walk. Lamphere denied making that comment. The investigation meanwhile continued, with answers coming to two questions. One, the hair found in Helgelein's hand was not Lamphere's. Two, a cablegram from Norway stated that a week's hunt had failed to find Belle in that country.

The rain had hampered the digging outside, but it was decided to examine a cistern under the barn floor and to remove the tool house's cement floor. Identifying bodies was going to take even more importance because the Helgelein survivors had filed a $3,000 suit against the Gunness estate for money Belle got from Andrew, and other confirmed deaths would likely bring similar suits from remaining relatives.

Even without the unearthing of new bodies or the tracking down of Belle, the case continued to inspire melodrama. Such was the burial of Andrew Helgelein, whose brother had been the instrument exposing Belle's murders. When this brother, Asle, had returned to South Dakota, he had left $200 for the burial of his brother's remains if identification was definitely established. This had now been accomplished, and those taking responsibility for the burial decided it should be done as secretly as possible and therefore under cover of night. The event was arranged quickly, with a minister procured, the funeral director notified, and the cemetery contacted. The funeral mourners consisted of Charles H. Michael, local hotel owner; Fred Pitner, to whom $200 had been given; E. A. Evans of the Chicago police department; and some newspaper reporters. At 10 p.m. the undertaker's "Black Maria" wagon left Cutler's morgue, and the carriages wound their way through LaPorte streets to Patton Cemetery. There, in the eerie torchlight, Andrew Helgelein's body was placed in a vault to await burial the next morning after a grave was dug. No tears were shed; no relatives said goodbye. At his burial, the only flowers were some violets sprinkled atop his casket. He was the first of the 14 dead to be buried.

Another occasion for drama occurred at the farm when Defense Attorney Worden stood in the middle of the ruins and loudly demanded that Sheriff Smutzer "find Mrs. Gunness." The sheriff's reply, patterned after the one that Prosecutor Smith was repeating, was that all that was left of Belle was in the morgue. The incident illustrated how sharply drawn were the divisions of opinion in this small town.

Just as the defense and the prosecution were unrelenting in their opposition, so were their partisans. On Saturday, May 16, the two sides clashed at a meeting of the LaPorte County Council. At issue was the disposition of money appropriated in connection with the case. Approval was given to spend a total of $9,000 for the investigation, including $2,500 for the coroner's expense; $1,500 for court expenses; and $5,000 for "apprehension of prisoners." Supporters of Mayor Darrow and the defense team demanded a reward for "the arrest of Mrs. Gunness." They lost the vote, but not before one councilman, John Matthews of Wanatah, became so angry he threatened to resign. Prosecutor Smith commented he almost wished they would offer a reward because then "it would be up to them to produce her."

The grand jury was set to begin its work on Monday, May 17, and most observers were betting that Lamphere would be indicted for both arson and murder. They were less sure of any ruling on Lamphere's involvement with Helgelein's murder. The witnesses were to be presented by Deputy Sheriff Leroy Marr, who did much of the detective work for the LaPorte authorities.

While the subpoenas were being isssued on Sunday, another crowd of sightseers gathered at the Gunness farm. The macabre festivities of the previous Sunday were repeated, with "Gunness Stew" offered in restaurants, picnickers eating within sight of the charnel house, and pennants proudly labeled "LaPorte". The only difference was in the size of the crowd, down from 15,000 to 10,000. By the time the next Sunday, May 24, rolled around, the excursion business was definitely off. The crowd numbered only about 3,000, even though the week between revealed its share of sensations.

During the week, doctors doing autopsies on two unidentified bodies raised the possibility that all four bodies found in one grave might have been killed on the same night. In addition, Dr. George Osborn and Dr. F. T. Wilson found that one body thought to be male was really female. What's more, there was the likelihood that Belle committed the four-person murders in 1906 on Christmas. The identities, based on what the investigators had so far learned, were a definite Jennie Olson, a probable John Moo, and two possibles, the man and the woman that Emil Greening had heard at the farm. The first two disappeared at Christmas of that year, and the two visitors were at the farm the last time Greening saw Jennie. Then, too, they were all found in one grave. The positive identification of Jennie allowed her to be buried on May 20 next to Andrew Helgelein. Jennie's brother and sister, Sigward and Sarah Olson of Chicago, were there for the burial.

Another possible identification was made on a body buried separately. Once again, teeth were considered a clue. This skeleton had only two inches of brown hair clinging to its skull. That this could be the missing Edward Canary was supported only because both he and the skeleton in question wore upper false teeth.

CHAPTER EIGHTEEN

On May 19, Belle's bridgework was found, and it came with its own set of mysteries. For one thing, the lower bridge was found along with Belle's upper plate of false teeth. How these two managed to stay together through three weeks of shoveling, poking, prodding, sluicing, and sifting was puzzling, to say the least. Then, the bridgework came attached to a natural tooth, thereby torpedoing any idea that Belle casually tossed it into the fire. This circumstance would give rise to a theory about the case put forth decades later. Also, the teeth and the gold had somehow survived a blaze that had melted the gold right off several watches. Plus, Joseph Maxson later testified that he and another man were working in the yard the morning of the discovery. He said Louis Schultz, the miner, pulled the plates from his pocket that morning and announced, "We have found what we are looking for." Strangely, Schultz could not be located for testimony at the subsequent trial. It was said he had gone out West somewhere.

At any rate, Maxson said Sheriff Smutzer was not yet present at the farm when Schultz made his announcement. The sheriff arrived about an hour later and took the teeth to the dentist, I. P. Norton, who promptly identified them as Belle's. Norton had not made the upper plate, which was done previously for Belle by some other dentist, but he identified that, too, from his general recollection of the plate.

This was enough for Coroner Mack, who now at last permitted Belle to be declared officially dead. But he withheld any official verdict on who the murderer was. It was not enough for others, however. Doubters sought to use the $5,000 appropriated by the county council "for apprehension of prisoners" to offer a reward for anyone bringing in Belle alive. The prosecution, which claimed credit for the $5,000 appropriation, continued its attitude: "Do your darnest but you're not going to find her because Lamphere killed her."

Another curious circumstance can be found in the coroner's inquisition records. Mack named the witnesses who gave evidence: Joseph Maxson, William Clifford, William Humphrey, Michael Clifford, Daniel Hutson, John Larson, Mrs. Nellie Larson, Frank Coffeen, J. Lucius Gray, and I. P. Norton. Each person's testimony can be read even today--except for Norton's, which is the only one missing. Mack's conclusion can be read: "It is my verdict that the body so viewed is that of Belle Gunness; that she came to her death through felonious homicide and the perpetrator thereof is to me unknown."

Mack also issued a report on five skeletons of the unidentified dead:

"Adult (presumably a male), found May 6 in cesspool in Mrs. Gunness' chickenyard. Bones bare. No flesh attached to them. Skull found lying on base near pelvic end of torso. The femurs were sawed off an inch or two above the knee. Light brown hair on skull. Through the skull is an opening about 2 x 3 inches, which removes a large part of the left temporal bone. The front border of the hole in the skull is straight, as if made with some cutting instrument and is through the front part of the squamous portion of the left temporal bone. Aside from the back bicuspid and back molar on the right upper and back bicuspid on the lower right side, all the teeth were found in the mouth. No fillings were found.

"Adult (presumably a male), taken from the fourth grave. In this hole were two other bodies. The body was dismembered. Each of the femurs had been sawed off or hacked off just above the knee. On the skull was dark short hair. No teeth at all were found in the lower jaw. Short dark hair, like a beard, was found on the front jaw.

"Adult (presumably male), taken from the same hole as the preceding skeleton. Short dark hair on the skull. Most of the teeth present in both the upper and lower jaws.

"Adult (presumably male). Last body taken from fourth hole in barnlot. Condition and description same as preceding skeleton.

"Adult (sex undetermined), taken from fifth hole. This is either skeleton of young girl or young man. The upper teeth are missing, indicating that the persons must have used a plate. The wisdom teeth are just coming through the jaw bone, showing the person to have been quite young. No fillings are found in the lower teeth. The fact that a pair of woman's oxford shoes and the metal clasp of a lady's purse were found in the grave might indicate that the dead person was a woman. The body had been packed in lime and then placed in a box, the sides of which had rotten away."

The idea that four had been murdered on Christmas day was now rejected because no four had disappeared at the same time. John Moo was now considered found in a different gravesite. As the grand jury continued to take the testimonies of from a half dozen to a dozen witnesses each day, the investigation continued to pursue the possibility of other accomplices in the murders. One lead that was followed up involved a man in Warsaw, Indiana, who committed suicide after reading about the unearthed bodies. A close scrutiny of the incident revealed that the man's despondency was instead over his poor health. Another lead came from Fred Hafle of Cleveland who mailed a small photograph of a woman that might have been a younger Belle. His accompanying letter explained: "Last August while waiting for a streetcar in our public square, I was approached by a man who began a conversation with me. He stated he was in Cleveland on a speculation and that cattle was his line. After some time, he endeavored to find out regarding my family, etc., and asked me if I was married. In a spirit of fun I said no, and he immediately began to tell me about a rich widow who resided in LaPorte, Ind., who was looking for a man. He claimed she was the owner of a large ranch, stocked with cattle, and that she was looking for a man. He also gave me a picture of the woman who was supposed to be looking for a husband, which I inclose herewith, and I do this merely thinking that might be of assistance in the matter of Mrs. Gunness. This man claimed that Chicago was his home. He was about 35 or 36 years of age, 5 feet 3 or 4 inches tall, and weighed about 160 pounds. He had a reddish complexion, smooth face, dark hair, and wore a black soft hat, blue suit, and had the general appearance of a man pretty well to do."

Speaking of well to do, one of the puzzles in the situation was the absence of Belle's money. At the time of the fire, she had only $700 in the bank. Yet calculations of funds she accumulated from victims was thought to be at least $51,000. The sources of that sum broke down this way: Mads Sorensen, Chicago, $8,000; Peter Gunness, LaPorte, $3,500; Andrew Helgelein, South Dakota, $2,900; Ole Budsberg, Wisconsin, $2,500; John Moo, Minnesota, $1,800; Henry Gurhat, Wisconsin, $400; Kerman Konitsberg, Chicago, $8,000;. Charles Erdman, Pennsylvania, $5,000; George Berry, Illinois, $1,500; suitors reported missing, $15,000; and three unknowns, $3,000.

Another close call was reported all the way from Chamber, Wyoming, by I.N. Youtsler, who wrote to Sheriff Smutzer that he had once spent the night at the Gunness farm. Enclosed with the letter was a razor that Youtsler said was given to him by Jennie Olson at the request of Mrs. Gunness. The bone-handled razor was made in Sweden and bore a scratched inscription, "T. Lind, Chicago." An Odd Fellows' emblem was scratched on the other side. Youtsler said he came through LaPorte as a peddler and found himself late one night near the Gunness farm. He approached the farm and asked Belle if he could spend the night, and she agreed. He thought the razor could perhaps be traced to some missing man, and he thought he escaped Belle's greed because he was poorly dressed, never hinting in appearance that he carried $600 in cash and $700 in drafts with him.

Another letter came to the sheriff from Thomas Williams of Mount Yeager, Pennsylvania, who, like so many others, was looking for missing men: "Since so much has been published about the disappearance of so many men from various parts of the country and so many have fallen victims to Mrs. Belle Gunness, I write you about two farmers who left our community within the past two years. They are George W. Williams of Wapwallopen, Pennsylvania, and Ludwig Stoll of Mount Yeager. Both left here as suddenly and mysteriously as though the earth had swallowed them. It is well known here that Stoll was always answering advertisements appearing in matrimonial papers. He owned a fine farm and it will be sold for taxes shortly, as he cannot be located. It is also well known that he had considerable ready cash. When he left here he told his friends he was going west to buy horses and that they need not be surprised if he returned with a housekeeper. It is this last remark that makes people hereabouts entertain the belief that he might have been in communication with Mrs. Gunness. George Williams farm was sold by the sheriff on May 2. Farmers in this section are of the opinion that he went West. Will you kindly inform us of the kinds of watches found on the premises and the numbers, for by so doing you will greatly oblige."

The sluicing was to end the afternoon of Thursday, May 21, now that the bridgework had been unearthed. That hunt was over, and the digging was set to resume, with the agenda to include the floor under the barn and the entire chickenyard. The sheriff said he also intended to drag the little pond. This prompted the Plymouth (Ind.) Democrat to write: "If they don't find another body at the Gunness farm pretty soon, the people will get back to politics and the market reports with their interest."

The next day, Friday, after four days of deliberations, the LaPorte County grand jury indicted Ray Lamphere for arson, the murder of five people, and an accessory in the murder of one person. He was charged with killing Belle, the three children, and Helgelein. He was also charged with being an accessory in Helgelein's death and with setting fire to the farmhouse.

Although the grand jury proceedings were secret, important testimony was thought to have been given by Deputy Sheriffs Leroy Marr and W. C. Anstiss, Daniel Hutson, William Humphrey, Fred Voorhees, Daniel Havens, and Mrs. Elizabeth Smith, the latter being the African-American woman with whom Lamphere said he spent the night of the fire. Subpoena records show that many other people also were called to testify. In his cell, Lamphere's reaction to the verdict was unremarkable and unlike his agitation upon learning of the discovery of the teeth. His reaction at that time indicted that he was as stunned as everyone about the discovery because he actually thought Belle was not in the fire.

One true bill handed down by the grand jury contained the unusual feature of indicting Belle, and it read: "The grand jury presents that Belle Gunness, late of the county of LaPorte and state of Indiana, on the 14th day of January, 1908, did unlawfully, feloniously, wilfully, and with premeditated malice, kill and murder Andrew Helgelein, the means and manner of such killing being to the grand jurors unknown." Attached to that indictment is the one accusing Lamphere as an accessory: "Lamphere unlawfully, purposely, wilfully, and feloniously did harbor, conceal, and assist Belle Gunness in the disposition of the body of Andrew Helgelein, with the intent that he, Ray Lamphere, might escape from detection, arrest, capture, and punishment, and Lamphere did assist Belle Gunness in the disposition of the body of Andrew Helgelein after he, Lamphere, well knew and was informed that Belle Gunness had killed and murdered Andrew Helgelein."

So now Belle was officially dead, and Lamphere was to be tried for her murder. That did not stop people from saying they had letters from Belle written after the fire, or they had seen her, or they had names of more possible victims. For example, Jacob Hoeckler of Elkhart, Indiana, had made two trips to LaPorte in search of his cousin, Justina Loeffler, who disappeared in 1902. Another inquiry came from Capron, Illinois, from where Olaf

Jensen had departed two years before to marry a rich widow in LaPorte. He was never heard from again. The scenario was tragically familiar. Jensen had met the woman through a matrimonial ad in a Scandinavian newspaper and withdrew a certain sum of money from his bank for a visit to the widow. A few weeks later, he returned to Capron and withdrew the remainder of his money, saying he was returning to LaPorte to marry the widow. After promising to stay in touch, he never wrote to anyone, even his relatives in Norway, with whom he regularly had stayed in touch.

On the day of the indictments, the sheriff and his crew resumed digging, unearthing a human skull from a cesspool. It was assumed to be female because of the long hair attached to the skull. No one knew if the body belonging to this skull had already been found or if it was still buried in Belle's graveyard.

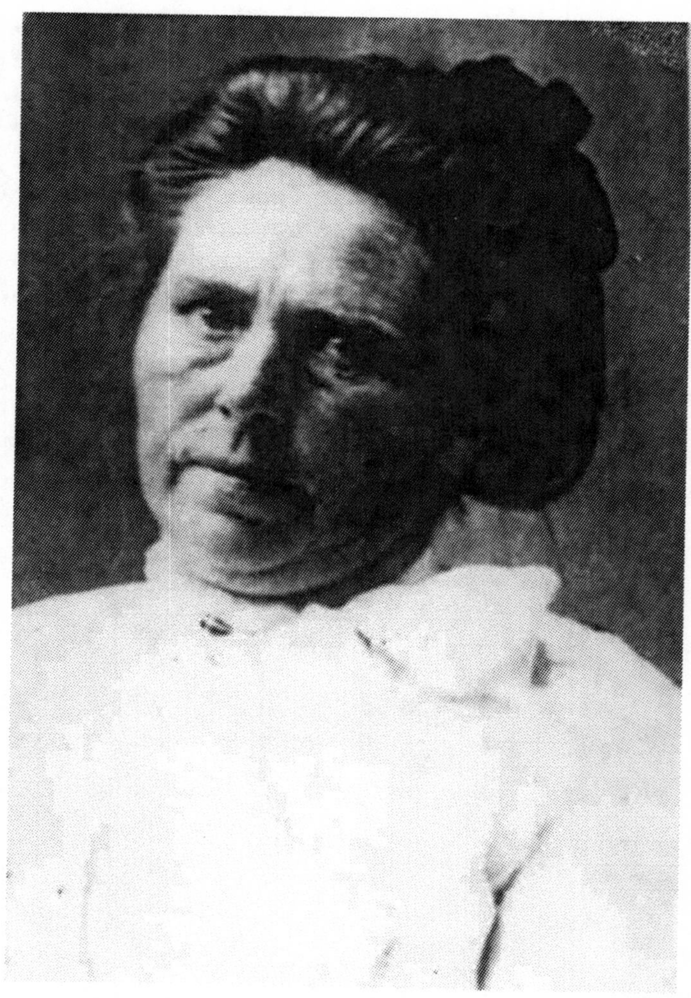

Belle Gunness

Belle with Lucy, Myrtle, and Philip

Ruins after the fire

Hillside where nine of the bodies were found

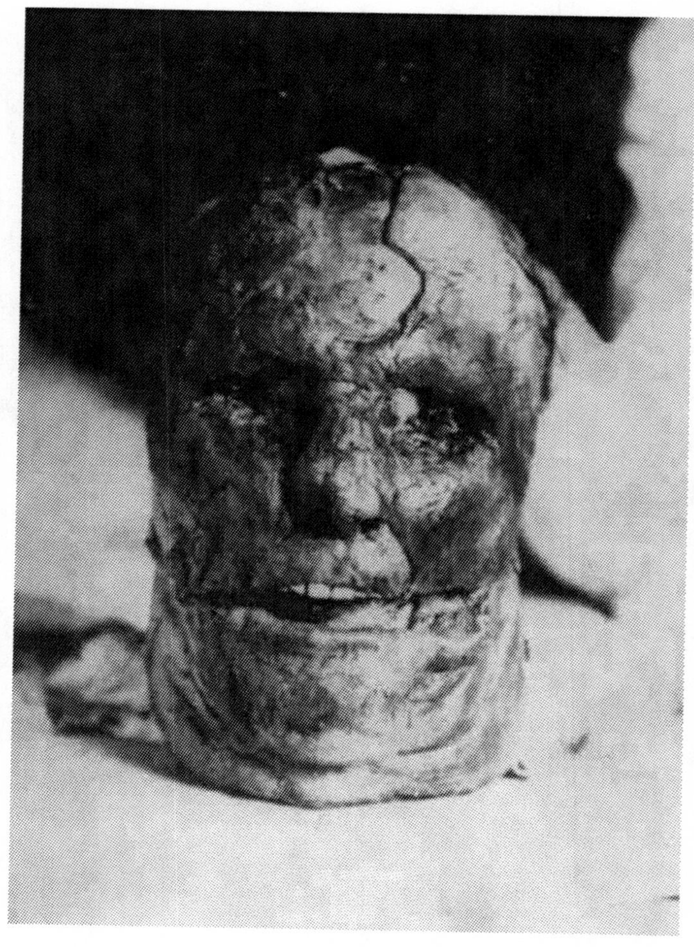

Andrew Helgelein's skull

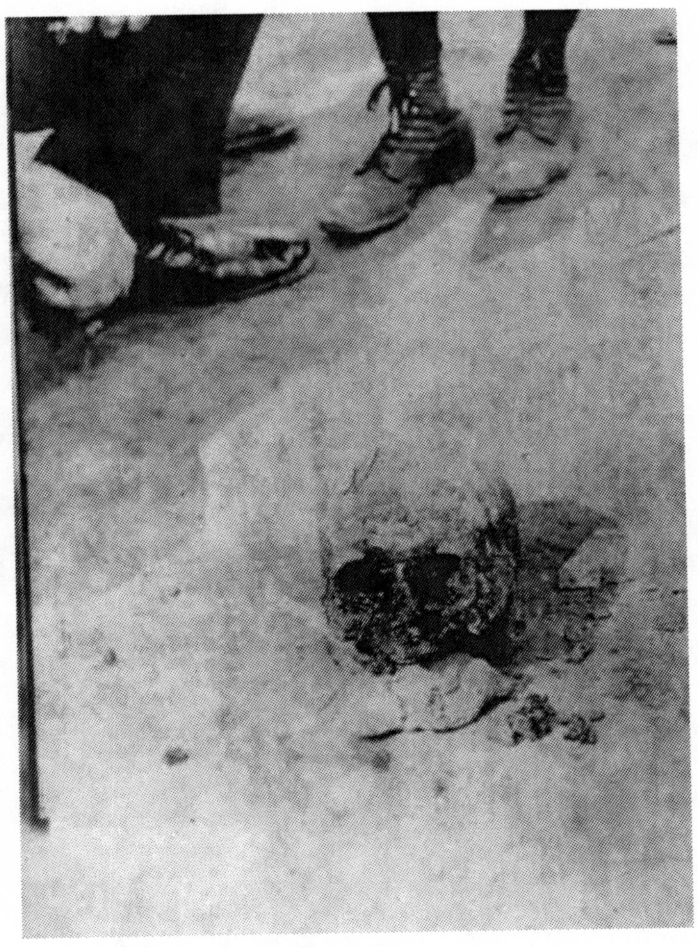

A skull retrieved from the barnyard

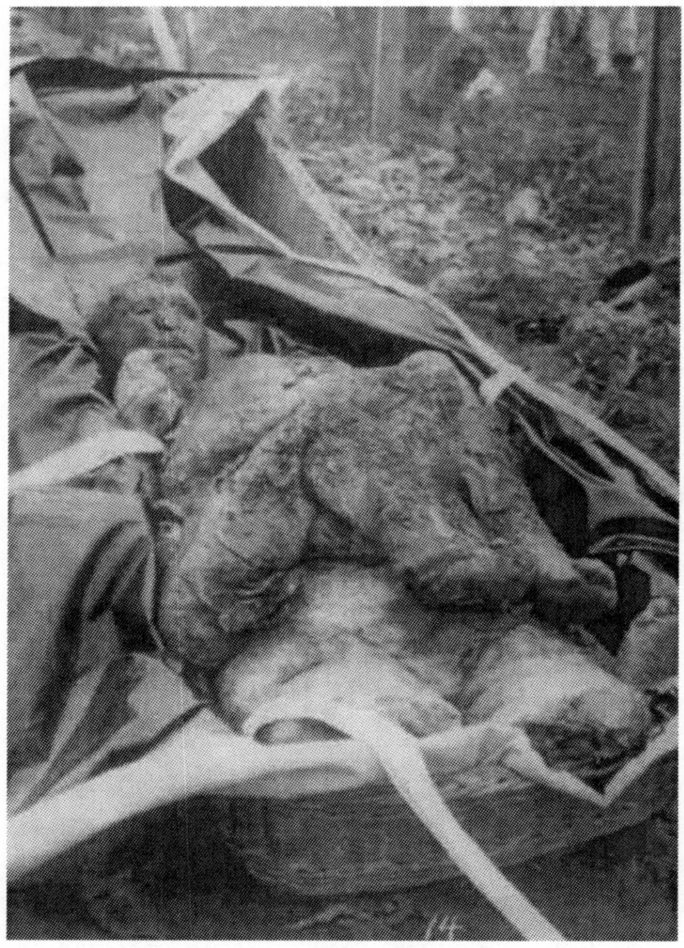

The remains of one body

Andrew Helgelein's grave

The unmarked plot in Forest View Cemetery

CHAPTER NINETEEN

Nature put on a display of impetuousness on the eve of the auction of Belle's earthly goods. Wind and rain unlike anything seen in years roared through LaPorte uprooting trees and blowing out windows. Roeske's flour mill gave up its roof, and Peterson's clothing store lost the plate glass window. In some places, like the interurban line, fallen trees had to be removed before people could get where they wanted to go. In the case of thousands, on May 29, they were heading out to Belle's place again.

Anyone who has gone to an estate sale and wandered among the relics of a life gone forever knows the feeling of sad fascination that comes from looking at tangible evidence that we really must leave all our personal possessions behind. Some items, like their former owner, lie lifeless and resigned. Others seem almost perky in their bid to catch the fancy of the new hands that finger them. Whatever the lure, more than 4,000 people came to the farm that Friday to buy a piece of sad history or merely to see what such a person as Belle called her own.

Long before the hour set for the auction to begin, people descended by bicycle, wagon, auto, buggy, and feet. After all, Belle's personal property was about to go on the block, and even those who couldn't afford to buy could afford to look. Early arrivals took all the choice parking spots, so late-comers had to hitch up to fence posts for a half mile stretch east of the farm. The proceedings were arranged by Wesley Fogle, Belle's executor; and Ora Bosserman served as clerk. The event broke with farm-auction tradition when A. L. Brownlee, the auctioneer, began with the sale of small items rather than farm equipment and livestock. The big items were saved until last. Brownlee enlivened the progress of the auction with commentary on the various items offered, and souvenir hunters were not disappointed. As expected, the prices paid reflected not so much the items offered as the former owner's notoriety. Everything sold for inflated prices, like the shepherd dog, which went for $107, and the pony, which sold for $250. This came as no surprise to people close to the case, who knew purchasers planned to exhibit some of their new acquisitions. Even before the auction, for example, the brother of Harry Thomas, the barber at LaFountaine's shop, arrived in LaPorte from Wanatah, Indiana, and bought the cat and four kittens that had lived in Belle's barn. George Thomas told Executor Fogle that the animals would be exhibited at the Butler Music Company in Wanatah. In all, the auction brought in about three times would it would have under normal circumstances.

The Rochester (Ind.) Republican newspaper registered its disgust: "One of the discouraging evidences of a lack of moral development in some people, and quite a large number at that, is the morbid avidity with which every conceivable article of value was bid in at the Gunness farm public sale ... It is certainly not the mark of a highly cultured mind to desire any of the possessions of a woman who was notably the arch fiend of the century. No better fate could have befallen the Gunness residence than its utter destruction by fire, which is nature's purifying agent, and if the barns, sheds, and property in them contained, could have similarly fared, it would have been an added blessing towards the upliftment of the community. Psychometry teaches that the walls, furniture, tapestry, pictures, etc. of the home, school, church, alms-house, jail or penitentiary, bear impress of the transactions of their inhabitants and may reflect their influence on succeeding occupants ... Were it generally understood that the personal effects of Mrs. Gunness transmit or reflect an ora (sic) of evil, though unknown and unseen, men would be about as keen to buy them as a mother would be to buy rattle snakes as play things for her children. Five hundred buggies at the public sale, bearing their burdens of humanity thither to buy relics, keepsakes, memorials of a she-devil whose like has not been known, is rather a sad commentary on the intelligence of those who spent the high dollar to obtain blood-spattered goods they should be ashamed to own, and which may some day lead them into folly."

While the auction went on, additional hubbub arose when some workers digging near the pond began unearthing bones. Onlookers crowded around, and suspense mounted as each bone was extracted from the dirt and placed on the ground. All this excitement dissipated quickly after the skull was removed and found to belong to a hog.

As May turned into June, there surfaced a tantalizing tale of complicity all the way from Texas. This tale, in fact, was so provocative that its existence was withheld from the newspapers until it could be either verified or discredited. The story began Thursday, May 21, when Prosecutor Smith received a letter from a man jailed in Vernon, Texas, who claimed to have assisted Belle and Lamphere in farmyard burials and who said Lamphere lost in a coin toss to determine which of them would set fire to Belle's house. The details in the letter were considered correct enough to send Sheriff Smutzer on May 22 to Texas to interview the potential accomplice. Although aware of this information, both The Herald and the Argus-Bulletin agreed to withhold publication until the confession was either substantiated or discredited.

The letter was finally printed June 1, along with information about the subsequent investigation that was said to disprove the confession. The letter's author was Julius G. Truelson Jr. using the alias Jonathan G. Thaw, and this is what he claimed:

"What I have to say and confess in the following paragraphs, I hope will be withheld from the press, as my parents are a respected family, and let me say I can withhold my guilt no longer and by turning state's evidence I hope leniency will be shown me.

"I have been an accomplice in crime with Mrs. Belle Gunness of LaPorte. I have just learned she and her three children are dead and Lamphere, another accomplice, is under arrest. Being equally guilty with Lamphere, I am man enough to take my medicine with him. I will be brief, for I don't believe in putting too much in writing, so will just state the affairs I had in the matter.

"I won't go into detail as to how, when and where I met her except that I met her on or in January, 1903, in Chicago, through a Swedish paper printed in Milwaukee, and from that time on we fell in together confidentially. On June 21, 1907, I brought my first victim to her place, a Mae F. O'Reilly of Rochester, whom I married and wanted to get rid of, and later a Frank Reidinger of Delafield, Wisconsin, whom she roped in by her ads. This was a month later, in July, I think. Lamphere and I buried these bodies in the same place, near the railroad tracks in the rear of the farm. After this, I went East and lay low, in the home of my parents. On March 2, 1908, I married again and went to Quebec, from where I wrote Belle to let me hear from her when I got to Montreal. In my letter to her I told her I had another to put out of the way and in her letter to me she told me to drop it as the climate was warm in her vicinity, and told me to hasten to her, as she wished to see me. Consequently I left this girl in Montreal on March 16 and arrived in LaPorte on the 18, 'o8. I arrived at her home about 10 p.m. and found Lamphere there. After a confidential talk, she told me one of her victim's husbands, or rather brothers, was coming to look for him and she wanted me to fire the place and go with her to Frisco. She wanted Lamphere and I to stay all night, but we thought best to go to town. Lamphere and I decided that we had to put her out of the way before she did us up, so we tossed coin to see which of us was to do the job. Lamphere lost and it was decided that he was to enter at night and knock Belle and her kids in the head and then set fire to the place to cover her crimes and ours. I left that night and went to Chicago and from there to St. Louis. Remaining in St. Louis for a few days I left and came to Ft. Worth, Texas, where I met Guy Waggoner, a rich ranchman, and I represented myself as J. G. Thaw, a cousin of H. K. Thaw, and he invited me to take a trip to his ranch, which I accepted. After being there a few days, I passed several checks and was arrested in trying to get away. I made this good to the bank and was bound over to the grand jury, which meets in September, in $1,500 bonds."

Truelson said his reason for confessing was his guilty conscience, which haunted him "most every night." He also said his parents and friends had disowned him.

Investigation into the Mae O'Reilly aspect of the claim led to the Rochester chief of police who believed the young woman had died within a year or two in the West. His information came from the woman's uncle, John Doyle, who owned a Rochester tavern, and who said Mae had already been involved in a murder trial in Rochester in 1902. This is the story Doyle told. Mae, along with Florence McFarlin and Lulu Miller worked together at Bell Telephone Company. A local businessman, Frank Young, became the lover of both Miller, whom he married, and McFarlin, whom he kept as his mistress. Lulu, knowing of the continued affair with Florence, attacked her with a razor until she bled to death. Mae felt her association with this case would best be forgotten if she left town, which she did, marrying a telegraph operator and moving West, where she died. Doyle's story, however, was refuted by his wife who claimed Mae was living in New York City but refused to give the address. In those days, that refusal was enough to create a dead end, even though her fate was crucial to the entire investigation. Truelson, after all, was claiming in subsequent interviews with Sheriff Smutzer that he took Mae to Belle's farm in June, where Belle murdered her with chloral hydrate. He said he would still locate the spot where he and Lamphere buried her in a field near the railroad track behind the house. As payment for her part in the act, Belle asked Truelson to help her dispose of another body, which they buried the next night in the same hole. Truelson said Lamphere told him the man's body was that of Frank Riedinger of Delafield, Wisconsin. When asked, Truelson rightly knew that

Belle had a wood wheelbarrow for transporting bodies rather than an iron one. He also could give a good description of Belle's horse and surrey. In addition, if he were inventing the story, how did he know so many details, considering he had been in jail since a month before the fire and therefore had limited access to newspapers that could have conveyed information about the case to him.

Truelson told Smutzer that he met Belle in early 1904 at the Sherman House hotel in Chicago after answering one of her matrimonial ads. The two of them then went to Belle's farm, where he spent the night. He was too poor and too young for Belle to marry. At 18, he already had been in trouble with the law for forgery and passing worthless checks; and she offered to hire him to dispose of bodies of people who died under her care as an illegally practicing midwife. He said she told him one man was already hired, but the job took two. Unwilling to take on this job, Truelson went back to Chicago and eventually to New York. He said he married Mae on August 4, 1904, in St. Peter's Church in Albany. After a two-week honeymoon at the Powers Hotel in Rochester, Truelson deserted his wife and eventually joined the Navy. After being discharged for desertion, he was convicted of passing worthless checks and sent to a reformatory. During this time, he had corresponded with Belle and was told that he was welcome to come to her farm, which he did after being paroled October 20, 1906. He claimed to have arrived on Christmas night and immediately assisted Lamphere in the burial of a girl. Lamphere said the girl was Jennie Olson, and Belle said she was a patient who had died after being treated unsuccessfully. When it was pointed out to Truelson that Lamphere did not become Belle's hired hand until 1907, he said Lamphere was working for Belle part-time in 1906 as a carpenter.

On the second night of his stay, he helped to bury a man that Lamphere said was John Moo. Truelson said that it was only then that he realized Belle was a murderess. After confronting Belle with his knowledge and refusing to participate further, he was lured by $50 to bury two more bodies, said by Lamphere to be an old man and a woman. This, too, had an element of believability in it because the autopsy of the two bodies in the grave with Moe and Jennie showed only that they were male and female and that their teeth showed that they probably were old. There then followed the episode with Mae, whom he had convinced to rejoin him. Truelson said he was later summoned from New York by Belle to help in the burial of Andrew Helgelein. After arriving at the farm the morning of January 14, he hid out in the house until Lamphere arrived back from Michigan City. At 9 p.m., a card game commenced with Truelson, Belle, Helgelein, and Lamphere. After Belle poisoned Helgelein's beer, the two other men carried him to a room where Belle refused to admit them. She later dragged out bags, which they buried. For his part, Truelson was paid $500.

Truelson said his last visit to the Gunness farm was in March, shortly before his arrest March 29 in Texas. He had married again and angered his father, a New York City piano manufacturer. He and his second wife, Sarah Vreeland, were at the Chauteau Frontenac in Quebec when he wrote to Belle at the farm on March 10, asking if they could visit her. Truelson said he had no intention of murdering this wife but only of staying at the farm until his parents' anger subsided. Belle sent her reply, as he requested, to him at the Palace Tiger Hotel in Montreal and told him that he had better come alone because the sheriff was making inquiries about Helgelein's disappearance. When he would not let his wife see the letter, she accused him of corresponding with another woman and refused to believe it was a business correspondence. So, Truelson went to LaPorte alone, where he entered into discussion with Belle and Lamphere about how Belle was going to deal with growing suspicion. He said Belle asked him to burn the house and flee with her to San Francisco, but he cautioned her not to panic and thereby draw suspicion upon herself. It was then that the events occurred that he related in the letter. Truelson said he went on to Chicago, St. Louis, and Texas.

Truelson, when led away from the interview and back to his cell, recanted the confession, saying it was all a lie and that during the time in question he was really in a New York reformatory or in government prisons for desertion. His letter of confession to LaPorte had been aimed at getting him away from the charges in Texas. For a 22-year-old, Truelson then had quite a talent for believable lying. Even his comments about the Frank Reidinger murder were surprising, considering how little publicity was given to this case in the newspapers. The name, however, had been mentioned in the press, and no one knew exactly how many newspapers Truelson had seen or which ones. In reality, Truelson's attempts to escape forgery prosecution led the Texas authorities to pursue what really happened to Mae O'Reilly. When queried, the Rochester (N.Y.) police said Mae had recently left New York for the home of her second husband's parents, by the name of Welch or Cowan, in Saratoga.

For his part, the jailed Lamphere adamantly denied knowing Truelson, which, of course, he would, since admitting knowledge would be tantamount to confession. As it was, he was housed all by himself in the unoccupied woman's section of the jail where he could not communicate with any other prisoners. He had the freedom of the corridor and all the reading matter and smoking tobacco he could want. A visitor to his cell described him as "very cheerful" and "the most contented and least worried prisoner in the county jail."

While that may seem to be peculiar behavior considering the charges against him, the behavior of Belle was still getting more attention. An Indianapolis attorney and native of LaPorte, L. H. Oberreich, had been interested in Belle ever since he served as stenographer at the coroner's investigation of the death of Peter Gunness. He could not be convinced that Belle burned her children and escaped. His reasoning was: "My father is in the jewelry business at LaPorte and he told me of a little circumstance which has made me believe that Mrs. Gunness did not kill her children and escape. She was fond of those children. About two or three days before the fire, Mrs.Gunness came into my father's store to buy her little daughter a ring. The child picked a $2.50 ring she liked. Mrs. Gunness finally bought it, though she had not expected to buy one that cost more than $1.50 and tried to get the child interested in one at that price. The next day she went to the store again. My father had seen the clerk waiting on her and knew she had bought a ring so he waited on her and asked if she had come to make an exchange. She said she had not--that she had come for a ring for her little boy. She said that the boy had felt hurt because the girl had a ring and he did not. Mrs. Gunness bought just the same kind of ring for the boy. I believe that she was really fond of the children and I don't believe that she killed them."

That she could have killed them was supported all the way from Italy by a man who later became recognized as the founder of modern criminology. Cesare Lombroso said in a statement printed June 3 in the New York World: "In criminal mothers, the maternal instinct, which is conspicuous in the normal woman, is not only suppressed, but reversed, as it becomes to them a pleasure to torture their offspring." Lombroso's theories are outmoded, but his contemporaries held him in high regard as a criminologist. He focused on the scientific study of crime with attention on the nature of the criminal, and his work was an embryo of what occurs today in the FBI's behavioral science work.

In his theory of the "born criminal," the villain is a throwback to primitive man; and his physical traits were like his ancestors. In 1881, he published the following analysis of criminal traits: "Prognathism (protruding jaw), abundant woolly hair, scarce beard, usually brown or dusky skin, oxycephaly (pointed or pyramidal skull), obliquity of eyes, small size of the cranium, development of the jawbones, receding forehead, huge and ansated (handle-shaped) ears, and muscular weakness."

Lombroso believed a trained observer could identify a "born criminal" on sight. A man was such if he had four or five of the mentioned traits; for a woman, it took only three or four.

At the time of the Gunness case, Lombroso was only one year away from his death and was a highly respected scientist. "There is no reason," he stated in the World, "to wonder that Mrs. Gunness used the knife, poison, deception, etc. Born women criminals often devote themselves to two different kinds of crime--poisoning and assassination." His examination of the details of the case led him to believe Belle had an accomplice, at least one and that one a man. Keeping in mind reports of Belle's strength, Lombroso still thought her too weak to carry out the murders and concealments. "Knowing that feminine criminals always mix eroticism with crime," he explained, "Mrs. Gunness must have used to obtain her accomplices besides the attraction of gain the attraction of sensuality. The enormity of the crimes, the exaggeration of energy which must be assumed to be in her, the extraordinary type of face, convince me that there must have been in her a strong inclination to hysteria and epilepsy, as there cannot be any great feminine crimes apart from these characteristics. It is not an unusual thing in criminology to find great ferocity and great dissimulation in women. They generally commit fewer crimes than men, but when they are criminal, they are considerably more so than men. It is not enough for a woman to murder an enemy; she wants to make him suffer, and she enjoys his death. But, however cruel she may be, a woman had not sufficient strength to commit alone a large number of murders of young, robust men, although repetition may have made the commission of crime more easy. It is therefore quite natural that there must be one, or even more, man accomplices."

Lombroso had a whole list of horrors committed by women from which he drew his conclusions. There was Fiburzia, who murdered a companion, bit off pieces of her flesh and threw them to the dogs; Chevalier, who murdered a sister-in-law by shoving scissors into her ear and into the brain; Enjalbert, who used her son to help murder her husband and sent her daughter into prostitution; Goglet, an arsonist, assassin, and thief; Bombard, a thief, a swindler, and a killer. He made particular mention of Weber: "Her own children and those of her friends, her neighbors, and even of strangers were strangled without any reason whatever in such a manner that the criminal hand could not be recognized at all. Her exaggerated and perverse sexual instincts manifested themselves in murdering beings who should have been most dear to her, and found, in this, strange satisfaction."

Belle was able to commit her crimes while deceiving those around her, he said, because "in doing evil mad persons are clever, more clever than sane ones." If, he said, "a superior intelligence for doing evil and carrying out are present; a born criminal appears and the woman will be more terrible than any man criminal."

It was only five years later that Lombroso's born-criminal theory was challenged. In 1913, Charles Goring published "The English Convict," with the results of his actual measurements of both criminal and noncriminal types. They showed there was no physical criminal type, and left the puzzle that was Belle still unsolved.

CHAPTER TWENTY

Although the Truelson story was considered self-serving rather than true, Sheriff Smutzer excavated the earth along the railroad track to prove or disprove the claim that two bodies were buried there. Nothing was found, as was the case in other digging ventures conducted by Smutzer and Deputy Sheriff Marr in suspicious locations throughout the month of June.

If Truelson's letter seemed to be worth following up, others certainly were not. One case in point came all the way from Wales in the form of an offer by Asberry Henderson, a cleaner and dyer in Maesteg:

"I observe from the Police Budget that you are offering a reward for the apprehension of the Gunness woman. I am able to tell you (but, mind you) I have the almighty to my back and I know it, and I have been like this ever since a boy large enough know anything. He has been a guide to me in my simple everyday life, of everything I do and I am now 24. I have waxed strong and nothing can turn me now. I was writing 12 months before time of a man inventing a flying bicycle in Yorkshire in the North of England and I in the south of Wales. You can imagine how I was laughed to scorn, but after 12 months, it was out on the public and the papers ringing with Asberry, then the laughing was stopped. Then again from Cardiff to India, I told a sailor in one night all about his family, as if I had been there. I told him two children died accidentally. It was not for them. It was meant for dogs and the children got hold of it. So this Gunness business will be a small matter for me to find out. I am also writing a book for a great thing, concerning the dead coming to life in the vault in Paris. In the 12 months when I go to Paris to take my place in the vault, the lady will come to life, after being dead so long. So this work makes the Gunness business very small. I think it would be best not to let my name out, for my name has been in all the papers not long ago of this mysterious work I am doing, and probably some of your enemies in this Gunness case have seen it or heard of it, and then see it in this case again, it will gave me two weeks of trouble, where it wouldn't take me a week. If you think it wise, send me her photo. If you accept my letter, let me know at once. When I get an answer from you giving me the job, I will start my work at once. Write down what you want to know about this woman."

Another "crank" letter came unsigned from Milwaukee stating that Belle was part of a gang operating in Chicago and Milwaukee. It claimed she also went by the names of Mrs. Cora Gibson, Mrs. Cora Buck, and Mrs. Cora Springer. An address was given for a Mr. and Mrs. Smith who were supposed to be members of this gang, and Belle was supposed to be in British Columbia. Belle was said to be in regular communication with her sister, a Mrs. Harrington of Milwaukee. After this information appeared in newspapers, a Mrs. Stella Smith, daughter of Mrs. Mary Harrington came forth denying the family had any connection with Belle and identifying the letter-writer as a man who had been harassing her. Whereupon, the man denied writing the letter.

There were, of course, people who were genuinely trying to help. Darrow and Worden of the defense were still actively searching for Belle and were offering $5,000 in reward money. One letter claimed the murderess was seen after the fire in Louisville, Kentucky. This letter, from Wallace W. Simms of that city, stated:

"It is a well known fact that Mrs. Gunness was in a resort on Green Street, this city, on May 1st. While here she wrote a letter to a man in LaPorte by the name of Fogle. This letter she gave to one of the inmates by the name of June, requesting the latter to mail it at the end of ten days, which was May 11th. The attorneys for Ray Lamphere are aware of the existence of this letter and intend to spring it as a surprise when Lamphere comes to trial. This will also account for the action of the county commissioners in withdrawing the funds to prevent you from further search for bodies. June, the inmate of the resort, declares Mrs. Gunness had a suitcase filled with currency while here. She also states that his man Fogle was the executor of her will and that she had seen several of the authorities in LaPorte and had things fixed to a queen's taste before she left LaPorte. June declares Mrs. Gunness had her hair dyed by Miss Rose Wilson, a hair dresser on Fourth Street, this city, on May 1, and it made a marked changed in her appearance. The defense of Ray Lamphere is holding back valuable information, which would lead to the apprehension of Mrs. Gunness if it were made known to the proper authorities. As to the authenticity of the statement made in this letter, I beg you to place yourself in communication with Chief of Police Hager who after a little investigating will vouch for the truth of them."

Another letter came from Mrs. A. Curtis of Minneapolis, who stated: "I saw an account of the crimes that Mrs. Gunness of your town was supposed to have committed and the description of Mrs. Gunness. A woman came here four weeks ago (early May) who bears the very same description. She is a large woman, weighs about 200 pounds, is large boned, gray hair, combed plain, dressed plain, a bold rather loud voice, large muscular arms, face somewhat wrinkled, and a dark upper lip, resembling a mustache just growing. She had a very masculine look and appearance. She cannot tell anything about herself or her family twice alike. She claims to have come here from her daughters in North Dakota but acknowledges to have lived in Ohio and Indiana. She says she had a husband and several children but that her husband and three children are dead. She calls herself Mrs. Sarah Parker here, but it has been noticed that she forgets to answer to that name sometimes and shows extreme confusion and fright if the name of Mrs. Gunness of LaPorte is mentioned and directly leaves the room before she can get her nerves collected again.

"The Catholic Home for the Aged, where she is stopping, had occasion to call the police wagon a few days ago to take a crazy woman away and the rest of the inmates did not know it until the wagon came. When Mrs. Parker, as she calls herself, saw the ambulance, she jumped from her chair and rushed in haste through three doors, looking very wild and frightened, as one would who expected somebody was after her. She is very careful to watch the ways and actions of the police who happen to come this way. All the inmates here are suspicious of her actions and believe she has had something to do with some crime. She came to the home for the aged some four weeks ago with a very pitiful story about her son-in-law turning her out of his house in North Dakota. She said she had come all the way to Minneapolis in the night and wanted the Catholic sisters to take her in, where she could be quiet and away from everybody. She seemed embarrassed when she found the doors were generally locked and no one could get out without asking leave, but was pleased that no one could get in without being let in. But allow me to tell you the way to get to her, if you want to. If you should bring some one with you who knew Mrs. Gunness, and should tell the doorkeeper that you are Mr. Jones or somebody else you could get in. This woman would not recognize the name, and be sure to come on a Sunday afternoon, for that is the only time that the general inmates of the home are all together. Tell the doorkeeper that you want to see me. I will help you to see her. She will never mistrust you if you are dressed in plain clothes. You alone could never arrest her. She is a strong, bold, desperate woman and we would all be glad to know if she is or is not Mrs. Gunness of your town. But we would not like to make a noise in the house unless we are sure of it for we are all friends of the sisters."

Although the letters were released to the newspapers, their claims were not investigated because the chief investigator, the sheriff, said that Belle was dead. Truelson's letter got attention in part because it supported the sheriff's belief.

Activity picked up in legitimate graveyards with the exhumation of one body, burial of others, and the transportation of the remains of the three children and woman found in the fire to their last destination in a cemetery west of Chicago.

The exhumation retrieved a body for viewing by Mrs. B.F. Carling of Chicago, whose husband had disappeared two years ago after meeting a rich widow. Like the body in question, he had a plate with three false teeth in front. Mrs. Carling, however, was left with uncertainty as she thought the body was her husband's but she was not sure enough to claim it. Meanwhile, the Coroner Mack permitted the burial of five unidentified skeletons.

Six weeks after their deaths, the bodies from the basement of the farmhouse were released for burial. Frank Cutler, the funeral director from LaPorte, accompanied them on their journey by train which began at 8:04 a. m. Tuesday, June 16. The train was met in Chicago by Andrew Larson, a funeral director in Austin, who was in charge of their burial at Forest Home Cemetery, a spot selected by Belle in her will. As the four were lowered into the ground, only the funeral director, his assistant, and the gravediggers were in attendance.

The identities of two other victims were tentatively announced in June. Smutzer was confident that one victim was Olaf Jensen, whose disappearance was being investigated by C.E. Faye, Norwegian consul in Chicago. The story had the same old story line. Jensen left Chicago for LaPorte to visit a rich widow, whom he had met through a matrimonial ad in a Scandinavian newspaper. He was never seen or heard from again. Faye sent a letter from the missing man's mother who lived in Norway and who quoted her son as saying the widow was from Trondheim, Norway. She also said he left Chicago with a large sum of money intended for investing in the widow's farm. Smutzer thought the other victim was Christen Hilkven of Eau Claire, Wisconsin, who disappeared in 1906 after selling a farm for $2,000. He had switched a newspaper subscription to LaPorte and had received mail at the Gunness farm.

The events of June also included plans by the two daughters of the late Peter Gunness to sue Belle's estate for the $3,500 she collected on their father's life insurance policy and even further evidence of the international scope of the Gunness story. Wu Ting-Fang, a member of the Chinese governmental delegation to the United States, interrupted a trip from Chicago to South Bend to visit the Gunness farm.

It was now decided, although both prosecution and defense claimed to be trial-ready, to postpone the trial until Fall. A civil suit would first claim the space in circuit court, and it was expected to last for from two to three weeks. Both sides agreed that conducting the trial in the middle of summer would be too hot.

And it was the hottest summer to date in the history of the weather bureau. The drought persisted throughout the summer and took over the headline space that had once belonged to the Gunness case. Medical experts at Rush Medical College in Chicago reported that traces of arsenic and strychnine were found in the bodies of the woman and three children found in the cellar and in Andrew Helgelein's body. And in August, the body of a well-dressed man about 40 years of age was found under a pile of rails a little east of Rolling Prairie, just east of LaPorte. He died of a shotgun blast to the head. He apparently had nothing to do with the Gunness case, but all identification had been removed from him, except a copy of the Minnesota Farmer.

CHAPTER TWENTY ONE

Summer and the record-setting heat came and went. The courthouse cooled and waited. September and October brought their own heat, an intensifying of the election campaigning; and still there was no trial. Obviously, the Gunness case would have to wait on more pressing issues--like who would have a job after the November election. When the votes were counted, Taft had given Bryan his third presidential election defeat. Locally, the political results were mixed. The Republicans retained the offices of clerk, recorder, and sheriff and gained membership on the county commissioners' board. The Democrats got the treasurer, prosecuting attorney, coroner, surveyor, and a county commissioner. The Gunness adversaries were still in place. Smith remained as prosecutor; and Sheriff Smutzer's right hand man, Anstiss, was the new sheriff, the first to occupy the new county jail now nearing completion.

Lamphere had remained in jail through the heat and the waiting. The only Belle yet found lay buried deep within a cemetery in the countryside west of Chicago. The case was set to begin the first Monday after the elections. Meanwhile, the prosecutor announced a change of plans. He scrapped his original idea of charging Lamphere with the murder of Andrew Helgelein. Instead, he decided to charge him with the murder of Belle and the three children. Smith said the switch was made to establish once and for all that Belle was dead and buried. "I am tired of this silly rot that she is alive, " he explained, " and I have therefore decided to take up the Gunness case proper and put Lamphere on trial for the murder of Mrs. Gunness and her children, through setting fire to the house, so that it will open up the channel for this discussion."

"I can prove without the shadow of a doubt to any man, who is not so unprejudiced that he will not believe anything, that the woman died the night of April 28th in her house and that her body was taken out and held at Cutler's morgue for several weeks before being finally shipped to Chicago for burial. I am going to put a stop to all this talk about her being seen in 40 different places in the country by every Tom, Dick, and Harry, who thinks he is a detective. Lamphere will have every opportunity to prove his innocence of setting fire to the house and thereby killing the inmates, and if the evidence does not show that he did it, I will be just as pleased as anyone, for I do not want to convict a man who is innocent. If it does show he is guilty, he should be punished and I will ask for the death penalty in that case."

Worden for the defense replied: "We will prove Lamphere innocent, without doubt. He was not guilty of setting fire to the house. We can prove he was not there at the time. Besides we are confident Mrs. Gunness is alive and so how could he be guilty of murdering her?"

Both men were entirely committed to their positions. No big money was backing the defense.

Forty witnesses were subpoenaed by the state. They were all found but one. That one, however, was about as important as a witness could get. He was Louis Schultz, the gold miner, who said he sluiced out Belle's teeth. He'd gone out West, and no one could find him.

On Monday, November 9, Case No. 1061 was called in Judge Richter's courtroom. Attorney Worden for the defense tried but failed to get the indictments quashed on the grounds that they were not specific enough. He also cited the "circumstancial evidence only" as insufficient to bring his client to trial. Again, he lost the point. At 9:45 a.m., Lamphere entered the courtroom with Sheriff-elect Anstiss. His face had a prison pallor, but he wore a new black suit. A reporter for the LaPorte Herald made this observation that first morning: "The keen eye of the defendant has gained an unaccustomed intensity during the long imprisonment. He seems to be oblivious of the fact that he is alone in the trial for his life ... There is no quailing, and his frequent whispered questioning with his attorney is his only change from the position of an interested observer of the proceedings. One cannot help wondering as he sees the Lamphere from the exterior what visions of the past must come before the Lamphere of the unseen interior. At least he was acquainted with the arch-murderess and his acquaintance gave him an opportunity to know something of the tempestuous spirit of that fiendish modern Lucretia Borgia. When the 28th of April is mentioned, does it recall to his mind the scene of a quiet morning made lurid with the flames of the smoking farmhouse, and resonant with stifled cries of innocent children, or does he reassure himself, in the consciousness of his own freedom from guilt of murder or arson, as now charged and being tried."

As jury selection began, it was anticipated to be a long process. Crucial questions to be asked were whether the prospective juror had formed an opinion about the case and what stance he had on the subject of the death penalty. It was a tedious business because few people in the county had no opinion on the case. Typical of the rejects were A. W. Fall, who had an opinion and had known Lamphere for 20 years; Herman Oberreich, who objected to infliction of the death penalty; W. P. Allen, whose opinion was so set it would require evidence to remove; George Rogers, who was personally acquainted with the defendant's father; and George Staiger, who admitted he could not try the case impartially. Juror after juror was excused because he had already formed an opinion on the case. At the beginning of the third day, there remained three jurors to be selected. The defense, led by Worden, changed its questioning thrust after learning that one of the state's witnesses would be instead a witness for the defense. Dr. Walter Haines of the Rush Medical College in Chicago changed sides after finding poison in the stomachs of the woman and two of the children found in the burned out basement. He found enough strychnine and arsenic to cause death.

Attorney Worden explained the defense's position: "The testimony of Dr. Haines will support either theory which may be adopted by the defense--that Mrs. Gunness poisoned her children, placed a cadaver with them, set fire to the house and escaped, or that she poisoned the children and then committed suicide, after setting fire to the house. The state will be unable to reconcile its theory that Lamphere set fire to the house with Dr. Haines' testimony and that is why we called him instead of the state. Of course, the state might claim that Lamphere set fire to the house at the same time that Mrs. Gunness poisoned her children and that they died from the suffocation and the fire before the strychnine and arsenic had time to act. Quite a coincidence, isn't it? Of course, we don't admit that it was Mrs. Gunness' body."

So now, some new questions were posed by the defense even to those jurors already selected: "If after the evidence has all been introduced, there was a doubt as to whether the persons whose bodies were found in the fire met death through fire or by poison, would you give the defendant the benefit of that doubt?" Prosecutor Smith vigorously objected to this "latitude of proof required of the state," and jury selection continued until completed at 4 p.m. that afternoon, Thursday, four days after the trial began.

The state began its case with an opening statement from Prosecutor Smith: "Gentlemen of the jury--There has been an unusual length of time consumed in the selection of this jury. It may seem to you that there has been a good deal of unnecessary questioning, but this matter is one of great importance. It has gained a widespread notoriety. I want to thank the members of the panel for their patience in the long and somewhat tedious examination. I anticipate that this may take longer than many of you may have apprehended. It is always difficult to tell where a lawsuit will end. I trust that you will give the same attention in the trial that you have in the selection of the jury ... It is not the business of the prosecuting attorney to abuse everybody. I want to ensure you that my partner, Mr. Sutherland, and myself feel that we occupy exactly the same position that you occupy as officers of this court. We have no animosity to satisfy. We have no axes to grind. We have no spleen to vent on anyone. We are not persecuting anybody. If sometimes we get zealous, it is because of our anxiety to fulfill our duty ...

"Gentlemen, a dark cloud has fallen upon our country. It is our duty to uncover the mystery and to punish the guilty, if possible. You occupy a twofold position. You are citizens of this county and officers of this court. Now, I want to set at rest any idea that we are of necessity trying to fasten the crime upon someone, no matter whom it may be. Somebody has been killed. Somebody has been murdered, and it is your duty to inquire into the matter and find, if possible, the guilty man. Every citizen of the county is interested in the manner in which you do that duty. There has been a lot of notoriety in this case--a lot of gossip has been spread broadcast to poison people's minds. Of necessity this must be gone into to a certain extent. It is going to be our effort to bring out every fact bearing on this incident ... The evidence will be largely circumstantial. There will be some evidence that is positive. People when they set out to commit a crime, such as the burning of a dwelling, do not start out to do it with a brass band ...

"The first element of our proof will show that Ray Lamphere set fire to the house. The second element of the proof will be that by reason of that fire, Belle Gunness and her three children were killed. You have said you would try this case according to the law and the evidence ... All we are required to show is that the defendant set fire to the house and that these occupants lost their lives by reason of this act.

"Along about six or seven years ago Belle Gunness moved out here on what is known as the McClung Road. Her husband, Peter Gunness, lived with her there some two or three years and then died under what seems to have been unusual circumstances. They had one child, Philip Gunness. Belle Gunness had two children by a former husband, she having been formerly married and lived in Chicago. We shall present evidence which will show that this husband died under peculiar circumstances. We are not here to defend the character of Belle Gunness, neither are we here to drag it down, but the evidence will disclose the fact that lots of folks were buried on her premises. The evidence will disclose that Ray Lamphere in June, 1907, began to work for Belle Gunness--that he stayed there until February, 1908. We shall show that in January of this year a man named Helgelein came to her home, and that Mrs. Gunness proceeded to lure and get his money from him.

"The evidence will show that on January 14 of this year Belle Gunness sent Ray Lamphere to Michigan City on some pretext or other, probably to leave some horses there for some one who was to call for them. In place of staying there that night, as she had instructed him to do, he came back on the street car and got off near the powerhouse, and the evidence will show that he made the remark to a man on the car that he was going over to see what the old woman was doing, that he went over, and came upon the scene while Mrs. Gunnesss was disposing of Helgelein and so assisted her in that job. He was 'Johnny-on-the-spot.' By putting Helgelein out of the way, she got $3,000 which he had received from a bank in Dakota on a draft which was cashed in the First National Bank in this city. The evidence will show that Lamphere received some part of that money and that it was over this amount that the two fell out, and a great animosity grew up between them.

"On February 3 they quarreled and Lamphere didn't live there any more. Some time before this, Mrs. Elizabeth Smith had had Lamphere arrested for not paying a board bill, and Mrs. Gunness paid the fine. Soon after this quarrel, Mrs. Gunness had him arrested on the charge of trespass--and it will be shown that she served a written notice upon him to stay off her premises; and when he was convicted in justice court for this offense, it was Elizabeth Smith who paid his fine. The evidence will show that a third time he was arrested and this time a bond for surety of the peace was made by him. Whether all this is true or not, it is true that there was an animosity between them. The evidence will show that he made the remark, 'I'll go to the old lady's house or make it hot for her.' We shall prove that he said, ' I can make the old lady get down on her knees to me' and numerous statements as to his getting money from the old lady ...The evidence will show that this business had caused a breach that was getting wider and wider between the two and that he kept constantly going there until the evening of April 27th. On the 27th, Lamphere was living at Wheatbrook's or in that vicinity and was making Wheatbrook's a sort of headquarters. On the afternoon of the 27th he came to town with Mr. Wheatbrook shortly after dinner for some trivial purpose, with the intention of going back with Wheatbrook. Wheatbrook missed him some way, and Lamphere spent the afternoon around town in the saloons until 5 or 6 o'clock. Then he went to Lizzie Smith's and after supper went down town again until 9 o'clock. At 9 o'clock he went back to Mrs. Smith's and went out and got a pail of beer after that. Lamphere set the alarm for 3 o'clock the morning of the 28th, according to his own statement, and probably 15 or 30 minutes after 3, he started from Mrs. Smith's.

"The evidence will show by Lamphere's own statement that he took the other road past the Belle Gunness place. He was on the spot. He was right at the house when the fire started and there was not another living soul at the place.

"When asked why he didn't give an alarm when he saw smoke from the house, he said, 'I didn't think it any of my business.' We next find him over where the Lake Erie tracks cross the road. The morning train was due here at that time at 5 o'clock and the evidence will show that the train was on time that morning. The train then probably passed that point at about 10 minutes of 5. Lamphere had left the Smith house at a little after 3 o'clock and here he was a mile and a quarter away one and one-half hours later.

"In place of walking along the highway, he jumped the fence by the cemetery and ran along the woods up to John Ross', getting there about 5:30 o'clock to get a broad axe. Along about 7 that evening he was arrested by the sheriff and the evidence will show that when the sheriff spoke to him and told him to get on his coat and go to town his first words were, 'Did those folks burn up in that house?' To this the sheriff replied, 'What house?' The foremost thing in Lamphere's mind was the burning of that house.

"Another phase of this case is the burden resting upon the state to prove the corpus dilecti. The indictment with reference to Belle Gunness lays the burden upon us to prove that she died and burned in that house. We do not want in any way to be released from that burden. There isn't anyone who stands for the freedom of American citizens more strenuously than I do. It is the privilege of every man to have a chance for his life. The evidence will show that one the night before the fire, one Joe Maxson was staying at the Gunness home as a hired man. On Monday in the afternoon, Mrs. Gunness went to Mr. Leliter's office and drew up her will and at Mr. Leliter's suggestion rented a safety deposit box in the bank and into that box she put the will and her private papers and some $700 in money. After that she went to Minich's grocery store for her week's supply of groceries and she also bought a supply of toys for the children, spending some $8 or $10 for necessaries of life and the comfort of her children. Maxson remained up until 9:30. The evidence will show that they had supper late that evening and among other things that they had for supper some beefsteak. I want you to remember this fact, for I shall return to this later. About 9:30 Maxson went to bed and at that time the mother and children were at the table in the home playing games and nothing unusual had happened. Now whatever this woman may have done, I don't believe anyone will say that she was other than a good mother to these children.

"About four in the morning Maxson was awakened. He was occupying the upper story of the frame part of the house. Mrs. Gunness occupied the southeast corner room with the little boy. It was the custom of the children to occupy the northwest corner room. Maxson heard them retire. He was awakened by smoke in his room. There was a gale blowing that night from the northwest. He rushed to the window and the whole interior of the brick was on fire. He tried to burst through the door but he was unable to do so. He grabbed his clothes and got down stairs and tried to go back and break open the door but the smoke was so thick he was compelled to go back. He ran around the house yelling like a wild man. He had heard no sound from the other part. The fire had evidently been started in the outside cellarway. Others came on the scene. They climbed to the room occupied by the children but there was no one in the room. The bed gave evidence of having been occupied.

"The evidence will show that the house burned down. One contention will be that Mrs. Gunness became suffocated and died. That the children were awakened by the smoke and ran over to their mother's room into the thickest of the fire and there were suffocated. About 4 o'clock that afternoon, 12 hours after the fire had begun, the sheriff got into these ruins--about 100 or 200 pails of water had been thrown upon the debris. He found the little boy lying in Mrs. Gunness' arms. The debris was from five inches to one foot under the bodies. A photograph will show a bed spring and mattress under the bodies and these were lying back down. The forms of the other children were near, lying face down. After the bodies were taken out, they were in charge of the sheriff and later a coroner's inquest was held. Let me say that up to the time of the discovery of Helgelein's body there never was any question as to the identity of the bodies ...

"That at the autopsy by the doctors, the coroner found on the hand a ring or rings belonging to Mrs. Gunness. We can prove by photographs taken before her death and by engraving that these were Mrs. Gunness' rings. There is a dentist here in

LaPorte who did some dental work for Mrs. Gunness, that he did crown and bridge work on the upper and lower jaws. There are not many more facts to be dealt with. There are some but these are the material elements of the case ...Did Ray Lamphere burn this house? Did he feloniously and wilfully do this? Did Belle Gunness and her three children meet death because of this act? If we prove beyond a reasonable doubt an affirmative answer to these questions and I believe we can, we shall expect a verdict accordingly."

CHAPTER TWENTY TWO

While the prosecutor was giving his opening statement, Lamphere sat up and showed interest. Because of his limited contact with the outside world during the last six months, much of what Smith was saying seemed to be news to him. A local newspaper reporter described Lamphere's reactions: "He leaned forward in his chair much of the time, particularly during the recital of the fire scenes and the manner in which Mrs. Gunness and the children lost their lives. His eyes were riveted on the speaker and he gripped the arm of the chair with his left hand in a sort of nervous grasp. His right hand tugged at his mustache, at times almost viciously. Several times it looked as though he intended to leap from his chair, but if he ever had such a thought, he restrained himself. His face paled at times, but during the greater share of the time he was flushed, the dark, and light shades chasing each other over his face as the blood surged to and fro."

For the first time, Lamphere's mother now made a public statement. Gray-haired and elderly, with her voice often quivering and her eyes often teary, she was allowed to break the silence that the defense had imposed on her. "I shall go upon the witness stand to help my boy in his fight for his life at any time they choose to call me," she said. " I shall do everything in my power to aid my son, and the few years that are left to me I shall devote to trying to clear his good name. I have not spoken heretofore merely because I was advised by his lawyers not to say anything to be printed in the newspapers. I obeyed this injunction, but I say now that it was against my own desires. My attitude has been entirely misrepresented. It has been stated that owing to my estrangement from my poor unfortunate husband, I had forsaken my boy in his trouble. A more cruel falsehood than this could not be uttered. No one who really knows me could, for a moment, imagine that I would leave my own flesh and blood at such a time as this. With my own fingers, I made all the clothes that Ray wore until he was 10 years of age. I sewed love into every stitch. He was my heart, my life, during his childhood. When my own difficulties came upon me, he was my refuge and my strength. It is true that I have not lived with my husband for years. He and I know why, and I think if you ask him, the squire himself will say it is through no fault of mine. Alone as I am in the world at my age, it makes my boy all the more dear to me. Every day that he has been in that jail my heart has ached for him, but I could not go to his cell and wrap him in my arms. Ray is innocent. God knows and I know that he is not guilty. He has written this to me, and he never told me a lie in his life, even as a boy."

The defense, to legitimize its contention that Belle was still alive, subpoenaed her. But because Worden could not supply an address for delivery for the subpoena, the sheriff gladly filed it away. That isn't to say people weren't still seeing her. She was "seen" near Milwaukee and "appeared twice" at an undisclosed location in Illinois. People also continued to remember past encounters with Belle. John Zach, a house mover, came to court looking for Judge Richter with a story about moving Belle's hog pen. Zach recalled how he moved the pen three times in April of 1907 before Belle finally approved of the location. Her anxiety over the exact position of the pen caused Zach to think she wanted to cover more bodies. Another possible gravesite was pointed out by D. M. Hutson, who remembered seeing Belle with a shovel coming away from a pile of fresh dirt on the hillside right after the visit of a stock buyer.

Meanwhile, Mrs. L.A. Heerin and her mother, Mrs. Lucy Burton, who were taken from railroad sleeping berths in New York when authorities mistook Mrs. Heerin for Belle, were each suing the New York Central Railroad Company for $30,000; and Asle Helgelein arrived in LaPorte from Aberdeen, S. D., to testify for the prosecution.

On November 13, the first full day of the trial, Attorney Martin Sutherland for the prosecution called the first witness, Coroner Mack. Mack testified that he had lived in LaPorte for 12 years and had been coroner for two years. The only surprising information he offered was his observation of a hole in the forehead of one of the children. In general, his memory seemed vague and uncertain. The state won its first victory when Judge Richter, over the defense's objections, allowed the coroner's verdict as evidence. The judge would later tell the jury to disregard the coroner's verdict that Belle was dead, saying the state would prove that fact through other evidence. This reversal, however, did not occur until the verdict was read to the court. The cross examination of Mack by Atty. Worden would produce an entire list of things the coroner did not know or did not do. He did not, for example, ever examine the hole that he found in the child's forehead, nor did he know which child's head had the hole or if any of the other children had holes in their heads. In response to Worden's questioning, Mack also did not know: whether a leg had been cut off or burned off, whether the arms were disjointed or not, or whether any vertebrae were missing along with the adult woman's missing head.

The next witness was Dr. Franklin T. Wilcox, who did the autopsy on one of the girls. "The front part of the head was burned away. The right arm was burned off at the shoulder; the left arm, at the wrist; both legs were burned off at the knees. The lungs were collapsed and the heart was full of blood," he testified. "The stomach was so badly burned that it was not preserved. The bladder was normal. The sex was that of a female. The measurement from the top of the head to the knees was 3 feet and 7 inches. I examined the brain and found no evidence of hemorrhage and the skull had no evidence of fracture. I was unable to determine the cause of death."

Wilson also said he helped remove some rings that were on the adult body. An enlargement of a photograph of the rings on

Belle's hands showed that those rings appeared to Wilson to be similar to the ones taken from the corpse.

Prosecutor Smith then took over the questioning of the next witness, Sheriff Smutzer. The sheriff told of reaching the fire scene at 5:30 a.m. and of searching for and finding the bodies. He said Belle had been in his office three or four times, and from those meetings he said he was able to say that the rings in the courtroom belonged to Belle. For this witness, the defense reserved its right to cross examination later.

Dr. H. H. Long, who conducted the autopsy on the younger girl, now took the stand to describe his examination, which showed similar conditions to those described by Dr. Wilcox for the older girl. In this corpse, the neck was so damaged that the head came off when the body was moved. Both girls had empty stomachs, which indicted to Dr. Long that they had eaten at least four to six hours before death.

Next came Dr. J. L. Gray, a former county LaPorte County coroner and coroner's physician in Cook County, Illinois. He did the autopsy on the adult female with the missing head: "The upper vertebrae were missing down to the seventh cervical," he explained. "The left arm was burned to the upper third. The right arm was disconnected at the shoulder. The right leg was burned off to the knee. The left leg was burned off at the ankle, and most of the flesh to the knee. The breast was burned, exposing the contents of the body. An adult right arm was with the body with the fingers tightly clutched. In this hand was a piece of cloth. There was a band ring on the second right hand finger. On the left third finger there was a small diamond ring with the inscription inside, 'P.S. to J.S.,August 27, '94. In the band ring was the inscription, 'P.G. to J.S. 3-5-95'. The length from the tip of the shoulders to the ankle joint was 49 3/4 inches. On making an incision the cardial sac appeared normal. The heart was dilated and all four compartments were filled with clotted blood. The lungs were normal but appeared cooked. The abdominal wall was about two inches thick. The stomach was empty. It was tied at either end and taken out. The liver was normal, as was the bladder and adjacent organs. On turning the body over, the back and chest were burned to the sacrum. The back of the legs was worse burned than the front. All the muscular tissue was burned off. The kidneys were normal as to size. With the body was a mass of clothing, which was difficult to classify."

When asked, Gray also described the items beside the body: "With the body there were parts of a felt mattress. There were remnants of a child's nightdress, and on this there were lace collar and cuffs ... There was a small night robe. This was badly burned. There was a boy's union suit of underwear. There were the remains of an adult undershirt, length 33 inches. There were the remains of a pair of drawers, fleece lined, the waist band only remaining."

The prosecution made strong points when Gray said the probable weight of the woman in life was about 200 pounds and the heat and fire had produced "very great" shrinkage. He also said the woman was about 5 feet and 4 inches tall, had 2 inches thick of fat at the abdomen, and had "fat and large" breasts. He also identified the rings and he said there was no decomposition of the body or its organs, a blow to the idea that Belle had murdered a woman and stashed her someplace until the fire.

During the cross examination by Worden, he tried hard to repair the damage done to his case by Gray:

Worden: Was the hand contracted in the right arm?

Gray: Yes, sir.

Worden: Did you ever know of such a postmortem condition in the hand being occasioned by death by suffocation?

Gray: Yes, sir.

Worden: Where?

Gray: A case of a Polander in Chicago, who was suffocated by coal gas. I was also present at the hanging of an anarchist, where the same conditions were present.

Worden: Have you read from any of your medical works that contraction is incident of death by suffocation?

Gray: Yes, sir.

Worden: Can you produce that authority?

Gray: Yes, sir.

Worden: Will you produce it?

Gray: Yes,sir. (The books were brought.)

Worden: Turn to the place in the book. In general rule of cases does the body become rigid in death by suffocation?

Gray: Yes, sir.

Worden: Are you familiar with the postmortem condition of a body when death has been caused by strychnine?

Gray: I have seen several.

Worden: State whether or not poisoning by strychnine causes a postmortem spasmodic contraction of the body.

Gray: Yes, sir.

Worden: It is the usual symptom, is it not?

Gray: Yes.

Worden: Isn't it a fact that when you made your examination and wrote a verdict, you stated it was impossible to determine the cause of death?

Gray: Yes.

In the cross examination about the size of the body, Gray told Worden the corpse weighed 73 pounds. He said he estimated that it had shrunk by about two-thirds "by comparing with other meat which had been cooked." To Worden's question about whether he had any vested interest in the case, Gray replied, "Absolutely not."

Also testifying was Dr. J. H. William Meyer, who did the autopsy on the little boy's remains, which he described: "The body was severely burned. The legs were burned off at the knees entirely. The forehead was burned away, exposing the brain. The back was badly burned, the spinal cord was exposed ... One of the arms was missing. The lungs were partially preserved by cooking. In cutting through the pericardium, we came to clotted blood. The heart was contracted, containing no particle of blood. All the organs were well cooked." Meyer said the corpse measured 2 feet and 7 inches "from top of head to stump of feet."

The first week ended with two important witnesses for the prosecution, I. P. Norton, a dentist; and Frances Flynn, a frequent visitor to the Gunness house. Norton had identified the bridgework handed over by Louis Schultz as belonging to Belle. After stating that he had seven years experience as a dentist, Norton described the work done on Belle: "She came to my office to have some teeth attended to. I extracted three lower teeth. Upon two cuspids I put two gold crowns and swung between these certain dummies in bridgework, the peculiar features. It was an unusual construction. There was 18k gold solder used to reinforce this. Afterwards I drilled through one of the dummy teeth and placed two platinum pins, riveted in the end." Over objection by the defense, diagrams showing the condition of the mouth before and after the bridgework were accepted into evidence.

The following exchange then took place between Prosecutor Smith and Norton:

Smith: Did the sheriff bring to your office some teeth?

Norton: Yes, sir.

Smith: When was that?

Norton: May 19, 1908.

Smith: I now hand you some teeth. Are these the teeth the sheriff gave you?

Norton: Yes, sir.

Smith: Did you ever see the teeth before?

Norton: Yes, sir.

Smith: Where?

Norton: I constructed them.

Smith: For whom?

Norton: Mrs. Belle Gunness.

When Smith then asked Norton how these teeth could have been removed, the dentist replied that the gold crowns would have had to be split and that the teeth could not have been pulled.

Then it was Worden's turn:

Worden: Did you keep a record of the work?

Norton: No, sir. It was a cash deal.

Worden: You made a diagram?

Norton: I made two.

Worden: What did you do with the other?

Norton: Gave it to Sheriff Smutzer.

Worden: When was that?

Norton: May 17

Worden: Which is the most flammable, a tooth or jaw bone?

Norton: A jaw bone in my judgment.

Worden: I show you the natural tooth and ask if you think the upper maxillary would be destroyed before this tooth, in passing through the fire?

Norton: Yes, sir.

Worden: Do you think a fire intense enough to destroy a skull would not destroy the tooth also?

Norton: It would not.

Worden: Why?

Norton: Because of it being protected.

The jaw bone that Norton had originally identified months ago as belonging to Mrs. Gunness, was produced. Norton now explained that this jaw bone, pulled from the ruins, had teeth pulled from the same side as Belle. But this wasn't as damning to the defense as were the portions of roots of two teeth that were still attached to the bridgework that had been sluiced out of the debris by gold miner Louis Schultz. That showed that the owner of the bridgework did not just toss it onto the ground deliberately so that it could be found and identified.

The next witness was Mrs. Frances Flynn, who lived on Pine Lake Avenue and frequently visited Belle at the farmhouse up to about a year and a half before the fire. It was at that time, estimated by Mrs. Flynn to be November 30, 1906, that Jennie Olson disappeared. In her personal observations of Belle, Mrs. Flynn said she was physically large, about 280 pounds, and emotionally maternal, being aways kind to the children. She recognized two of the three rings found as those worn by Belle while alive. Mrs. Flynn also said she had witnessed the discovery of the bodies in the cellar ruins and saw some sort of bed and mattress beneath the bodies. Hers was important testimony for the prosecution because she had no known reason to lie.

CHAPTER TWENTY THREE

As the trial began its second week, the cross examination of Mrs. Flynn brought out only her contention that Belle's rings were so tight that the only way to remove them would be to file them off. The prosecution also presented its version of the motive for the crime, Lamphere's jealousy. This they attempted to do with a series of letters from Belle to Asle Helgelein, brother of victim Andrew:

"LaPorte, March 27, 1908--Mr. Asle K. Helgelein: "I have your recent letter in which you wish to know where your brother Andrew keeps himself. Well, that is just what I would like to know. He came here about the middle of January. When he left here, he said he wanted to find his brother who had kept a gambling room in Aberdeen. He thought he was in Chicago or New York, or possibly had gone to Norway. Bella Gunness."

"LaPorte, Ind., April 11, 1908--Mr. A. K. Helgelein: "Your letter I have received some days ago, but have not been able to answer in regard to your brother Andrew. I have tried every which way to find some trace of him. The man who told me he is in South Dakota is named Lamphere, who worked for me for a while. He said he had heard it from someone he knew in Mansfield, and he also had probably told them about the $10,000. I knew right away that it was a lie. But this Lamphere began to find so many wrong things to talk about until at last they arrested him, and they had three doctors examine him and see if he was sane. They found him not crazy enough to put in a hospital. But perfectly sane he is not. He is now out under bonds and is going to have a trial next week, therefore, there is no foundation to the stories told, but one thing I am sure of is that he in one way or another has taken the letter from Andrew he had sent me. Others have told me that Lamphere was jealous of Andrew and for that reason troubled me this way, but to me he did not say anything and I did not mention it to him when

Andrew left. This Lamphere drank so much and I got the impression that he was not quite right, and others say the same. Andrew had sent to him a lot of money when he was here. Some of this I got for a mortgage which he had made over to him and a lot of cash money, but I do not think it was so much but he had alot of checks, but as far as I know I think they were all payable to himself, and he had other valuable papers. I knew he had the mortgage he got from me and alot of others, but I did not pay much particular notice to them and therefore did not know what they contained. He did not say anything to me in regard to the farm or creatures, but I think it would be best for you to sell the farm and creatures as soon as you can and come here in May. When Andrew comes up there again, which he no doubt will some time, be sure and do not tell him that I told you this or do not tell it to others either. Bella Gunness."

"LaPorte, Ind. April 24, 1908--Mr. A. K. Helgelein: "Your welcome letter I have received, for which I thank you. It is a wonder to me as well as for you as to where Andrew keeps himself. It is strange he should go away without his belongings. However, I will tell you all that I know, and you can be sure that I am telling you the truth. I cannot remember the accurate date he left on the 15th or 16th of January. Two or three days afterward I had a letter from him in Chicago, saying he had hunted for his brother but did not find him, and that the next day he would look around the board of trade and see how it was, also to get track of his brother. If he could not find him he would go to New York and find out if he had gone to Norway. If such was the case I think he would go to Norway too. That Lamphere was here, and he probably took the letter, but that part of a letter which I spoke of we found in the barndoor in the evening when he was around. I will send it to you. I recognized Andrew's writing, and I think you do, too, and I believe that the letter was addressed to me, as I do not think Andrew would write to any other woman. I assure you I will do all I can if you will take a trip down here to see what we could do to find him, but I don't understand what keeps him away so long. Bella Gunness"

This was the fragment referred to in the letter:

"My Best Friend: I am well and the spring is here, as the snow is going fast. My creatures, most of them, slept outside yesterday and tonight without cover. The cows who have calves, I have them inside, also those who expect to 'calve' soon. I am happy every time I write you. I think I can come to you in the month of May."

CHAPTER TWENTY FOUR

The letters entered into evidence were only three out of 75 that the prosecution had in its possession. They had been translated from Norwegian and checked for accuracy by Asle Helgelein. That they were written to a man whose brother she had already chopped up and buried just illustrated further how cunning and coldblooded Belle really was. Never duped by Belle, Asle Helgelein had shocked the court by testifying to his belief that Belle had buried 50 bodies in her yard. Listening along with the others, Lamphere had lost most of his previously displayed agitation but still appeared nervous as his name was mentioned in the letters. "The others" were growing in number, with most of the standing room taken in the aisles and along the sides. People seemed surprised that so many of the spectators were women, but the height of interest in this trial was so great that even people passing through LaPorte wanted to drop into the courtroom for a while. Once they did, they often prolonged their stay. Those who had to stay, the jury members, were sequestered but taken for walks and other outings and dinners.

The prosecution proceeded to weave its web around Lamphere by using his words and whereabouts as described by witnesses. M.E. Leliter, the attorney who had drawn up Belle's will, testified that Belle and Lamphere had argued about wages. But on cross examination, he admitted his knowledge of the controversy was only hearsay. He did score one point for the prosecution, though, by saying that Belle often signed her name "Bella P.S. Gunness," thereby showing that the "P.S." inscription on the rings could apply to Belle. Clyde Martin, a civil engineer, testified that the most direct route from where Lamphere spent the night before the fire to where he worked on Wheatbrook's farm was down McClung Road and past the Gunness house. Eli Hoover, however, who had known Lamphere for many years could not identify a man he saw walking and then running through a field near the scene of the fire on the morning of the fire. This man was wearing a dark overcoat, and Lamphere was seen at 6 a.m. that morning wearing an overcoat at the home of John Ross, his cousin, where Lamphere told Ross about seeing the fire and asked to borrow a broad axe. By 8:30 a.m., Lamphere was at the farm of Jacob Warnick, where he worked for three hours before complaining of feeling ill and leaving. While there, he did not mention the fire. When Lamphere was arrested he was at John Wheatbrook's farm, and Wheatbrook testified that Lamphere told him about the fire, saying he first thought it was another house but a closer look showed him it was Belle's place. Lamphere told Wheatbrook he heard someone "holler" in the distance but didn't know if anyone escaped from the house.

On Tuesday morning, a defense theory became apparent when Worden asked Wheatbrook this: "Do you remember in the trial at Stillwell if it was not a fact that her first husband was killed by poisoning?" An objection by the state was overruled by the judge. Worden explained his reasoning: "My idea is, that we are attempting to show that Mrs Gunness had certain ideas in her mind, and these questions affected her, convincing her that the attorney knew of her former experiences, and thus furnishing a motive for suicide." After the overruling, the witness answered in the affirmative. However, when Worden went more deeply into the hearing on Gunness' death, objections were raised and sustained.

A new insight into Belle's personality surfaced on November 17 when Peter Colson, a farm hand, testified. It probably partially explained why this large, ordinary-looking woman was able to keep a hold on the men she had attracted into her web. Colson went to work for Belle in March of 1903 and left when Belle's cruelty to Jennie Olson became unbearable. In the meantime, though, he had fallen in love with her. "I loved Mrs. Gunness in spite of myself," he said. "I didn't want to, but I couldn't help it. She caressed and purred like a cat and then I couldn't resist her. All the time that I was submitting to her there was something about her that seemed to be pulling away."

Colson repeated the following conversation he had with Lamphere: "I asked him if he had heard Mrs. Gunness say anything about Jennie Olson and he said she had a letter from her. He said he worked there and said she owed him money and he said he would get even with her. I told him he would never get ahead of her. She claimed that she would pay him or he would make her get down on her knees to him. He said the man who had been there in the winter from Minnesota he had driven away and Mrs. Gunness got down on him for that. He said he knew something else about her. I asked him once why he didn't sue her. He said he wouldn't tell what else he knew then."

On cross, Worden asked, "Why did you quit work there?" Colson replied, adding information about a confrontation with Belle: "There is a good deal about it. She said to go West and get a farm and get cattle and ship to Chicago. Then there was a sort of a love affair ... One of the horses was lame and there was a pile of old clothes and I took a piece of old shirt, and when she saw it, she called me down pretty sharp. I told her I would buy a couple of shirts if she would not say anything. I had been doing chores two or three days and was staying in town. She talked better and I asked her for some money. She was angry. She asked me to go upstairs and said I would feel better in the morning." Colson said he was afraid to stay there, though, and slept at a neighbor's. This made him, along with Lamphere, one of the few men known to survive Belle's charms.

Along those lines, a remark was made causing "a demonstration among the spectators" that prompted Judge Richter to threaten to clear the courtroom. The remark came during testimony of William Slater, who had employed Lamphere right after he left Belle's. Prosecutor Smith asked Slater: "Did Lamphere tell you that he slept with Mrs. Gunness?" The answer: "No, he said she slept with him." Slater said

Lamphere was jealous of Helgelein, and that the intimacy between Belle and Lamphere was initiated by Belle.

Lamphere's boasting about his power over Belle was also heard by Bessie Wallace, one-time resident of McClung Road now living in nearby Michigan City. She testified the defendant asserted he "would get even" with Belle if she did not pay him any money. The cross examination questioned the veracity of the testimony, honing in on the type of "house" Wallace lived in on McClung Road, which had a number of houses that weren't homes. A saloon keeper then testified adding his Lamphere quote: "If that woman does not let me alone, I will send her over the road."

The prosecution lost a point in its attempt to tie Lamphere to the murder of Helgelein. Witness John Rye said the gun and overcoat thought to have belong to Helgelein and seen in Lamphere's possession were already in the defendant's possession before Helgelein's disappearance. Rye did say, though, that Lamphere said he was going to the Gunness farm the night of January 14, the night thought to be Helgelein's death date. He had gone with Lamphere to Michigan City late that afternoon, about 4:30 p.m.; and on their way home, Lamphere left him, saying, "I am going to get off and go over and see what the old woman is doing." Lamphere did not meet Rye later, as promised, at Smith's saloon, but did see him the next day, when he told Rye the story about drilling a hole in the parlor floor to overhear the conversation between Belle and Helgelein.

While the prosecution was playing coy about whether Dr. E. A. Schell, the minister-confidant of Lamphere during his early days of confinement, would return to town to testify, the defense was concentrating on strategy to offset the testimony of Norton, the dentist. The teeth were the key ingredient in the puzzle. Even Coroner Mack refused to declare Belle dead until that bridgework was found. Now the defense needed to cast doubt on the genuineness of that bridgework and to introduce the idea that this "evidence" might have been planted after the fire. It needed to find experts who could debunk the idea that all those teeth could survive an inferno.

On Nov. 18, all the news was made by Sheriff Smutzer, who many years later would be implicated in the mystery in a new way. Smutzer testified to his belief that Lamphere killed Belle because she would not give him his share of the money taken from Helgelein. The sheriff said Lamphere came to him with a tale about Helgelein being wanted for murder in South Dakota. Lamphere wanted Smutzer to know that Belle was harboring a criminal, as a sort of retaliation for firing him from his job as hired hand. Smutzer also said Lamphere obviously lied when he said he saw Helgelein board a 5:10 a.m. train with a suitcase, when in actuality Helgelein was dead. About his own relations with Belle, the sheriff gave an example. One day Belle came to him and complained that Lamphere had been following her. The sheriff said he confronted Lamphere and asked for an explanation. Lamphere, he said, did not answer.

Other witnesses included Austin Cutler, a funeral director for 12 years, who said the four bodies taken from the ruins were at his mortuary for about seven weeks before being taken to Chicago; Frank Pitner, cashier at the First National Bank of LaPorte, who described the efforts of Belle and Andrew Helgelein to cash in bank drafts and Pitner's subsequent interview with Belle to query her on the whereabouts of Andrew at the request of his brother, Asle; George Wrase, grocery clerk, who testified that Belle purchased two gallons of kerosene in a five gallon can the day before the fire; and D. M. Hutson, a neighbor across the road from the Gunness farm, who assisted in the excavation of the bodies from the basement ruins and estimated about two feet of rubbish atop the bodies and six to ten inches underneath them.

CHAPTER TWENTY FIVE

The defense had reserved its right to cross examine Sheriff Albert Smutzer, and that time was approaching. But first, the prosecution brought the sheriff back to the stand to explain his close involvement with the case. It was, of course, already known that he was firmly in the prosecution's camp, that he was the first to finger Lamphere as the villain, and that his voice was among the loudest proclaiming that it was Belle in the ruins.

In describing his movements for the prosecution, Smutzer said he spent April 27, the day before the fire, in Indianapolis, returning home around midnight. At about 5 a.m., he and Sheriff Anstiss (at that time a deputy sheriff and now sheriff-elect) went to the fire. His first actions were to get permission from the coroner to search for victims and to get the fire chief to tear down the remaining walls. Men hired to dig in the ruins began work at 9 a.m. in the northwest corner of the basement where the debris was the shallowest. The hottest, most debris-filled spot was the northeast corner, he said, and that is where the bodies were found. Smutzer supervised the removal of the bodies, and these are the details he recalled: Arms and legs were attached until moved and then they broke away. The first two bodies, the girls, were lying face down. The boy was found under one of the girls and lying in the adult's left arm. The boy had a small hole in his head, and the adult was missing a head and right arm. He was emphatic that the bodies were in the hottest place in the basement and the head was in the hottest part in that place. Portions of a bed and bedsprings were found on both ends of the bodies, which lie atop debris about 10 to 15 inches deep. He also mentioned mattress pieces under the bodies and a burned quilt between the girls and the boy. Smutzer also identified a revolver found in the ruins and various bones, including the jaw bone, and he described the finding of Helgelein's body.

During this recital, Smutzer referred to the adult body as the "mother," to which the defense voiced an objection, which was sustained. The day ended with Smutzer still on the stand and scheduled for more direct examination the next morning.

On Thursday, the witness explained how 10 bodies were found from May 5 to 9 and how subsequent attention then turned to sifting the ashes in search of Belle's bridgework. To assist in this hunt, Louis Schultz was hired to construct and operate a sluice box. Smutzer said he did not know the present whereabouts of Schultz, the man who found the bridgework. These were identified along with other items such as watches and jewelry.

It was now time for the defense to face off with the sheriff who had exercised more control over the day-to-day unfolding of the case than anyone else. One line of questioning concerned Smutzer's relationship with Belle. The sheriff denied that his car was frequently seen at Belle's house and he told Atty. Worden that she had visited him only three times--each visit with the purpose of complaining about Lamphere. Another was the bodiless head found in the vault, a point of interest since there was one body without a head. Could they be paired? Smutzer said this head was nothing more than a skull with no substantial hair attached. It would then seem to be too old to belong to the headless body in the ruins. Then there were the questions about the amount of digging done, whether there had not been enough. Smutzer said that even during a trip to Texas, he left instructions that digging should continue in any suspicious locations.

When it came to the diagram of the teeth that Norton, the dentist, said he gave to Smutzer on May 17, Smutzer remembered the date as May 19, the day the teeth were found. Two days difference, but perhaps it was Norton that was wrong. The sheriff testified that the teeth were found about 15 minutes after his return from the dentist to the Gunness farm.

Worden hammered away at the idea that authorities had made a "rush to judgment" by honing in on Lamphere, refusing to believed that Belle was still alive, and thereby doing far less than they should of to try to track her down. Smutzer's response was that he had done his best, including the hiring of the Pinkerton agency.

Worden also asked, "Have you any interest in this case?" To which the sheriff replied, "No, sir. No more than anyone else."

A couple of other witnesses were recalled briefly: Joseph Maxson, who did not see anything in the defendant's hand the night he was spotted by Maxson at Belle's; and Austin Cutler, who said a greasy substance coated the oil cloth that bore the adult female body to his morgue. Then it was time for Deputy Sheriff LeRoy Marr, who testified about his trip to the Wheatbrook farm to pick up Lamphere. As he approached the farmhouse, Lamphere came out of a door. The following conversation took place:

Marr: Ray, get on your coat and go to town with me.

Lamphere: Did those three children and that woman get out of the building?

Marr: What building?

Lamphere: That building near town.

On the way to town, Lamphere talked about seeing the fire.

Lamphere: When I got along by the house, the smoke was coming out of the windows and around the roof.

Marr: Did you see any one around the house or on the place?

When the reply was negative, Marr asked, "Why didn't you yell?" To which Lamphere replied, "I didn't think it was any of my business." The only other comment made by Lamphere on the way to the jail was, "Did you think I meant the Gunness road? I meant the other road past the city park."

On cross examination, Worden was interested in the prosecution's acquisition of Lamphere's trunk. In response to questioning, Marr said he and Prosecutor Smith went to Lamphere's room at Wheatbrook's farm at night because they learned of the trunk's existence in late afternoon. He said he knew nothing about forcing a door lock to get into the room, but he did know the trunk was delivered to Smith's office.

The next witness was Sheriff-elect Anstiss, whose most damaging testimony concerned the confrontation of Lamphere with accusations that he had lied in previous statements. Anstiss said that at one point Lamphere was ready to confess to arson but changed his mind because he did not want his mother to suffer with the knowledge of her son's guilt. Anstiss also said Lamphere did not deny witnessing Helgelein's death but instead refused to talk about it because "I wouldn't be fair to my lawyer."

Anstiss pressured Lamphere about his behavior the morning of the fire--his hiding behind a railroad tower when people approached and his fleeing across a field. The sheriff-elect also saw an attempt to derail the Helgelein investigation in Lamphere's statement that he had seen Helgelein leave town with a suitcase. Most of Anstiss' testimony concerned the defendant's jailhouse conversations:

"Lamphere told me that on the evening before the fire he stayed all night at the home of Nigger Liz, setting the alarm clock for 3 o'clock and leaving the house a twenty minutes past 3 or half past at the latest. He said he went to the corner near the Erie crossing, where he saw a man and woman coming with a baby carriage. He told me he hid behind a signal man's tower until they had passed. Then he claimed to have gone out Park Road. He said he left Park Road and hid in a small clump of trees, then crossed to a stone road, leading by the Gunness farm. According to the story he told me, he first saw smoke coming out of the Gunness house at this time. He said that finally he left the road and went across the fields to John Ross and the Wheatbrook farm.

"After I had investigated his story, I went to Ray in jail and said, 'Ray, you've been lying to me. You'll put your foot in it this way. When you went to that clump of trees you passed through it and went over a rail fence, didn't you?' Lamphere answered yes. I asked him whether he wasn't running when he went down a slope and Ray answered, 'Yes, I guess I was running.' When I wanted to know why, he said he was in a hurry to get to his work. I told him he did not take the stone road as he had said because a man was working there and would have seen him. Then Lamphere said he went only a short distance on the stone road. His explanation for hiding behind the tower was that he didn't want anybody who was acquainted with him to see him coming from Nigger Liz's house.

"Another talk I had with Lamphere was about the night of January 14, when he made the Michigan City trip. He told me he was sent by Mrs. Gunness with orders to meet a man named Moo with whom he was to trade horses. Mrs. Gunness told him to stay all night. Lamphere said he stayed all night in Michigan City, but Moo did not show up. I said, 'Ray, this is pretty bad business. Didn't you take the 8 o'clock car for LaPorte and get off at a switch near the icehouse? John Rye says so.' Lamphere admitted then that he had lied but said his horse had stayed all night in Michigan City. Then I asked him: 'When you could have saved trouble by telling Sheriff Smutzer and me you saw Mrs. Gunness kill Helgelein, why didn't you do it?' Lamphere replied, 'Bill, you've always acted pretty fair, but you are a deputy sheriff.' 'You won't deny you saw her killing Helgelein?' I asked. 'No, but I don't want to talk about it,' was Lamphere's answer. 'It wouldn't be fair to my lawyer.'

"I had a conversation with Lamphere about the cellar door at the Gunness house. Lamphere said he made the door and that there was no lock for it. He said the Gunness house had a peculiar square room in it which could be entered from the frame part of the house. The brick part of the house was kept tightly locked by Mrs. Gunness, Lamphere said."

Worden, in cross examination, demanded to know whether Anstiss had told a newspaper reporter that he doubted Lamphere's guilt on the arson charges. Anstiss replied: "I said I was positive about his having seen the killing of Helgelein, but that some things that had happened made me less positive of his guilt on the arson charge."

"That was when you heard about there being poison in the bodies taken from the Gunness house, wasn't it?" asked Worden.

"Yes, that was it, but I understand that matter now," was the answer. Anstiss also testified that he had asked Lamphere several times whether he had torched the house and that Lamphere had denied it each time.

Worden posed the same question of self-interest that he had asked the sheriff: "Are you interested in any way in this case?" He received the same answer: "No, sir. No more than anyone else." Then Worden asked, "Are you interested in trying to prove any theory in this case?" The answer came back, "No."

With the conclusion of Anstiss' testimony, the state rested its case.

CHAPTER TWENTY SIX

When the prosecution rested at 9:50 a.m. Friday morning, November 20, it caught the defense by surprise. Worden asked for a recess until Monday morning, but the request was denied by Judge Richter. There was nothing Worden could do but go ahead with his opening statement, in which he outlined the defense's case: The body retrieved from the ruins was not Belle's; Belle was seen by a neighbor and two girls in July; the teeth, crowns and bridgework identified as Belle's could not have gone through the fire; and the four people found in the ruins died from poisoning. In the statement, called strong even by his opponents, Worden contended, "The real issue is whether Ray Lamphere is guilty of burning those bodies found in the ruins of the Gunness fire. That is the ultimate question to be determined. In order for the state to prove its case the first thing necessary is to prove the corpus delicti, that is, the identification of the bodies.

"Now we have our ideas as to whether it was the body of Mrs. Gunness," he continued. " We believe our evidence will show you that it was not her body. Whether it was or not this does not in any way determine the question of the guilt or innocence of Ray Lamphere ... Our evidence will show that Mrs. Gunness is still alive. She had motive to set fire to the house and escape."

Worden talked with first-hand knowledge about Belle's growing realization that people suspected her of murder. He had been part of the trial at Stillwell concerning the question of Lamphere's trespassing. "In the cross examination there," he explained, "she was asked if it was not true that her first husband, Mads Sorensen, was poisoned and that she drew the life insurance." He also pointed out that she was reminded of her questioning after the death of her husband, Peter Gunness; and she was asked when Jennie Gunness would return.

"I believe that the evidence will show that on April 27 there was a crisis in her life," he continued, "that she was expecting Helgelein here to investigate about his brother, and that she thought that Ray Lamphere knew more of these things than she would have him know. All these things culminated at this time. Our evidence will show that Bella Gunness had reason to commit the crime that was committed. The evidence will show that she did commit the act. On the afternoon before the fire she went to Minich's grocery and bought an unusual quantity of kerosene, more than she was in the habit of buying. The evidence will further show that down near the First National Bank on Main Street she was heard to say to a man, 'It will have to be done tonight and you will have to do it.' ... Evidence will be introduced that Mrs. Gunness has been seen alive since the burning of the house. A man who has been on the witness stand, who lived across the road from her, who helped Sheriff Smutzer dig in the ruins, will testify that he saw her at the Gunness place on the 9th of July about 4 or 5 in the afternoon. He could distinguish her features. He could describe her dress, her horse, and her buggy. There are two children who knew her intimately, who saw her pass them on the road."

Worden said that a man who had seen Belle every day since her arrival in LaPorte and who took charge of the adult body taken from the ruins would testify that it was not Belle's body. He promised to show that a fire hot enough to destroy the head of a body "could not possibly leave teeth in the condition of those exhibited to the jury." Teeth that had gone through such heat, he said, would have become brittle and crumbled away. "The chemical composition of the teeth renders them more easily burned than the jaw bone," he explained. "The reason is that there is more mineral than animal matter in them. There is 98 per cent mineral matter in the enamel. The tooth is of three parts, the enamel, the outer covering, the cementum, the body of the tooth, and dentine, the inner part of the tooth. Dentine is more easily destroyed than bone. The composition of the cementum is the same as that of the jaw bone, 33 percent animal and 67 per cent mineral matter. Heat that would destroy the jaw bone would destroy every vestige of the teeth. In at least one of the watches, the gold case had melted so that the metal ran into the works in globules."

"You have already had a statement that where the head was was the hottest place in the whole fire. Along the line of Dr. Norton's testimony, we will show you that it is utterly impossible from a jaw bone to tell the sex of the person. It is impossible to tell the age from the angle of the jaw bone. We will show that it is possible to remove the teeth from the mouth in various ways. These teeth were not found until the 19th day of May, 21 days after the fire. We think we will be able to show you that Mrs. Gunness committed the crime of killing Helgelein. That the stomach was sent to Dr. Walter Haines of Rush Medical College for examination. That in this stomach there was strychnine and arsenic in fatal quantities. We expect to have Dr. Haines here and he will testify that in the stomachs of these bodies found in the fire there was also arsenic and strychnine in fatal quantities. It was his opinion that death was caused by poisoning. We expect to show that this test of Dr. Haines was made for the state. You have not heard that testimony. We shall show from this testimony already introduced that it would have been impossible for Ray Lamphere to have gone there and administered poison, set the house on fire, and been where the state has tried to show he was at the time they have said.

"There are several theories. One is that Mrs. Gunness administered poison to the children and placed the adult body with them and escaped. If this be true, Lamphere could not be guilty. Another theory--if that was her body and she came to death by poison, then Lamphere could not be found guilty. I am confident that after the evidence is all in, that you will be satisfied that Ray Lamphere had nothing to do with the committing of this crime."

Because of the prosecution's unexpected closing, the defense could round up only two witnesses on quick notice. The first was John Ball, a former funeral director who went with Austin Cutler to pick up the four bodies and returned them to the morgue. Ball testified that the Belle he saw standing in a street about four years ago weighed about 215 pounds. The adult female body that was in the morgue was handled by him five times in three weeks. Worden asked, "From your knowledge of dead bodies and your acquaintance with Mrs. Gunness, was that the body of Mrs. Gunness?" The state, however, objected on the ground that this called for a conclusion by the witness. Judge Richter sustained the objection, and Ball was not allowed to answer. The second witness was Charles Russell, a retired businessman, who had said that he saw Sheriff Smutzer at the Gunness farm on the day the bodies were found. When Worden attempted to impeach part of Smutzer's testimony, the time and place of a certain remark could not really be determined so Russell was excused without testifying as the court broke for lunch. When he was recalled after lunch, however, Russell said Smutzer told him there was no mattress under the bodies, a direct contradiction of what was stated in the prosecution's case.

While the defense was trying to pull together its witnesses and learning that a chief witness, Dr. Haines, would not be available until Monday, a side issue arose that grabbed the attention of LaPorteans temporarily away from the evidence in the case. This issue came, of all places, from the pulpit.

CHAPTER TWENTY SEVEN

On Thursday night, the pastor of the First Christian Church in LaPorte, took on the city's women. At his midweek service on the "Beginning of Family and Business Life," the Rev. M. H. Garrard came down hard on those women who had crowded into the courtroom to hear the Gunness case. These were his feelings on the topic, which were printed in a local newspaper on Friday for all to read:

"I have been thoroughly disgusted with the way women have flocked in large number and at all hours of the day both morning and afternoon into the court room to have poured into their ears all the filth connected with the notorious trial now in progress in our city. It seems that these women have 'camped out' near the cesspool and mean to stay there until it is drained of its rot. I am told that many of the officials who are compelled to listen to this stuff would gladly stop their ears to it all and get away from it if they had their own way in the matter, and I am confident they mean what they say. It is bad enough to see so many men there, but when I see the women sitting up right in front, as near to the filth as it is possible for them to get, I presume they are there out of fear that one of the rotten words or scenes might be missed were they further back.

"I say when I see this thing I am at a loss to know just how to adequately describe it. It is a strange thing that women, under no compulsion whatever, are found in large numbers in every notorious trial everywhere, and the more dirty the trial the more women will usually be found in attendance. LaPorte has its trial where in all manner of dirty, rotten stuff is recited, and LaPorte also has in large numbers the women who will give anxious, eager ears to it all. What are we to say of such women? Of their modesty? Of their refinement? Well, I make no attempt to bring the adequate charge. It is mild to say that they are not of the genteel type. I went up to the court room one afternoon and also one morning to look over the crowd, and while I deplore the number of men who are constantly there, yet I feel we have a right to expect more of the women.

"What one sees is sickening in the extreme. One young woman was comfortably located near where all could be heard and seen and gave evidence of her very great pleasure in being so fortunately situated. She was artistically squashing a big piece of gum, her cheeks bulging out on both sides with the fat cud, and her head bobbling like a cow's. One could easily see that this particular young woman was a pastmaster in this business. Well, many other things could be said, but I have more pleasant things to say. I hope that all decent women, who are not compelled to be at that trial, and very few if any are compelled to attend, will keep away and frown on all those who go. Let modest, refined, wellbred ladies keep away from the very appearance of evil."

As the trial began on Saturday morning, fewer women were in attendance. People wondered, had the pastor's message shamed them or were they simply doing Saturday chores? It was perhaps the latter because the court's afternoon session attracted even more women than usual, now giving rise to the idea that the women were angry at the criticism and determined to show their defiance. One woman wrote this rebuttal:

"I think the Rev. M.H. Garrard has desecrated his pulpit and his own profession by casting the slurs which he has upon the women of LaPorte. I have attended the Lamphere trial several times and have seen the very nicest and most refined ladies of town there and have heard nothing said by anyone in the court proceedings which contained one-tenth part as many obscene words and low phrases as the selection from his sermon, which was published. He is making a broad statement when he says that the genteel type of women do not attend. And what worse slur do the women want than that which he gives them when he says that, when the worst stuff is recited, the women come in thicker numbers and crowd the more closely for fear of losing a word? Perhaps he forgets that his mother and wife are women, even if they have not attended the trial. I am sure the ladies who have attended, and whose characters are far above reproach, are extremely complimented at the hint that they are not decent. As far as I can learn, his brilliant (?) flow of eloquence has made no 'hit' but only excited ridicule upon his own head. From a minister of the gospel, at least, we naturally expect 'Charity for all and malice toward none.' This is not an age nor time when women are kept underfoot and in ignorance. A mere desire to see justice done, and to learn the ways of justice, should not be construed into an appearance of a gratification of evil tastes, by such a distinct outsider in this case, as the Rev. M.H. Garrard."

The response, unsigned, was sent to a local newspaper and printed on Saturday. This did not daunt the pastor, who came up with these remarks in his Sunday sermon: "I certainly would not keep down the liberty of women, but liberty does not mean license. So far as concerns a profound interest in learning the ways of justice by attending the Gunness trial, I have little faith in it. I repeat my belief and say: God made man and woman. He made man the stronger and set him over a particular field. He gave woman a peculiar nature and set her in the home to be the presiding spirit there. Her powers are represented by gentleness, sympathy, purity, devotion to principle, and love. I say to you that if woman is to conquer she must do it with these weapons. If she does it in other ways, she only brutalizes man, and instead of being his complement, as divinely intended, she becomes his worst enemy. Her power becomes weakness. Witness multitudinous divorce proceedings due to woman's attempt to conquer by weapons God never intended for her use. God give us more Puritan homes and fewer women who will seek the court rooms when these notorious trials like the Gunness and the Thaw cases are called."

The Thaw case referred to the trial of Harry Thaw, accused of killing Stanford White, a prominent New York architect. The whole premise of Garrard's contentions on the proper role of women has created controversy that has outlasted both cases.

CHAPTER TWENTY EIGHT

Meanwhile, Friday afternoon in the courtroom saw the defense attack a wide variety of prosecution testimony, including the identification of the teeth, the starting time of the fire, and the conduct and relationship of the sheriff and prosecutor during the investigation. But the first witness of the afternoon was N. D. McCormick, the courier who took the jars containing the stomachs and their contents from Coroner Mack to Dr. Haines in Chicago. He testified that the jars were sealed, and he had received a receipt for his delivery. This evidence was presented to stop any future prosecution moves to taint the testimony of Dr. Haines by suggesting the possibility of evidence-tampering.

With that out of the way, Worden then called Dr. George Wasser, a dentist and graduate of Northwestern University. His testimony was totally at odds with that of the local dentist, Norton:

Worden: I will ask you if you have made any comparative tests as to the effects of heat upon bone and teeth?

Wasser: I have. The results were that at the end of four or five minutes the bone showed a good deal of resistance, while the tooth was about collapsed.

Worden: I will ask if in your opinion a head had been consumed and all the jaw except the jaw shown you, could the teeth have been left in the condition of these teeth?

Wasser: No, sir.

Worden: Could you state from this piece of bone whether it is the jaw bone of a human being or not?

Wasser: No, sir.

Wasser also testified that the jaw bone gave no clue as to the age or sex of its owner. Even in the estimation of the opposition, Wasser was an excellent witness for the defense. The following testimony came during cross examination and redirect:

Sutherland (for the prosecution): If a tooth covered with a 22-karat crown were exposed to the same heat, which would be destroyed first?

Wasser: The exposed part.

Sutherland: Before the teeth would be exposed to the flame it would be necessary for the flesh and bone protecting them to be burned away, would it not?

Wasser: Yes, sir.

Sutherland: Do you believe these teeth have been worn in the mouth at some time?

Wasser: I believe they have been.

Sutherland: Was the articulation perfect?

Wasser: It was about as good as usual.

Sutherland: Were they of the same shade?

Wasser: There was a slight difference in one of the side teeth from the rest. In general the color was the same.

Worden (for the defense): Crowns could be removed without burning or destroying them, could they not?

Wasser: Yes, sir.

Sutherland (for the prosecution): Do you think these were removed that way?

Wasser: I do not know.

Sutherland: The teeth might have been burned off?

Wasser: Yes, sir.

Sutherland: Do you think they have been in fire?

Wasser: Yes, they have been through a fire.

The defense now attempted to show that the time of the fire's start was before Lamphere was even out of bed at Wheatbrook's. Mrs. George Wright, who lived near the Gunness farm along the Lake Erie tracks, said she saw the blaze arise from the center of the brick portion of the house just as her clock struck 3 a.m. Her husband also testified that she awoke him because of the fire and that he could see it just beginning to show through the roof. When his wife handed him his watch, he saw the time was 3:15 a.m.

Next on the agenda were the relationship and behavior of the sheriff and prosecutor in the conduct of the case. The episode selected for exploring this topic was the two men's involvement with a small trunk. To delve into what was now being hinted at as mysterious behavior, the defense called the prosecuting attorney, Ralph Smith. The story that came out from the testimony of Smith, John Yorkey, and William Ball was that Smith and Deputy Marr went out to the Gunness place one night last spring and without permission hauled away a trunk from the carriage shed. Yorkey testified that he drove the two men out to Gunness' and that they brought back a trunk. Ball was the night watchman at the time of the visit, and he pried his way into the shed because he had no key, and let the men in. At the time, Smith told him to "keep mum" about the events of that evening. Recalled to the stand on Saturday morning, Smith said the trunk was still in his office, and Judge Richter told the bailiffs to bring the trunk into the courtroom so that the jury could see what was in it. This accomplished, the opened trunk lid revealed neckties, books, and letters, none of which had any relation to the case.

The defense now called O.P.M. Squires, a jeweler, who told of his experiments on the melting of porcelain and gold. In one experiment, for example, he put soup bone marrow inside a gold crown. In another he wrapped meat around platinum and gold teeth. Then he put these in a wood-fire stove for 1½ hours. The results were not allowed into testimony, though, because they were not conducted by an expert.

Next was another dentist, Dr. W. S. Fisher, who had practiced for 21 years and said he was familiar with the amount of heat needed to melt gold and porcelain. He thought it impossible that the teeth survived a fire hot enough to melt a head. They had, however, been subjected to fire of some sort. He also said that the plate and bridgework seemed to match and that they had been worn. He also agreed with Wasser that it was "utterly impossible" to determine the sex or age of the owner of the jaw bone in the exhibits. On cross examination, the witness said the teeth did not appear to have been removed by force, but that it was possible that they had been clipped off.

On Saturday afternoon, Justice of the Peace Robert Kincaid was called to the stand. He had presided the previous April in the State vs. Lamphere and recalled that Belle had been asked about the deaths of her two husbands. Also called was Fred Rickman, who had worked for Belle several times. One of his jobs was digging a hole about five feet long and five feet deep. Belle was in town at the time and two anticipated men arrived in an automobile. As instructed by Belle, he told them the house key was under the mat. There followed some drinking in the house, and Rickman suspected he was doped because he became unconscious on his way home after accepting a glass of wine from the visitors. He also testified that one of the men gave Belle the money to pay him for his work. This hole was near where a shed now stands and brought up the possibility that someone might be buried under the shed, which had never been examined.

The defense also presented three witnesses who testified that they saw Belle alive at the farm on July 9. They were D. M. Hutson, the farmer across the road, and his daughters, Evelina, 11, and Eldora, 9. Although Hutson swore it was Belle, he admitted under cross examination that the woman, in the company of a grey-haired man, wore a black veil. He said he recognized her from her build and walk.

John Anderson was called to the stand to support the defense's contention that Belle had lured another women to the farm, poisoned her, and placed her body in the cellar. "I saw Mrs. Gunness on the Saturday evening before the fire," claimed Anderson, who lived on McClung Road near Belle's acreage. "She stopped and asked how the flowers were getting along. There was a strange woman with her. She was a little smaller than Mrs. Gunness. I never seen her since. I told the sheriff about her." The sheriff also was approached by William Miller, a county commissioner, who was present when the bodies were taken from the ruins. He observed that the adult body was headless but told the sheriff he also observed fresh digging in one location and a large stone in the vault. Upon subsequent visits, Miller saw that the stone had sunk somewhat and then that it had disappeared altogether. John Ball returned to the stand to say he was present when the vault was investigated and that a skull without a lower jaw was found.

On Monday morning, the defense produced a parade of witnesses, beginning with Louise Gackle, who lived on Park Street and who testified that she saw an automobile going south at about 3:30 a.m. the morning of the fire.

Joseph Maxson returned to the stand to describe the sluicing operation of Louis Schultz. The first time he saw the recovered teeth was when Schultz pulled them out of his pocket and announced, "We've found what we've been looking for." Another witness, Peck Algrever, who had helped shift the ashes, backed up Maxson's testimony about the teeth coming out of the pocket.

A former crematory attendant, W. H. Ludwig said his experience showed that small bones burn first. The skull, he said, is the last to burn. Then C. L. Replogle, who was present when the bodies were found, said he saw no debris or bedsprings under the body. The absence of bed springs also was recalled by John Burlingame, who held the board on which the adult body was rolled from the cellar. Mrs. Rachel Lyons said she saw only a small amount of ashes under the bodies. She did see, however, the remains of a piano on top of the bodies. On cross examination, though, she said perhaps six inches of ashes might have been under the bodies.

The defense informed the court that Dr. Haines would not be able to testify until Tuesday afternoon. So, a 24-hour recess was declared until this last witness for the defense could appear. After his testimony, the defense would be close to resting its case.

CHAPTER TWENTY NINE

As all awaited the arrival of Dr. Haines, it seems that the furor arose by the Rev. Garrard personally riled another LaPortean, this one a man and a husband. In a letter to the local press, this anonymous scribe let out his anger:

"'A new preacher, a new hell' says a certain blunt proverb. The combination is in our midst. The women of our town have heard from it. My wife attended the Gunness trial, as did large numbers of other women, and now bobs up the Rev. M. H. Garrard and says that she and all the others are virtually not modest, refined, nor genteel: In short, not respectable ladies, if you please.

"Well! Well! Talk about arrogance, presumption, and the old criticaster's trick of 'curving a contumelious lip'--all that is a mild sort of stupidity compared with this. Since when was this man commissioned to sit in judgment on the question of our women's modesty, refinement, and gentility? Representative women, if you please, sir, of all clubs, circles, and churches were there.

"When I read that scurrilous and ungentlemanly attack on the good women of our city, my mind instinctively turned away from its unspeakable offensiveness to the noble tribute our girls by that fairer critic, Mr. Kipling, in his 'American Notes.' Kipling says 'they are clever, they can talk--yea, it is said that they can think. They are self-possessed, without parting with any tenderness that is their sex-right; they understand; they can take care of themselves; they are superbly independent.'

"Yes, indeed, I glory in this American girl's ability and spunk. We all should be proud that her noble attributes of mind and soul do not break, like blown glass, before the various little naughtinesses of every day life. If so sensitive and fragile as that, they would have been shattered long ago. And I submit to any knowing man or woman whether the 'racy' and unseemly words, unavoidably spoken in the Gunness trial were really any more vulgar, rotten, and suggestive than those that oft come from preacher's lips in the pulpit, when discussing dancing, the white slave traffic and kindred delicate topics. As many fair faces have been 'put to the blush' from the pulpit as in the court room. And they were words which were spoken unnecessarily and apparently with a certain secret delight in the helplessness and unpreparedness of the hearers.

"Where, then, is woman to go? Is she safe in the grinding babel of the street? Is she safe at the club, the church-ball or the lake side? Is the 'grave and comely damsel called Discretion, who answers the bell at the door of the house beautiful' always going to keep her indoors to bake and stew and darn and be the mere idle plaything of some squeamish man? Faugh! Ugh! The sort of mock modesty, refinement and gentility with which this minister would endow our women would close their eyes to 'the rosy blush of love' and their ears to 'the sound of the church-going bell.' Away with such false virtues as that.

"I consider that woman's curiosity, her desire to see and hear and learn is as legitimate a part of her life as of man's, and that if her refinement and modesty are of a genuine and sensible quality, they will withstand all the necessary indelicacies of the rough world all about her and outlive that hot-house sort that stays at home with its nose turned up at the horridness of things, and then sneaks around the back way to get a whiff of it to found a sermon on.

"For my part, I have faith in the modesty, refinement, and gentility of my wife. She went to that trial a good woman, and she came home from there a good woman still. True virtue can be trusted anywhere. I am not afraid to trust my wife. And Mr. Garrard is not qualified or commissioned to sit in judgment over her. The good women who attended that trial were as safe and secure from evil as the women who remained away, and it was a bit forward and presumptuous for some self-appointed critic to rise up and virtually say, 'I can conduct you, lady, to a low but loyal cottage, where you may be safe,' as if the women had to have a guardian of their security, their refinement, and modesty. In conclusion, I think the young lady described as sitting well in front 'artistically squashing a big piece of gum' was engaged in a much better business than the immoderate Mr. Garrard spitting out unholy and gratuitous insults on the character of our women, thereby dragging the pulpit down to a level with the scandal-mongering street. Verily, from such attacks as that 'the white wonder of dear Juliet's hand' is safe."

CHAPTER THIRTY

Tuesday, November 24, was the last day of testimony, and it was dramatic. The long-awaited appearance of Dr. Walter Haines, professor of toxicology at Rush Medical College in Chicago, began at l:30 p.m. with his recital of impeccable credentials: 32 years on the faculty of the college and 7 years in association with the University of Chicago. To begin, Haines described his receipt of the three jars and their contents--one jar contained three stomachs, another contained one stomach, and a third contained stomach contents. Then the following exchange took place:

Worden: Did you make a chemical analysis of the stomach which was alone?

Haines: I did.

Worden: I will ask you to state the result of that examination.

Haines: I found arsenic and strychnine in the Helgelein stomach. I examined a third of the stomach and found a little less than one third of a grain of strychnine. In the entire stomach, there were one and one-half grains of strychning.

Worden: How much would cause death?

Haines: One-third of a grain has been sufficient to produce death. I also broke the seal of the jar of the other three stomachs. They had almost run together so that it was in material like a thick mud. A few fibers from the original wall were observable. The only possible analysis was by using the mass together. I found an abundance of arsenic and a quantity of strychnine. There was enough strychnine to cause the death of three persons. The most common appearance of strychnine poisoning is a violent contraction of the muscles. Death results from strychnine poisoning at varied periods, sometimes in a short time and again as long as 11 hours. The most common symptoms are severe pains in the stomach and bowels, nausea, and vomiting. Acute vomiting is the rule in arsenical poisoning. When the two are administered together at the same time, strychnine would appear first and perhaps would have killed before the arsenic would begin its work. Convulsions in strychnine poisoning are developed by a touch or any physical activity. I have examined many dozens of embalming fluids. In former years they contained arsenic and corrosive sublimate. In later years the embalming fluids I have examined are made up chiefly of formaldehyde. There are no antiseptic preservative properties in strychnine."

The cross examination was damaging to the defense because Haines could not say whether the poisonous material was put into the bodies before or after death, or even whether the poison was inside or outside the stomachs. As further rebuttal, the prosecution called Austin Cutler, the morgue owner, who said he used a formaldehyde solution and 10 or 15 pounds of arsenical powder upon all the bodies before the autopsies were conducted. While that left the presence of strychnine unaccounted for, Cutler pointed out that about 200 people had access to the bodies before the autopsies, leaving open the possibility that poison was introduced in the morgue. It was with this uncertainty hovering over the cause of death of the four in the cellar that the defense rested. The strychnine problem was predicted to be a key element in the next day's arguments by both sides and the judge's instructions to the jury. The instructions were expected to be extensive on the subject of reasonable doubt.

On Wednesday morning, Atty. Sutherland began by defending the sheriff against the defense's criticism: "The defense has sought to belittle the sheriff in his zeal in doing his duties. I presume that they would have you believed that a law should be enacted reading something like this: 'Be it enacted that the sheriff shall be confined to his office when a crime has been committed and only seen by his family and that when he seeks to find a criminal, he must give 10 days' noticed and be followed by a brass band.' I am not attempting to be humorous but to set forth and by exaggeration to show the attitude of the defense."

Sutherland called on the jury's "common sense" in believing that the four bodies found in the ruins were "those who inhabited the building." He pointed out that Maxson, the hired hand who escaped the fire, described the evening before the fire as quite routine; and Sutherland contended that nothing in Belle's past showed her to be anything but "a good and tender mother to her children." He then outlined the prosecution's belief that Helgelein had replaced Lamphere in Belle's household, thereby creating a jealousy in Lamphere that led him to return early from Michigan City, which resulted in his complicity in the death of Helgelein. The prosecution believed that Belle promised to pay Lamphere to keep quiet. "From receipts it was evident that there was no money due him for labor, yet his whole cry was that she owed him money and he would get even with her," Sutherland stated.

In explaining the evidence behind the arson charge, Sutherland said: "On the afternoon before the fire, he (Lamphere) dogged her steps, following her into Minich's grocery, glaring at her, following her out. He began to fear her, and on the morning of April 28, he put into execution his threats. The difference in time of the fire was not over one hour by all the witnesses. Here was a fire at an unseemly hour, and Lamphere's own statement he was there on the spot at the time the fire started. The evidence shows that he was seen running through a field away from the fire about 5 o'clock. He told Anstiss a man was working on the road and he did not want to been seen and so ran through the field. He concealed himself before the fire. He was avoiding being seen. What does common sense teach you? From all the facts, we ask you to sum up the whole matter and use your good common sense."

Sutherland next criticized the defense testimony about the identity of the female body in the ruins. He said that one defense witness tried to show that the bridgework was clipped off and left in the fire but another said it was not Belle's bridgework. He said the fact that the body's back was burnt to the spinal cord showed that the body did not start out on the basement floor. As to the expert who found poison in the stomachs, Sutherland said the embalmer testified that poisonous fluid was used on the bodies.

The defense's response was handled by Attorney Weir, who pointed out that Belle had purchased two gallons of coal oil the day before the fire. Prior to the fire, that can was placed in the frame portion of the house, he said, but after the fire it was found in the cellar near the bodies in the brick portion of the house. "Whatever theory you may take, it is merely a guess, and you cannot guess this defendant into the penitentiary, nor hang him by guessing," he added. "There has not been a scintilla of evidence outside of Dr. Norton that there was a portion of the head left. Yet Dr. Norton not only identified the jaw bone as that of a human being but the sex and age as well. Six or seven other physicians could not tell what it was. I do not charge Dr. Norton with falsifying but rather as being ignorant."

Weir said the prosecution's failure to produce Schultz, the gold miner who found the bridgework, meant that the most important witness was not at the trial. At this point, he explained the defense's suspicions about the bridgework: "The teeth were shown to witnesses in the morning about 8 o'clock and they were not shown to Smutzer until about 11 o'clock. I believe that Dr. Norton is mistaken. The plan was given to Smutzer two weeks before they were found, and they could have been made and substituted."

The defense attorney agreed that the undertaker had used arsenic powder on the bodies, but pointed out that did not explain the large doses of strychnine also found in the bodies. He attacked the prosecution's scenario about Belle and Lamphere as partners in crime, calling it "a flight into the realms of fancy." He then attacked the time frame that pointed to Lamphere as the arsonist: "For Lamphere to have done this crime, it would have been necessary for him to have gone into the house and administered the poison and have carried them to the cellar and set fire to the building. We have the testimony of George Wright and his wife that the fire was at 3 o'clock and others that they saw the fire about that hour. If he saw Mrs. Blackburn at 4:20 as stated in his so-called confession, he could not have been present at the house in time to have set the house on fire. Mr. Anstiss testified that at first he believed Lamphere guilty but later did not know what to think."

As he wound up his response, Weir repeatedly voiced his belief in the innocence of the defendant. He emphasized Belle's cleverness in her criminal behavior and the defendant's significantly lower mentality. To him, everything pointed to a devious Belle who made a getaway while framing Lamphere. He ended with a plea to their emotions: "You will go home tomorrow (Thanksgiving) to the hearts of your families. This man, if condemned, will have nothing before him."

The closing statement for the defense was given by Worden, who began by saying that the defense and the judge were not in agreement on the law applicable in the case. Worden's opinion was that the jury had only two choices, either guilty of murder in the first degree or a verdict of acquittal. "This case is one in which every point connecting the defendant with the crime is circumstantial evidence," he stated. "The evidence must show that there is no other reasonable hypothesis than the one presented in the indictment. Mr. Smith, in his opening statement, stated that he wanted to introduce all the facts. And yet the evidence of Dr. Haines secured by order of the county commissioners was not introduced ... The state has made an excellent case against Mrs. Gunness. I used to have some doubt about it, but I believe now that she is alive. She had abundant motive for the commission of the crime."

Worden talked about the Stillwell trial on Lamphere's sanity and the luring of Andrew Helgelein into Belle's clutches. He talked about her shrewdness and how her will mentioned the disposal of her property in the event of the death "of all the children." Then he dangled a new notion in front of them: "I am of the opinion that Joe Maxson knows more than he has been willing to tell. I believe he had his clothes on all night. There was no yelling, no cry of fire, no calling of the neighbors." He then made these points:

. The impossibility of four bodies falling from the second floor into the cellar and landing in a row.

. The impossibility of a first-floor piano falling atop bodies that originated on the second floor.

. His belief that the rings had not been definitely identified.

. His further belief that Norton, the dentist, was prejudiced.

On the last point, Worden reviewed the testimony of the defense's dental experts and stated: "I say to you that these teeth never went through the fire from the manner in which they were found and the condition in which they now are. The head found in the vault had no lower jaw and the only portion found in the fire was the supposed jaw bone. Is this not significant? I am honest in saying that I believe the statement of D. M. Hutson and the two little girls."

Worden disputed the testimony of Rye, who said Lamphere went back to the Gunness house January 14. He read Lamphere's statement that denied this. He also questioned the testimonies of Anstiss and Marr and closed with these words: "Suppose you agree that Lamphere lied to Anstiss, would you hang him for lying? Then we all must prepare for death. I believe if you act as your conscience dictates and according to the law and the evidence, there will be no question about your verdict."

Next, it was Attorney Smith's turn to close for the prosecution:

"I am not here to make a political speech. I want to talk to you a little bit about this case. I appreciate the fact that for 14 or 15 days you have been closely confined. I am not trying to throw bouquets to you but merely trying to express a recognition that is due you. It is sometimes hard to do your duty when you see it. Officers will always have the criticism of people. I shall not be led astray in defending the officers by the attorneys of the other side. I am going to show you beyond a reasonable doubt that Lamphere set fire to the house and burned up those people. I cannot conceive on what theory the defense is trying this case. One moment they say she is alive and the next that she is dead. Now, when men start out to burn houses or commit crime, they do not give notice nor go around with a brass band. We agree with them that the fire started with the kerosene can. No one knew how to get to it but Mrs. Gunness and Ray Lamphere."

"They cannot paint Mrs. Gunness any too black for me. She was rottener than hell itself and Lamphere was going to marry her ... Where is there any evidence to show that Dr. Norton told anything but the absolute truth? When the dental experts for the defense testified, they stated that the teeth were made for and had been worn in the same mouth and further that they had been through fire."

After going through the prosecution's position on the sighting of Belle by Hutson in July and the connection of Lamphere to the disappearance of Helgelein, Smith looked at the defendant and asked: "What did you tell Louis Roule that you would put the old woman behind the bars for? Why did you tell Deputy Sheriff Anstiss and the prosecutor of this county that you would plead guilty to arson were it not for the sake of your poor old mother? And when you were being tried in the justice court at Stillwell, who was it sat beside Attorney Worden and told him to ask Mrs. Gunness whether she had not murdered her husbands? It was you, wasn't it, who knew about these things? What were you running around the Gunness place at nights for, and then pleading guilty to being out there, and paying fines for trespass? What did you tell John Rye you would get even with the old woman for? ... They say we have a feeling in this case. We have a feeling when three innocent children are slain by a man who stays with a black woman and hides behind towers and slips along and sets a fire with such consequences."

"Where is Schultz, they ask? Where is Nigger Liz, we ask? Why don't they establish an alibi by her? What was the defendant doing during the one hour and forty-five minutes which according to his own statements was consumed in going a mile and a quarter? If the time that has been stated is not correct, why don't they bring in Nigger Liz? She knows. Why don't they bring her in? I say to you that if you don't believe that Lamphere is guilty beyond a reasonable doubt, then do not bring a verdict of guilty. I do not ask you to vindicate the bad woman, but I have a right to plead in the name of God in behalf of those three little innocent children. Don't let us waste our tears on a man who had black and white paramours and who sets fire to dwellings and burns up innocent children, but let us save our flowers for someone more worthy."

The prosecution had now displayed all its cards, and the defendant had had his day in court. Now, all awaited the next move, the instructions to the jury by Judge Richter.

CHAPTER THIRTY ONE

Before Judge Richter instructed the jury, the opposing sides got into a intense argument about one of the possible verdicts. The prosecution submitted to the judge, and he accepted, an instruction to the jury that they could find the defendant guilty of just plain arson. This instruction was bitterly fought by the defense but to no avail. In their final form, the instructions provided for these choices:

. Guilty of murder in the first degree--Death.
. Guilty of murder in the first degree--Life Sentence
. Guilty of murder in the second degree--Life Sentence
. Guilty of manslaughter--Two to 21 years
. Guilty of arson--Two to 21 years
. Not guilty

The following are excerpts of what the jury heard from the judge:

"The indictment in this case charges the killing of four persons; and if you believe from the evidence beyond reasonable doubt that any one or more of the persons alleged to have been killed in the manner and form as charged in the indictment, you may convict the defendant, although you may believe the remaining persons charged to have been killed and met their death in some other way ...

"Under the indictment in this case, it is prerequisite that the state should show beyond a reasonable doubt that the persons alleged to have been killed shall be proven to have been killed beyond a reasonable doubt and by and through the commission of arson; or if you should entertain a reasonable doubt as to the manner in which they met their death, then you should acquit the defendant of murder ...

"It is alleged in the indictment that Belle Gunness, Myrtle Sorensen, Lucy Sorensen, and Philip Gunness met death by being burned in the dwelling of Belle Gunness. If you should believe that these parties met death in any other way than that alleged in the indictment, still you may find the defendant guilty of arson under this indictment, provided you believe beyond a reasonable doubt that the defendant burned the said dwelling and that said dwelling was of the value of more than $20 or upwards.

"The jury are instructed that if they believe from the evidence, beyond a reasonable doubt, that the defendant Lamphere set fire to the dwelling house owned by Belle Gunness, as charged in the indictment, then you can find the defendant guilty of arson, regardless of whether or not any human being was killed as a result of such burning."

Much of the other instructions concerned definitions of reasonable doubt and the rights of the defendant. On the subject of circumstantial evidence, the judge stated: "The jury are instructed that circumstantial evidence is to be regarded by the jury in all cases and is many times quite as conclusive in its convincing power as direct and positive evidence. When it is strong and satisfactory, the jury should consider it, neither enlarging nor belittling its force. It should have its just and fair weight with you; and if when it is taken as a whole, and fairly and candidly weighed, it convinces the guarded judgment, you should convict, and on such conviction, you are not to fancy situations or circumstances which do not appear in the evidence; but you are to make those just and reasonable inferences from circumstances proven which the guarded judgment of a reasonable man would ordinarily make under like circumstances. And if in connection with the other evidence before you, you then have no reasonable doubt as to the defendant's guilt, you should convict him, but it if you then entertain such doubt, you should acquit him."

It was after 5 p.m. when the jury left to begin its deliberations. Six hours later, it went to bed without agreement on a verdict. It was Thanksgiving Eve.

The jury had a mighty task. Interest in this case was tremendous, with one local newspaper calling it the most famous murder trial in the history of the world. "In every city, every town, and every hamlet, and even at the crossroads, in fact, places no matter how remote in which the telegraph, the mails, and the newspapers had access, the people were watching the trial," the newspaper claimed. "They had followed the case from its beginning. They had devoured everything printed by the newspapers, and they had formed theories of the various features of the case. They wanted to know the outcome as soon as the jury reported. The newspapers and the news associations were wild to get all the news that was to be had."

When the jury left the courtroom late on Wednesday afternoon, most of the pundits thought the members would disagree. And when the jury members went to bed without a verdict and knowing they would be confined even on Thanksgiving Day, rumors of dissension grew. The next morning at 11 a.m., the jury requested additional information on specific aspects of the case. They were informed, however, that all they could get was a rereading of the instructions, which they were given. Second-guessers were busy watching the faces of the members and trying to figure out their positions. Rumors were going around that 10 jurors were for conviction and two were for acquittal, and court watchers wondered who the two were. The instructions over, the jury once again retired to deliberate; and everybody thought it would be just a short time before a verdict was rendered. The afternoon contained only two notable events. First, the jury once again requested information on a particular topic, and once again it received a rereading of the instructions. Second, a false alarm went out into the streets of LaPorte that a verdict had been reached. In fact, all that happened was that Sheriff-elect Anstiss took some out-of-town friends into the court room and turned on the lights. Seeing the lights go on, people in the street assumed the jury was back and flocked into the courthouse, only to be turned away in disappointment. In fact, the entire afternoon came and went without a verdict. Then the jury went to supper.

It was only 15 minutes after returning from supper that the jury told the bailiff that it was ready to report. Judge Richter was called and the lights were turned on. By the time the judge and the attorneys appeared, spectators filled the seats, stood in the aisles, and lined the walls. Lamphere was summoned, and the jury filed into the room. When asked if they had reached a verdict, Henry Mill, the foreman, said they had but requested permission to read a statement to the court before rendering the verdict. The judge denied the request, saying he could hear such a statement only after the verdict was read. The atmosphere in the courtroom was described as "a painful silence" as the white verdict sheet passed from Mill to the judge, who entered the finding onto the docket. Judge Richter then looked up and read the words "guilty of arson."

As for the defendant's reaction, "the colors seemed to chase each other over the face of Lamphere," observed a local reporter. The observer noted that Lamphere's attorneys apparently took the news harder than the defendant. Weir, in fact, refused when asked to give the judge Lamphere's age, which was necessary to determine where he would be imprisoned. Prosecutor Smith, however, supplied the age of 38, which meant Lamphere was going to the prison in Michigan City. Judge Richter then sentenced Lamphere to from two to 21 years in prison, fined him $5,000, and disenfranchised him for five years. When the judge asked Lamphere if he had anything to say, Lamphere's only reply was, "I have none, now."

As the jury finally had the opportunity to submit the special statement that it had prepared, what it concluded, unrequested and on its own, was a short but startling opinion: "We, the undersigned jurors, and sworn in the case of the State of Indiana vs. Ray Lamphere, hereby say that it was our judgment in the consideration of this case that the adult body found in the ruins of the fire was that of Belle Gunness, and that the case was decided by us on an entirely different proposition." Each of the

12 jurors had placed his signature below this extraordinary document.

Throughout this proceeding, no vocal reaction came from the crowd. It had been warned that it could show no approval or disapproval of the verdict. Worden's reaction was harsh and he was angry as he then called the verdict "ridiculous" and supported by "no grounds and no evidence." Later, he announced his intentions of calling for a new trial the next Monday. If that was denied, Worden said he would take the case to the Supreme Court. As it turned out, there were several reasons against an appeal. One was the cost, $500 alone just for a transcript of the trial. Lamphere had no one willing to put up any more money for a process that would take two years, which was the minimum sentence already pronounced and at which time Lamphere's supporters could work toward a parole. Then again, if an appeal reversed the case, the prosecution could try the second case on the Helgelein murder, with the possibility that Lamphere could receive a harsher sentence in this instance.

After the verdict, Lamphere was taken back to the county jail until his removal the next day to the prison in Michigan City. That last night in the county jail, he had a conversation with a reporter from the LaPorte Herald, where a story about that talk appeared the next day: "He (Lamphere) did not appear very downcast over the sentence of the trial, for as he expressed it, it might have been much worse. 'I have no particular complaint to make. The evidence was pretty strong against me and so I am willing to take my medicine, but my conscience is clear and that helps some.' He had hoped for an acquittal. 'Why didn't you arouse the people when you saw the fire that morning, if you didn't set it?' he was asked. 'Well, I suppose if I had realized what was going to happen and had known what I know, I think I would have done so. I wasn't any closer to the fire than the city park pond. I got scared and did things which I shouldn't have done and that made it look bad.' 'Do you believe Mrs. Gunness is dead or alive?' was another question. 'Oh, she is dead, all right. That was her body and the children they found in the fire.' 'What did you really see the night you returned from Michigan City, the night Helgelein disappeared?' 'I didn't see anything.' Efforts to draw him out on that point failed. Likewise, it was impossible to get details regarding what he knew about Mrs. Gunness, his answers being evasive. He was told that it mattered but little now, since he had been convicted, but Attorney Worden had instructed him to make no admissions and so he was following these instructions as carefully as he could."

The next morning, Lamphere was cheerful and rested. His mother arrived from South Bend to see him before his trip to prison. "The scene between mother and son was pathetic," wrote a reporter, "the mother giving way to tears as she embraced her boy, but Lamphere, save for the glistening in his eyes, stood the ordeal well."

CHAPTER THIRTY TWO

If it hadn't been an election year, if the people involved had not been political opponents, if the newspapers of the time had been less partisan, what might the outcome of the case have been? One thing is certain. There would have been far less suspicion both then and now. As an example, there was the LaPorte Herald, a newspaper favoring the prosecution and Republican Party. Its counterpoint was the LaPorte Argus-Bulletin, which favored the defense and the Democratic Party. In the Herald, the day after the verdict, Friday, November 27, was an editorial that was very restrained in its tone, although editorials are the legitimate place for opinion. In contrast, the news columns, which are supposed to be impartial, carried such comments as the following:

"No greater bugaboo was ever sprung than the claim that Mrs. Gunness is alive. Upon no reasonable hypothesis could such a conclusion be reached that she escaped that night. This talk of automobiles was more bosh; and so far as Hutson and his daughters seeing Mrs. Gunness and recognizing her 'through a double veil', it was so ridiculous that the jury gave no consideration thereto."

This same article heaped praise upon Smith, Smutzer, Anstiss, and Marr, whom the writer seemed to think needed defending. They were lauded for the "able manner in which they handled the case" and "they should be commended and complimented by the people." The article complained, "The people who are censuring these officials are the people who put their faith in the yellow stories published and played up by some papers that Mrs. Gunness was alive."

Defense Atty. Worden, though, was given credit for his skill in saving Lamphere from the gallows. And Weir was called "one of the keenest lawyers in Indiana."

Prosecutor Smith considered the verdict a compromise. Ten of the jurors wanted wanted to convict Lamphere of murder but the other two, Charles Nelson and Henry Mills, stood unwavering against this. They couldn't justify a murder conviction when strychnine was in the stomachs of the burned bodies. To them, the fire could not have caused the deaths of people already poisoned. All, however, believed the defendant guilty of arson; and so the compromise was reached rather than settling for a deadlocked jury. Smith, too, congratulated Smutzer, Anstiss, and Marr in a letter he sent to the Herald. "It is largely through their efforts," he wrote, "that this mass of circumstances and evidence was obtained." He, too, seemed to feel the need for some sort of vindication: "I have no axes to grind and feel no personal gratification in the conviction of any person."

After saying goodbye to relatives, Lamphere began his trip to prison, during which he was said to have been quite talkative. To his escorts, including Sheriff Smutzer, his comments came just short of a confession. Smutzer, a biased source, reported the conversation to be such:

Lamphere: I didn't do any more than hundreds of other persons would have done had they been in my place. A preacher came to me and said that whatever I told him would be like telling a Catholic priest. From what came out, it seems he wasn't true to me. I don't feel kindly toward him now, and I feel that he did me dirt.

Question: What was the scene you witnessed the night you bored a hole through a partition in the Gunness house when you were working for Mrs. Gunness?

Lamphere: I ain't going to say anything about that ...If I hadn't been a drinking man, I never would have been at the Gunness place. The old woman drank considerable herself. It was whiskey and bad company. But it wasn't whiskey that got me directly into this case.

Question: Why did you say after your arrest that you burned the house and would confess before it came time for a trial?

Lamphere (denying he made such a statement): I'm going to prison with a clear conscience.

As the prison walls appeared in the foreground, Lamphere reportedly said, "I'm lucky to be here. I'm mighty lucky. Why, I might have been chopped up and put in a hole in old woman Gunness' chicken yard."

Soon after, at 3:50 p.m., Lamphere became Convict No. 4140. No one, of course, knew at the time; but he wouldn't turn out to be so lucky.

On the following Monday, Attys. Worden and Weir filed a motion that asked for a new trial. The motion was based on their belief that law prohibited the permission given to the jury to convict of arson only. The verdict, they maintained, was itself against the law. Judge Richter denied the motion, and 30 days was given in which to file an appeal.

The out-of-town newspapers that had covered the trial, and even those who had not, contained their pronouncements on the outcome. Much of it was critical:

Chicago News: If Mrs. Gunness had been on trial, perhaps the Lamphere jury would have fined her for not having secured a license to conduct a graveyard.

Lafayette (Ind.) Journal: The uncertainty that marks a jury trial was clearly shown in the case of Ray Lamphere, charged with the murder of Belle Gunness, the matrimonial agent, and her children. The jury found the defendant guilty of arson and sentenced him to prison for an indeterminate sentence of from two to 21 years. The result of the trial, is peculiar. Lamphere was charged with murdering Mrs. Gunness and her children. The burning of the house was supposed to be a part of the crime in order to hide the murder. The state alleged that Mrs. Gunness' body was found in the ruins. If Mrs. Gunness' body was found, it follows that she was either burned to death or else murdered and her body burned. If Lamphere burned the house, it would seem that he is guilty of her murder. The verdict allows many deductions. Evidently the average opinion of the jury doubts the death of Mrs. Gunness.

Florence (Ala.) Herald: The Northern press is condemning the South because of the apparent cheapness of human life here. The Northern papers are ever forgetful at the proper time. They should not forget that the North is the place (LaPorte, Ind.) where old Mrs. Belle Gunness ran a private morgue for revenue, the assassination of the three Presidents, Lincoln, Garfield, and McKinley was on Northern soil, the murder in cold blood of Stanford White, the more recent attempt to assassinate a prosecutor in San Francisco, Albert Patrick who plotted to murder and did murder for money William M. Rice, the riot at Springfield, Ill., this summer. Cases might be multiplied hundreds upon hundreds. The only difference between the South and the North is that once in a while a murderer is hung in the South and they rarely ever pay any penalty in the North.

Elkhart (Ind.) Review: The result of the Lamphere trial to establish the responsibility for the burning of the Gunness home and for the destruction of four lives was about what might be expected. In deed, nearly all the evidence was circumstantial, and as long as Lamphere keeps his own knowledge to himself, it is not likely that any further facts about the crime will be known. The criminal and the victims are all silent, the one for self-preservation, the other in the confines of the tomb. It is to be hoped, however, that the full 21 years will be measured out by the accused for the crime he is convicted of--the burning of a house in which lives were endangered if they had not been destroyed before the fire; and if they had, the punishment is none too severe. When a man commits a crime that puts human life in jeopardy, the penalty should include the jeopardy as well as the original crime.

Hammond (Ind.) Times: It is to be hoped for Indiana's sake, if not for LaPorte's, that the last has been heard of the Gunness case, unless Sheriff Smutzer decides to dig up that cement floor.

The legal system was not yet done with Belle. There was still the estate to be settled. The will that Belle signed on April 27, named Wesley Fogle her executor and was witnessed by M.E. Leliter and Neva Line. This is what it said:

"I, Bella Gunness, of LaPorte County, Ind., being of sound mind and memory, and realizing the uncertainty of this life, do make, publish, and delare this as and for my last will and testament.

"Item 1. I direct that my executor shall pay all of my just debts, expenses of the last sickness, and funeral expenses out of the first money coming into his hands.

"Item 2. I hereby give, devise, and bequeath, to my three children, Myrtle Adelphine Sorensen, Lucy Bergliat Sorensen, and Philip Alexander Gunness all my property, both real and personal, wherever situate, share and share alike; provided that, however, in case of the death of any or said children without issue before my death, the survivor or survivors shall inherit the whole of said property; and, provided, also that in case of the death of all three of said children without issue that the whole of my property shall go to the Norwegian Children's Home in Chicago, Ill.

"Item 3. It is my wish that I be buried in The Forest Home Cemetery at Oak Park, Ill."

The estate had accumulated an unusual number of claims. Some were the standard expenses one would expect to encounter, such as Fogle's claim for $400 as executor. Others were a tad unusual, such as the $18 paid for an auctioneer and the expenses for the men who dug up the bodies and guarded the remains at night. The caskets for the four cost $300; their transportation from LaPorte to Forest Home, $44.50; and the opening of the graves, $15. Andrew Helgelein's estate sued for the money Belle took from him and was awarded more than $3,000, including 6 percent interest. The Norwegian Lutheran Children's Home Society renounced any claim to the money, leaving the way clear for Belle's heirs to collect whatever was left of the money from the auction and $5,000 for the property paid by Edward A. Rumely. Eventually, $3,238.81 went to Peder Paulsen Moen, a brother in Selbu; Brynhild Larsen, the sister in Chicago; and Peder Paulsen Storseth, an illegitimate child of a deceased sister in Selbu.

CHAPTER THIRTY THREE

The verdict settled nothing. The drama was about to suffer more twists and turns as people tried to unravel confessions and rebuttals. Lamphere made at least two detailed confessions. The first was heard by only one man, but he was a man of the cloth and talked to the defendant even before an attorney was summoned. The second was an account of Lamphere's deathbed confession. Again, only one man heard the story, but several men heard sworn testimony of this hearsay account. There was no logical reason to doubt either man, and yet the facts of the confessions were completely opposite. The prosecution, which preferred the first confession, even questioned some of it. The defense, which leaned toward the second confession, doubted some of that. Many years later, the uncertainly got, if possible, worse. California authorities thought they had arrested a murderess who might be Belle. The poverty of the Depression prevented anyone from LaPorte from going there to prove or disprove this possibility; however, two former LaPorteans, now Californians, were called upon to visit the lady. She, however, died before they could get to her. Viewing the deceased, they pronounced her to be the missing monster. A photograph was taken and sent back to LaPorte, where Attorney Worden disputed their opinion. Each eagerly awaited development brought disappointment until all concerned just got weary of it all.

The first post-trial excitement came when Lamphere, who had been languishing away in jail with tuberculosis, died on Dec. 30, 1909. The wake was held Sunday, January 2, in the home of Lamphere's sister and brother-in-law, the H. L. Finleys. Officiating was the Rev. C. R. Parker of the First Baptist Church, who chose his theme from Genesis 18, which tells of Sodom and Gomorrah, and asks, "Shall not the judge of all the earth do right?" In its account of the funeral services, the LaPorte Argus-Bulletin philosophized: "The necessity is laid upon us often to make judgments, and even more often do we assume the role of judge and pass that final sentence not only upon the substance of human action but the motive which we assume prompts it. The futility of human judgments is apparent. The knowledge of the facts for a basis is insufficient and the spirit is often biased by blinding prejudice. It is a comfort that in the final outcome, we are to be judged by one who knows the facts and whose final verdicts will be right and will be based on abundant compassion. To such a One in hours of grief we go. Our deep, anxious, heartbroken cry is answered by Him who is slow to anger and plenteous in mercy. If one were born into the world with a physical deformity, the sympathy and assistance of all would be at once vouchsafed to relieve the handicap. May it not be that in the moral handicaps that have proved an unfortunate inheritance, there is a need of a broader sympathy and a more charitable judgment. 'That the judge of all will do right' we may have abundant assurance." Lamphere's mother, sister, and brother were at the service; and his elderly father was given a chance to view the remains before burial in Rossville Cemetery.

Lamphere was not even in the ground before pressure was applied to the Rev. E. A. Schell to reveal what Lamphere had confided in him right after his arrest. The pastor had always treated those conversations with the same confidentiality as a confessional. Now, with Lamphere dead, the clamor arose for disclosure. Schell, now president of Iowa Wesleyan University, consulted with three ministers, a bishop, and a judge before--once again--refusing to talk, except to give his reasons for refusing. He did not, for example, want to bring more grief to Lamphere's sisters, he said. When asked whether relatives of Belle's victims did not deserve to know the truth about her fate, Schell replied: "I did not know there was any doubt that it was Mrs. Gunness who perished in the fire which burned her residence at LaPorte. I thought that was settled when Lamphere said publicly after his conviction he was certain that the body found in the ruins was hers. It is a minister's duty to hear confession and to plead with the criminal to make restitution or to urge him to make his statements to the courts. If I should reveal this confidence, the ministry would be discredited and would lose some of their power to do good by hearing confessions. I expect to be criticized whether I decide to reveal this statement or not. The ministry and churchmen will criticize me if I reveal, and others of the public will criticism me if I do not. I would give $500 if I had not heard the story told me by Lamphere."

Commenting on Schell's refusal was this editorial from the Chicago Inter-Ocean: "Lamphere's confession might throw some light on one or two of Mrs. Gunness' crimes. But we may rest assured it would be of no help in explaining the abnormal character of this remarkable woman who seemed to have more in common with jungle beasts of prey than with humankind. Mrs. Gunness, we are told, had an amiable expression, a kindly glance, a pleasant smile. Her neighbors constantly used the word 'mother' to describe her. She was, indeed, a tender mother to her three small children. Nothing in her appearance, it is said, gave the faintest index to her murderous ferocity. She crooned her babies to sleep nightly. When needed a chicken for dinner, the hired man must wring its neck. She was too soft-hearted for the task".

The next week was filled with statements and counterstatements, still trying to find the truth of what happened on McClung Road. On Thursday, January 13, a St. Louis newspaper printed a story saying that Lamphere had talked to Prison Warden James Reid before he died. Reid, according to the article, relayed what he heard from Lamphere to the prisoner's brother-in-law, H. L. Finley. This was a detailed account not only of Lamphere's activities the night of Helegelein's death but also the night of the fire. While this might have been welcomed with open arms as a final closure of the mystery, it was denied by Reid the next day. He said he never received any such information from Lamphere. The story, as printed in the St. Louis Post-Dispatch, announced that Belle was dead, chloroformed along with her children by Lamphere, who also chloroformed Jennie Olson that night. In this account, Belle used chloroform to subdue three men in whose burial Lamphere assisted. The men were Helgelein, possibly Ole Budsberg and Tonnes Linne, the latter perhaps Belle's third husband. At first, Belle tried to tell Lamphere that Helgelein had suddenly left and gone to Norway; but Lamphere confronted her with his knowledge of hearing her arguing with Helgelein after she said he was long gone. This argument purportedly was overhead the night that Lamphere sneaked back to the farm after being told to stay overnight in Michigan City. Helgelein was begging Belle to send for a doctor until he collapsed, then Belle killed him with an axe.

According to this story, Lamphere and a woman entered the house that night and administered the chloroform in order to search for money. They illuminated their search with a candle, which evidently had ignited a spark that burned the house. The two thieves came away with less than $70 and a backward look was the first they knew that they had started a fire. In this story, neither the fire nor the deaths were planned. That was why, when arrested, his first question concerned the safety of the children.

The Post-Dispatch maintained that its information came from an impeccable source and asked Pastor Schell to verify its authenticity with his own knowledge gained from Lamphere's talks with him. Reid denied any part in this latest development, and the details themselves were totally foreign to anything so far advanced. Jennie Olson, for example, was never thought to be in the fire, which occurred about a year and a half after she was last seen. In the newspaper's version, Lamphere's answer to this was that she had been away but came back. Also this was the first time that anyone had heard of Tonnes Lińne, who was said to demand certain rights before agreeing to pay off Belle's mortgage. Hence, Lamphere's idea that they might have married. Sure enough, Tonnes' brother Samuel said he had heard nothing in two years from his brother, who had left Minnesota to marry the widow Gunness. Still, despite the tantalizing details, Reid denied any part in the transmittal of such information.

Evidently, all this was too much for Pastor Schell, who on Friday, January 14, broke his silence, saying that Lamphere admitted accidentally killing Belle and the three children but denied setting fire to the house. His accomplice was Elizabeth Smith, the black woman known as Nigger Liz, with whom he had spent the night before the fire. Schell said he had been asked by Prosecutor Smith to visit Lamphere in the hopes of getting a confession. "I found him agitated in the extreme, beads of perspiration were on his brow, his hands twitched, and his nervousness was plainly noticeable," the pastor explained. "I stated that I had come to see him, feeling that a conversation with someone might relieve his feelings and help him to calmness. He said that he supposed they would hang him, but that he was innocent of murder. He denied that he had set the house on fire and related to me how he had slept at the house of a negress until 3 a.m. that morning, then had started for the home of a relative in the country; and in passing by the Gunness home, had seen that it was burning, but being angry at Mrs. Gunness and no longer working for her, he hurried past. He then said he reached his relative's place in the country, some four miles farther, at about 4 o'clock."

"Early after dinner of the same day, I called again and told him I had learned he had not reached his relative until after 6 o'clock that morning. He said that on thinking it over he remembered that he went back to bed after waking up, and that the negress got his breakfast about 4 o'clock a.m. and that he did not start as early as he thought, as he remembered that the Lake Erie train went by just as he crossed the track north of the lake. He also said that instead of going directly by the house, as he had said in the morning, he had taken the road farthest east and on the other side of the lake, and only saw the house at a distance.

"I kindly accused him of falsehood and advised him, if he wanted my sympathy, prayers, and help, to remain silent or tell the exact truth. I promised not to tell the prosecuting attorney; and after some two hours of general conversation about Mrs. Gunness, he told me the story of the night as follows: 'I had been intimate with Mrs. Gunness from June, 1907, while as carpenter and man of all work, I was around the house. Three times at her request I purchased chloroform, and once I dug a hole in the hog lot for her and helped her put in the body of some one who she said had died suddenly about the house, and she thought the easiest way was to cover him up and say nothing about it.' Lamphere went on to say that he had no suspicions of Mrs. Gunness having murdered any one until one night when he returned suddenly from Michigan City and having bored some holes through a wall, saw her administer some chloroform to a man and hit him in the back of the head with a hatchet. Fearing her after that, he had quit working for her and returned to the house only occasionally to get his wages still due.

"I then told him that he had been known to stay at the house after that and that I did not believe his story and that it was contradictory in too many particulars. He then said he had taken money from Mrs. Gunness several times, making her 'dig up', or he would tell on her. Once she gave him $50. At another time, $15; and again, $5. He would then go to the saloons and when he was sober once more, he would find the money all gone. She had him arrested once for trespass and once for being insane, fearing he would tell on her. He bought the chloroform she used before she killed Helgelein, 'the Swede', as he called him, and slept in the Gunness house on the night previous to the burning of the house. At that time, she refused to give him more than $1, and he told her that he would get even with her.

Lamphere's confession to Schell stated that he and Elizabeth Smith were drinking the night before the fire and decided at about 11 p.m. to go to the Gunness farm to rob Belle. They had a key and they were quiet to keep from disturbing Maxson. With some chloroform he had stolen from Belle's supply, he drugged all four of them, Belle and the little boy in bed with her and the two girls in another bedroom. When Schell asked him to explain how all four bodies were found together, Lamphere confided only that he was very drunk and maybe his memory was faulty. The two intruders then searched the house for money but found only a small amount. His whole motive, he said, was getting enough money to have a "big time." As for the fire, he denied that he had set it, although he admitted that his companion, as drunk as he himself was, might have done it. After they left the house, they looked back and saw the flames, at which time they split up and Lamphere ran away.

Schell said he asked Lamphere to tell his story to the prosecuting attorney, to spare the county the cost of the trial and his sisters the cost of defending him. "The next day, Saturday, I called again, taking with me two sheets of paper on which I had written the statement which he had made the previous afternoon," Schell said. "I told him how he had been seen alone in the field and cautioned him that the negress ought not be be brought into it if she had not been with him and told him that Attorney Smith had scouted the idea that the negress had gone with him, and she had accounted for herself the whole night through. I also said that no one would believe that he had not set the house on fire and with some slight variation, he repeated the story as I had written it down, agreeing to sign it."

Schell explained that, after leaving Lamphere, he told Prosecutor Smith that Lamphere was going to confess; but the pastor refused to acknowledge that the prisoner had already confessed to him. Schell, however, did advise Smith to arrest the black woman; but the prosecutor took no interest in that advice. The next day, Schell left LaPorte for Baltimore to attend a Methodist church conference that lasted throughout the time of the discovery of the barnyard murders.

"It was several times suggested that I visit Lamphere after my return, but I refused to go," the pastor said. "I still feel that the communication was privileged, that I owed it to his sisters to refuse to make it public until now ... and that failure on my part to keep the confession secret might deter others needing the encouragement of a Christian preacher from opening his heart to some man of God."

What happened to the statement he wrote and gave to Lamphere in jail, he did not know. Nor did he hear anything from Lamphere about Jennie Olsen. Interesting, though, that this confession has Lamphere and Mrs. Elizabeth Smith wandering drunkenly around the house without Maxson hearing anything. Absolutely astounding is the revelation that Schell knew Belle was a murderess, by way of Lamphere, even before the first body was unearthed in the farmyard.

CHAPTER THIRTY FOUR

Once again, opinions split into two camps. Attorney Worden said he knew what Lamphere had told Schell, and it wasn't what the pastor claimed. Worden said he confronted Lamphere with the rumor that he had confessed to Schell. Lamphere, according to Worden, laughed at this and repeated to Worden what he had told Schell: That he returned from the January trip to Michigan City and heard noisy voices, which alarmed him to the point that he left the farm and returned to LaPorte. Lamphere insisted that was all he told the pastor. This statement was made also in the presence of Attorney Weir.

Prosecutor Smith believed the confession to be authentic. Smith's belief was based on his conversation with Schell right after the pastor's talk with Lamphere. "I know it's authentic," Smith explained, " because there are remarks in the story which Schell made to me, quoted exactly. Schell told me to arrest a certain negress. He didn't tell me why, but now I know. Lamphere lied to Schell, in my opinion, when he told that this colored person went to the Gunness house with Lamphere and assisted him in the murder of the woman and her children. I think this person helped plan the thing, but she was too wise a girl to go to the house with Lamphere and assist in its execution."

Even Smith, then, did not believe Lamphere's entire story; but he did believe Schell. Worden, on the other hand, hung his hat on what Lamphere had told him. If Smith believed all but the negress part, that meant he accepted the part where Lamphere denied setting the fire, which was the only action he was convicted for and for which he had been imprisoned. Ex-sheriff Smutzer got into the debate by commenting, "I always thought another person was mixed in it that way."

On Monday, January 17, the LaPorte Argus-Bulletin interviewed three physicians, who remained anonymous but unanimous in their doubt that Lamphere chloroformed the four found in the cellar. In one doctor's opinion, the story was "the most ridiculous thing I ever saw in print." The doctor explained: "It's practically impossible that Lamphere and a negress could have chloroformed Mrs. Gunness and her three children without awaking them. And if Mrs. Gunness had been awakened, there would have been screaming. And Maxson could have heard it. It's always been a mooted question as to whether a sleeping person could be chloroformed without being aroused. Authorities have decided that such is possible but Ray Lamphere couldn't have done it, not knowing anything about the anesthetic or its usage. No matter how deep might have been their sleep, it's impossible that Ray Lamphere and the negress could have chloroformed Belle Gunness and her three children without awaking them."

Another physician put it this way: "It's very, very improbable." Chloroform, it was said, feels at first very suffocating to the inhaler. This provokes the person to struggle against it. One possible way to overcome this would be to use a very gradual drip method, but a drunken Lamphere does not seem a good bet for this arrangement. And Belle, big as she was and possessed of strong vocal cords, would never have been subdued silently or without leaving marks on her assailant.

Of course, once again a sort of politics figured in this. Schell gave his version of the confession to the Chicago Tribune and later wrote a letter regretting that he had not done so to the two local newspapers, the Argus-Bulletin and the Herald. He said he was getting ready to mail his statement to Smith when a Tribune reporter appeared at his door. Or maybe he thought the Tribune would have no axe to grind.

Meanwhile, Mrs. Elizabeth Smith, or Nigger Liz, was arrested, questioned, and jailed. Although she put up no resistance, she vehemently denied any part in the Gunness case. She bailed herself out on a $500 bond awaiting an appearance before the grand jury charged as a material witness. She was, however, unable to appear at the grand jury because she was sick with fever and chest pain. The mention of chloroform also gave Smutzer a reason to reintroduce the Truelson confession of a conspiracy between himself and Lamphere, which was obtained by the sheriff in Texas. Smith was not mentioned in that confession, but it was intriguing that Truelson had said Lamphere chloroformed the four found in the ruins. Truelson made his "confession" while in jail at Vernon, Texas, on May 29, 1908, in front of Smutzer and a federal judge. Truelson later said it was a lie told to extricate him from his problems in Texas.

Out on McClung Road, the Gunness property was sold to the Rumely Company, which owned some adjacent land and was going to test plows on the site. It was the only bidder for the property and paid $5,000.

When Belle Gunness was reported to be working as a housekeeper in Wilmar, Minnesota, LaPorte sent a representative to investigate. Shortly after his arrival, he telegraphed back, "Nothing doing--no resemblance." But this was only the first of such incidents that would continue into the 1930s.

In fact, pretty much everything about Belle ended in the 1930s, but not before a few people made a last effort to set the record straight. One such effort came from a newspaperman whose recollections about the case were published posthumously. Another came in a 25th anniversary newspaper article. Still another was presented in a speech by Attorney Worden to LaPorte High School history students.

In July of 1930 the Indianapolis News printed a long article on the Gunness case that revealed what Lamphere reportedly told his nurse as he lay dying in prison. This article had been written in 1924, shortly before the death of its author, longtime News staff reporter William Blodgett, who had covered the Gunness mystery almost two decades earlier. Blodgett said this deathbed confession was repeated January 6, 1910, by Harry Myers, the inmate-nurse, in a sworn statement in the presence of the late James Reid, then prison warden; the Rev. O.D.

Kiplinger, the prison chaplain; defense Attorneys Worden and Weir; and James Kennington, notary-stenographer. In its thirty-some typewritten pages, the statement says Lamphere helped Belle to escape by taking her to a rendezvous with another man who was named in Myers' statement but omitted by Blodgett and who was to accompany her to Chicago. He then returned and set fire to the farmhouse, where four already-dead bodies awaited their role in the mystery. Myers said Lamphere told him Belle had poisoned the four and cut off the woman's head so that no one could prove it wasn't Belle's body. This woman had been recruited by Belle as a housekeeper after being seen by Belle in a Chicago store on State Street. She had arrived at the farm on Saturday and was killed on Monday, according to the statement, which does not answer how she existed for that period of time without Maxson knowing of her existence. The head was given to Lamphere, who wrapped it in a piece of carpeting, put it in a box, and buried the whole thing in a rye field. Belle's reason for killing the children was that they were talking too much about the male visitors and Lamphere's night-time digging activities. He said Jennie Olson was killed because she knew Belle had murdered Gunness with a meat chopper. Lamphere admitted he helped bury a number of bodies, including the burial of one at an adjacent farm. Belle, he said, always did the killing and dismembering.

Even when he knew he only had a few hours to live, Lamphere insisted to Myers that he had transported Belle in a pony-drawn two-seated rig to a spot nine miles from LaPorte where another man was waiting to pick her up and drive her away, presumably to Chicago. Her luggage consisted of a small tin basket, where she carried her money, and two valises.

In his article, Blodgett explained his reasons for writing the details of this information almost two decades later: "The passing years have not effaced from the public mind the awful details of the series of murders that stamped the woman as the most monstrous person of modern times--murders that for diabolical fiendishness and systematic brutality have no parallel in the criminal annals of the United States. The woman killed from pure lust of gold, luring her victims to the farm, stupifying them with drugs and when in this stupor, she put them to death with a heavy axe or hammer, cutting off their heads to prevent identification and amputating their legs and arms that they might be more easily buried in the yard of her home."

Myers swore by affidavit that his information was just as Lamphere had related it. He said he was in prison at the time of the Gunness case and had no knowledge of its details other than those that came from Lamphere. The weight of this revelation, however, was somewhat lessened by the fact that Lamphere had told so many versions of his relations with Belle and their final parting. Authorities tended to think that some of what he told Myers was probably true but that some of it came more from Lamphere's imagination than memory.

A similar conclusion was contained in an article that appeared in the LaPorte Herald-Argus on April 28, 1933, the 25th anniversary of the fire. Written by Robert F. Coffeen, it began by introducting the facts to those readers unfamiliar with the case. It then went on to add something new:

"Today for the first time in 25 years the Herald-Argus has information pointed to a definite answer to the question. That answer is: Belle Gunness never died in the fire. Belle Gunness fled from the scene before a torch was applied to her house and the man who took her away was Ray Lamphere."

What was new, the article stated, was the certainty of the escape and the positive identification of the man who helped in that escape. The source of this information was Attorney Worden, who was said to be closer to Lamphere than any other person, except Lamphere's fellow prisoner who nursed him in his final days as he was dying of tuberculosis. "For the first time today," Coffeen wrote, "Mr. Worden made public information given by Lamphere in his last illness. Lamphere, dying day by day, was in prison to stay even if he had been a well man. He had obviously nothing to gain by not telling the truth. So when he realized that death was imminent, he made a statement to the man who served as his nurse. The statement was witnessed in the Michigan City prison by Attorney Worden, his law partner Attorney Ellsworth Weir of LaPorte, the warden of the prison and the man who served as nurse.

"Lamphere's confession stated that he took Mrs. Gunness by team and wagon away from her home before the fire. This was on the morning before the fire. He admitted that he returned early on the morning of April 28th and set the fire to the house. In his statement he refused to tell where he took Mrs. Gunness other than to a railroad station 12 to 14 miles away from LaPorte. Lamphere confessed that the body of the woman found in the fire was not that of Mrs. Gunness."

Lamphere's statement explained that the missing head of the woman in the ruins was placed in a box made by himself of some heavy planks from a manger at the farm. This box was then buried in the orchard at the farm. After Lamphere's death, a secret search for the box was fruitless; and it was thought that the nurse, who was not familiar with the property, was not much help in offering directions. The box, if there was one, was never found.

Worden told Coffeen that he questioned Elizabeth Smith, the black woman in the case, many times. The only answer she would ever give was, "When I know I'm going to die, Mr. Worden, I'll send for you and tell you what I know about this case." When that time came and she was seriously ill, she asked twice for Worden. At the time, however, he was in the Southwest, and she died before he could return.

The article continued: "Police records of all the world contain to this day descriptions of Mrs. Gunness. Assuming that Mrs. Gunness escaped from the fire, it is doubtful if she would be alive today. Twenty-five years ago, she was a woman well past 40 years of age. LaPorteans to whom the case is a clear memory include former Judge J.C. Richter, who presided at the trial; Mr. Worden, defense counsel of Lamphere; and R. N. Smith, now judge of the Appellate Court, who was LaPorte County prosecutor at that time. Dr. Charles S. Mack, the coroner, passed away a few years ago. A short time after the case, Sheriff Smutzer left the city, never to return here to live, and little is known of him today.

"Today there is nothing on the old Gunness farm to remind one of the terrible happenings which once took place there. Scoffing at ghosts of the past, John Nepsha, a farmer living on McClung Road, now owns the property and he is building a brick bungalow there. If one can forget its associations, the place is most pleasant. Mr. Nepsha's little house is on the crown of the knoll, just where the Gunness home years ago crowned it when the little knoll was "Murder Hill." A modern concrete highway curves by in front; a short distance to the east and north sparkles Fish Trap Lake. And all about the house are cedar and fir trees which whisper--and whisper."

Unknown to Coffeen, sometime around that 25th anniversary, Smutzer had taken up residence with one of his daughters in LaPorte. When approached by two Herald-Argus reporters in May of 1934, he talked freely about the case, saying flatly that it was Belle that died with the three children in the fire. Claiming that the belief that Belle escaped after placing a decoy in the house was the brain child of a newspaper reporter, Smutzer told this story:

"There were 45 correspondents in LaPorte at the time of the case, and not one of them believed that Mrs. Gunness escaped. Everyone in town also believed that she died. Then one night, Al Pegler of the Chicago American came to me and said, 'Sheriff, I know Mrs. Gunness is dead, but I'm going to send in a story saying she didn't die in the fire, just to give the case a new angle.' When I protested, he told me I was 'a good sheriff but a poor newspaperman.' The next day, the story was spread over the entire front page of the American, and it was then that talk of

Mrs. Gunness' escaping started. It had its origin in the mind of one newspaperman."

Smutzer, who had been elected sheriff in 1904 and re-elected in 1906, was proud of the fact that he had been the only Republican sheriff to serve two consecutive terms in 72 years. He denied that he had left town right after the Gunness case: "I continued to live right here in LaPorte until 1917. There were a lot of ridiculous rumors that have cropped up about my leaving, but that has been only newspaper talk." Smutzer said he did leave LaPorte in 1917; and before his return in 1933, he worked in construction in Chicago, Fort Worth, Tucson, and several other locales. Smutzer continued to live with his daughter until his death at age 74 in October, 1940, in LaPorte's Holy Family Hospital. Anstiss, who had replaced him as sheriff, had been dead since 1929, when a heart attacked killed him at age 60. In Anstiss' obituary, no mention was made of the Gunness case but his political activities were. He had been "for a quarter of a century prominent in county and city politics" and "one of the most colorful political figures in the county's history."

CHAPTER THIRTY FIVE

In 1934, Worden was elected to the bench in LaPorte County and he served as judge until his death from a heart attack in 1943. He was one of those people whose involvement with the Gunness case was so personal that he was never free of it. Even his obituary mentioned that he always believed that Belle used the fire to cover up her escape. Five years before his death and thirty years after the trial, Worden spoke about the Gunness case to the students in the history class at LaPorte High School. On that day, Dec. 7, 1938, he reviewed the facts of the case, once more expressing his belief that Belle felt suspicion closing in on her for a variety of reasons, including her fear that Lamphere talked too much. When her attempt to get him declared insane failed, she had him charged with trespassing; and Worden was Lamphere's defense attorney.

Worden said that before the trial, which was held southeast of LaPorte at Stillwell, Lamphere told him things about Belle that made him suspicious. For example, Lamphere believed Belle had killed Peter Gunness; and he was skeptical that Jennie Olson went to California. Worden then told the history students about his cross examination of Belle:

"I asked some questions of Mrs. Gunness I really had no right to ask. Among some of them, I asked if it wasn't a fact that a sausage grinder had hit her husband. I watched Mrs. Gunness very carefully during the trial so as to see if Ray's suspicions were true. I next asked her if it wasn't true that she had the grinder in her hand when it hit him. The court objected. I then asked her about the insurance which her husband had carried on his life. I also asked her about her adopted daughter, Jennie Olson. I said that I understood that she, Mrs. Gunness, had sent her to California ... 'Do you ever expect her to come back?' I asked. I wouldn't have wanted to be alone with her in the same room at that time. I believe that this trial was one of the reasons for the fire at the Gunness farm ..."

In his comments about the controversial bridgework, Worden pointed to the absence of Louis Schultz, the gold miner, at the trial, saying Schultz "was supposed to have found a small piece of bridgework consisting of two human teeth with some porcelain teeth and gold crown work in between." He described how two dentists testifying for the defense ran tests on a jaw bone that they wired with similar bridgework. "This was placed in a blacksmith's forge and burned until the jaw bone could be broken easily," he explained. "The human teeth crumbled between fingers while the porcelain teeth were checked and the gold crowns somewhat melted." He pointed out that in the bridgework produce by Schultz, there was no checking or melting.

Worden then turned his comments to the female body found in the ruins: "There were oval marks on the foreheads of each of the children found. Doctors state what when the human skull has been crushed in a certain spot, that spot will show up when burned. Their heads were there. Why shouldn't the head of the adult body be there? About a week prior to the fire, Mrs. Gunness went home with a woman. This woman was somewhat shorter than Mrs. Gunness and had black hair, whereas Mrs. Gunness' was sort of a dirty brown. Several people had seen her about for a few days and then she had disappeared. When these bodies were taken out of the fire, the body of this adult person weighed--without a head and a foot, which was also missing--only 75 pounds. I do not believe that a body of some 210 to 225 pounds would shrink that much.

Worden talked about the fatal quantities of poison found in the stomachs of Helgelein and the four charred bodies in the ruins. He also told of being called by the prison warden after Lamphere had died and of talking to Harry Myers, the prisoner who had nursed Lamphere in his final days. Myers said Lamphere told him he had taken Belle just before the fire to a railroad station about 12 or 14 miles from LaPorte. Worden also repeated the story about the box with a head buried in the farm orchard but never found. "I arranged for the parole of Harry Myers," Worden said, "and employed him and some other men to dig in the orchard for the box. Although considerable time was spent on the farm in digging for it, the box was never located. It was a difficult task to begin with and merely a matter of guess work.

"Whether Mrs. Gunness is dead, I do not know. We have heard numerous stories of her having been located in this town and that. When she was reported having been found in California, I communicated with the authorities out there. They felt convinced after extensive questioning of her that she was Mrs. Gunness. I decided to take Tom McDonald (the sheriff) and fly to California to see this woman. The papers, however, got hold of the news; and, since they had, I changed my mind and did not go. However, there were two LaPorteans residing out there who had been in LaPorte at the time the Gunness case occurred and knew Mrs. Gunness. I wrote them, asking them to see her and to send me word whether they thought it was she. The woman was suffering from a disease and had been removed to the hospital. When the two men arrived there, they found she had died. They did go, though, to look at her; and they claimed that it was Mrs. Gunness, beyond the shadow of a doubt. The authorities had sent me a picture of the suspect. Her hands were on either side of her face. Why the picture was taken that way, I do not know--but from that picture, I did not believe it was Mrs. Gunness. Perhaps the way the picture was made had changed her appearance. So, perhaps she is dead; and again, she may not be. We do not know."

CHAPTER THIRTY SIX

When the jury convicted Lamphere of arson, not murder, and went out of its way to convey that its members believed that it was Belle in the cellar, that could only mean that they believed Belle committed suicide. To them, Lamphere could not be guilty of murder even if he torched the house because Belle and the children were already dead. To them, Belle dosed herself and the children with arsenic and strychnine.

Despite the smallness of the charred adult body, the absence of a head, and the additional absence of anything in Belle's background that would indicate a propensity toward suicide, the jury had one hurdle that it could not jump if it were to consider Belle still among the living--Belle's teeth. How did Belle's teeth get into the ruins if she were still alive? Not just bridgework, which could have been planted, but a bridgework of porcelain teeth attached to the charred stub of a real tooth, one that came out either with or without its owners permission. At the time, it was said that this piece of evidence, found so belatedly three weeks after the fire, could not have been removed from a living person without splitting the crown. Since real teeth which support bridgework are routinely pulled today, the belief that such an action was considered impossible back then is perplexing. To accept that belief means only one of two things--either Belle was dead or the bridgework wasn't hers.

The only one who could identify the bridgework was the dentist who installed it, Dr. Ira P. Norton. Defense Attorney Weir when questioning this identification took pains not to accuse Norton of anything other than ignorance. Worden called him prejudiced. There is nothing either before or after the case to suggest any complicity on the dentist's part. He insisted he had given a diagram of the bridgework to the sheriff several days before the teeth were found, while the sheriff thought it important to claim that the diagram had been given to him right on the day the bridgework was found, which he also tried to move up a day or two. Norton was the son of a medical doctor and studied dentistry at Rush Medical College in Chicago. After a brief time practicing in Chicago, he came to LaPorte in 1903. And he stayed there the rest of his life, dying at age 72 in 1940. His testimony before Coroner Mack at the inquest on the adult female body in the fire, however, is strangely missing while all others are there.

If that avenue toward solution of the Gunness mystery is thwarted, then there is the second scenario--Belle was dead. This idea gained a certain following of people who began to theorize how Belle could be dead if it wasn't her body in the cellar. After all, the teeth were there. This thinking evolved into the idea that Belle plotted her escape, took her money, and found an accomplice in this flight who then murdered her. It makes a nice fit. This accomplice found himself in the company of a woman with a great deal of money who would soon be officially dead in a fire. No one yet had dug up any bodies in the yard. There is no reason to think there will be any complications in doing away with this woman and taking her money. In this theory the teeth are easily explained. When it seemed that people, including the coroner, were loathe to declare Belle dead, a return to Belle's corpse would supply the bridgework. Gruesome work, but not for a person accustomed to corpses from a previous job as an undertaker. Add to that the fact that such a person was almost totally in charge of the evidence-finding and had met with Belle on numerous occasions. Then, again, while most people connected with the case remained in LaPorte or thereabouts, this person took off on various business ventures that left some people wondering where he got the money. The sheriff fit all those possible circumstances, but there never was or will be a way any accusations can be proved. There were others who thought such accusations were nonsense and cried "politics". There is always, too, the possibility that Lamphere might have accused him merely for revenge.

Whenever the sheriff was taunted with any accusations, he would just smile and mention Lamphere's reputation for lying. Basically what is wrong with the Belle-was-murdered theory is that such a person could have had the bridgework in the ruins much sooner. No need to wait three weeks.

If it is accepted that the teeth could have been taken from a living person, then the necessity for producing the bridgework could have been hinged on an eagerness to get a declaration of death. Perhaps that was Belle's condition for monetary payment. When the uproar over the missing teeth arose, someone who knew where Belle was could have asked her to send them. This person may then have needed the diagram to ensure that Belle had complied. Once the teeth were found, the coroner made the required declaration. That would be one way someone could suddenly possess money without committing murder. When the bodies were found in the farmyard, perhaps the game plan was threatened. It was suddenly harder to prove her dead, yet Belle held off payment until this demand was met. Bridgework--either the real thing or a close replica--would have needed to be found. That there was hanky-panky with the bridgework was considered back then. The LaPorte Herald wrote about the remaining "skeptics" on May 20, 1908: "Their arguments are that the woman was too smooth to meet an accidental death or be caught napping, or that when she escaped, she pulled her teeth, both artificial and real, from her mouth and threw them in the fire. The limit, however, is reached by those who argue that Prosecutor Smith had two sets of bridges made identical with those owned by Mrs. Gunness and threw them in the ashes." The "two" referred to were both Belle's upper plate and lower partial, which were discovered together in the ruins.

One or more of the "sightings" of Belle may have been genuine. There certainly were enough of them in Chicago; however, Fort Worth, Texas crops up an unusual number of times. Truelson, although jailed in Vernon, Texas, had been staying in Fort Worth, before his confession. A conductor and station master were convinced Belle was the woman whose ticket of origin was New Albany, Indiana, by way of St. Louis, and who was then in Fort Worth. The sheriff made several trips to Texas and many years later admitted to spending some time in Fort Worth. California was another possibility. Two former LaPorteans swore she died in jail as Esther Carlson in California in 1931. This woman was in jail for murdering a man named August Lindstrom for his money. From a photo, Atty. Worden couldn't see the resemblance. The face, in general, is not similar. But take a magnifying glass and compare the individual features of this woman and those of Belle in the picture with her three children.The fingers are similarly thick and long, the same forehead crease is there. The eyes are alike; but the ears, oh, the ears can hardly be denied. Belle's earlobes are long and the ear openings are high. Esther Carlson had that same earlobe peculiarity. Truelson's tale has her wanting to go to 'Frisco. And an anonymous writer from Omaha, who said he visited Belle several times at her farm, claimed to have met her in Ogden, Utah, shortly after the fire, where she told him she was headed for California to visit Jennie Olson. Norway? Authorities there looked but could not find her. Many leads were scoffed at by the constabulary, who insisted Belle was dead. Very few were even given second thought.

One of the most perplexing puzzles is why Lamphere's confession was kept secret so long. If Harry Myers repeated it January 6, 1910, why wasn't it front page news? Especially when newspapers were then exploring the credence of the Rev. Schell's version of a confession. While people were trying to mesh Schell's revelations into the known facts of the case, the five people who heard what Myers had to say were mute. The defense perhaps would not have wanted it known that it had rescued a murderer from his just punishment. Attorney-client privilege may have played a role in the silence. The warden's job was no doubt a political one. Myers probably swapped his silence for parole. What about Schell? On May 12, while he was in Baltimore, he was refusing to make public what Lamphere told him; but when pressed, blurted out, "I do not think the woman is dead." An Associated Press wire service story at that time had Schell saying he believed Belle was alive; but that he had no special knowledge of that, just a personal opinion. Then after Lamphere's death, he says that Lamphere confessed to him right after the fire that he had killed Belle and the children. In addition, according to Schell, Lamphere's accomplice in this risky and demanding endeavor was a black woman, whose age was figured at about 70.

One fact was known. Lamphere had no money. So if he killed Belle and the children for money, where was it? If it existed, it was never found. Money would have had to be the motivation. Because she shared in them, he would not fear disclosure of their night-time burials. They were joined at the hip--to protect themselves they had to protect each other. So, if Belle was setting Lamphere up to take the fall for the arson and cellar murders, she had to hedge her bets that Lamphere wouldn't talk himself--and her--into a murder charge. She had to get him in a place where any accusation of her was a condemnation of himself. He didn't talk. He sat in court, not knowing if he would be sentenced to death and said not a word about Belle's nefarious activities, because hers were his. In one way of thinking, he might have held back thinking he had a chance to escape the charges of murdering the cellar corpses so would not admit to any other murderous proclivities. Once he was convicted only of arson, why admit to anything else?

Lamphere helped her get away, stood pat when faced with a death sentence, feigned surprise when bodies were dug up, and felt relief when convicted only of arson. Once again, she used him. She needed him for the first leg of her escape because the dogs would not bark at him. Somebody had to bring back the buggy so that no transportation mode would be missing the next morning from the farm. The second man, therefore, would know more about her destination than Lamphere did. Would that second man have let Lamphere see him? Maybe not. Lamphere was just sneaky enough, however, to hang around and find out. So would this second man do anything to call attention to Lamphere, who just might turn around and implicate his accuser? Lamphere admitted she promised him a $500 team of horses and probably threw herself in with the bargain. No doubt, he thought he would be sent for by Belle even when he got paroled. So he kept his mouth shut. For her part, she had a week to get away before her murderous ways were unearthed. When dying, Lamphere still insisted he escorted Belle to a rendezvous with another man.

Lamphere has been described as a rather simple man, and a drunk. Belle was not simple and not a drunk, and she got away with murder primarily because people could not really believe the truth. It was too depraved. Her murders of Sorensen and Gunness were clumsy. She almost got caught. The others she buried in her own yard. Her ego was exceeded only by her cunning. Her letters to Helgelein are masterpieces of manipulation. She reeled him in by appealing to a multitude of emotions from jealousy and greed to a common nationalistic dislike for "Swedes." What would those haughty "Swedes" think when they saw him to prosperously ensconced on her beautiful farm? Would they not quake with envy? Oh, she was clever. One can see her, dangling $500 in front of Lamphere to help in her escape, and adding a bonus--the promise of meeting together with all the money when the fire cooled off. This would be a further incentive to keep him quiet. This two-part trip would enable her to bind Lamphere further to her and yet prevent him from knowing where she went. Once jailed, he could hope for parole in perhaps only two years. Maybe they would join forces again, if he kept his mouth shut. Belle, of course, had no intentions of involving herself permanently with Lamphere again. She had told Asle Helgelein to come to LaPorte in May. She knew she'd be gone by then, and she faced the fact that the whole truth might come out. She was a planner, and an anticipator--explaining to a neighbor that a bad smell might come from the pond because a dead dog was buried there. Cautioning Helgelein not to tell people of his plans, all the better to surprise them when he turned up as master of a prosperous farm.

Decent people have tried to figure out Belle. It is difficult to understand the pathology. While the case was still front-page news, the Chicago Tribune made these comments editorially:

"Her attitude of mind is beyond the comprehension of the ordinary mortal. The latter may be aware of his own little moral weaknesses and lapses but knows he could not deliberately kill a fellow being and cannot understand one who does. Such creatures as Mrs. Gunness are fortunately so exceptional that they become infamously conspicuous in the world's history and are held in popular execration, yet they are not without a certain psychological interest as showing to what humanity--the highest type of life, as we fondly boast--can descend. No one says of Mrs. Gunness that she was insane--the excuse often put forward for those who have committed especially dreadful crimes. On the contrary, she was regarded by her neighbors as an especially level-headed and intelligent woman, and that she possessed certain agreeable qualities is shown by the ease with which she attracted her victims. Her criminal instincts were successfully hidden. She was seemingly possessed of a feeling of avarice so overweening that she could permit nothing to stand between her and coveted possessions.

"To get money she was as ready to kill a man as a cat and apparently regarded the act with as much indifference, barring the necessity of concealing it from prying neighbors who held different views. She was monstrously abnormal, but not by word or sign had she given the people with whom she had daily dealings for years reason to suspect her quality. It is not worth while for men and women to look askance at their neighbors because of her, for her like is seldom found, but her case emphasizes anew the truth that 'man knows little of the world and least of himself' and as little of the people round about him."

Monstrously abnormal as she was, she was not totally unique. There have been others like her. The most recent was a 41-year-old British woman named Rosemary West, who was sentenced to life in 1995 for killing 10 people, most of them dismembered and buried around her house in Gloucestershire. Among the victims were a daughter, a stepdaughter, the teenage lover of her husband, Frederick, and seven girls murdered for sexual thrill. Her husband, also accused, committed suicide before he could stand trial. Rosemary West has a youthful and innocent face.

Belle's material cravings were not unusual, only the lengths to which she would go to satisfy them. That such self-serving attitudes are prevalent on a less-bold scale is evident in most of the others concerned in the case, whether it was their jobs or their reputations at stake. They forever muddied the water.

LaPorte has not forgotten Belle Gunness, and it never will. The LaPorte Public Library has a permanent file on the case, and the LaPorte County Historical Museum has a Gunness special section. There visitors can see a piece of charcoal wood from the remains of the fire and a brick from the house's foundation. There are many photos of the participants in the drama, from victims to those involved in the resolution of the case. Sheriff Smutzer's granddaughter donated the watch chain worn by the sheriff at the time of the crimes and trial. It is in the shape of a lady's shoe. And there is a letter, in the original Norwegian, from Belle to Andrew Helgelein. The museum is a fascinating place, and Belle's portion of it lives up to this standard.

LaPorte's main street is called Lincolnway. By taking the juncture of Tipton Street north, visitors can reach McClung Road. It is over the railroad tracks, beyond the old Kingsley Furniture Company, past closely built homes, and on to a stop sign where McClung goes west of Tipton. There the homes become sparse, and Clear Lake glistens on the left. The old roller rink is passed and so is Fox Park. At last the infamous hill is seen. There's a house on its crest and neighbors on both sides. The fir trees are the only items that remain--at least to the human eye.

There are evergreen trees, too, lining the drive that leads into Patton Cemetery, far from McClung Road but sharing its Gunness memories. For it is here that the body thought to be Jennie Olson is buried and also the man who was secretly interred in the dark of night--Andrew Helgelein. Belle has an official burial spot, just where her will requested, in Forest Home Cemetery in Forest Park, just north of Roosevelt Road in Chicago's western suburbs. By going to the cemetery office and requesting the location of the grave of Belle Gunness, directions lead to Area 17, Lot 29. A visitor might be cautioned to look closely for the nearness of the Schmidt stone, which is near Lot 29. That is the only way to be sure of the right location because the graves in Belle's plot have no stones. Belle wanted a monument. About a year before the fire, she stopped by to inquire of B.A. Franklin, a LaPorte monument builder, about the purchase of a monument and the cost of shipping a body to Chicago. She never followed up on this. Eight people are buried there in a corner plot under an old maple tree. The vegetation covers the ground so that there is no evidence of graves there. Records show the woman buried as Belle lies between Mads Sorensen and Myrtle Sorensen. Lucy is on the other side of Mads. In another row lie Philip Gunness, Alex Sorensen, Caroline Sorensen, and Jennie Gunness. Even this is evidence of the mystery surrounding this case. Jennie Olson, who is buried at Patton Cemetery in LaPorte, was also known as Jennie Gunness. Who is the person in this grave? How did this extra "Gunness" person get into the Sorensen plot? It is believed that many more people were killed by Belle than are actually known. Who is this, though, who deserved burial in the family plot? When the Gunness case broke, this fourth body was discovered and temporarily added to the growing pile of unanswered questions. Years later, an examination of death records showed that there really was another, little-known Jennie Gunness, one of three daughters of Peter Gunness in his first marriage. When Peter married Belle, Jennie was only seven months old; and so he brought her with him into the marriage. She lived only one week and was buried at Forest Home where there was plenty of room in the Sorensen plot.

No one in that cemetery office knows Belle's story, so a thank you for the directions might bring the retort, "Sure would be nice, if someone put up a stone." Maybe. Only seven of the eight--a man and six children--can be identified. The woman who lies with them is not Belle. Is it to be believed that woman of Belle's extraordinary boldness committed suicide? Or that her survival instincts let her fall prey to a murderer? If so, then a woman who weighed more than 200 pounds shriveled to 70 in the fire. Belle's private hole in the ground is somewhere else--this author believes it is in California, where a woman who died as Esther Carlson had the fingers, the forehead, and the ears of one of this country's pioneer female serial killers..

##

Statement of Belle Gunness on the death of Peter Gunness

Q.: What is your name?
A.: Bella, my first name, Bella Gunness.
Q.: How long have you lived here, Mrs. Gunness?
A.: We moved in here the last part of November, then went to Minnesota for a visit and didn't come back to live before the first part of this month, but we had our things here the last part of November a year ago.
Q.: You lived here with the children at first alone, didn't you?
A.: All alone until the first of April, I guess it was the 29th of March he came down here.
Q.: Who?
A.: My husband.
Q.: Peter Gunness?
A.: Yes.
Q.: And you married then?
A.: Married him the first of April. He came down Saturday night and we were married Monday.
Q.: How long did you know Peter Gunness?
A.: Well, I knew him in Chicago in World's Fair year, kept a store in Chicago; and he made a visit to the old country and came back and stayed there for some time. He worked there.
Q.: Worked in your store?
A.: No, he worked down at the stockyards some place.
Q.: You knew him first then in the World's Fair year?
A.: Yes, sir.
Q.: Now, since you were married, you have always lived right here?
A.: We always lived right here on this place.
Q.: Was he a good man? Did you get along nice together?

A.: He was a very nice man. I wouldn't have married him if I had not thought he was nice because I didn't only want a nice man for me but a nice father for my children. I never heard him say a word out of the way so long as he was here.

Q.: Now when did he die?

A.: What time in the night, do you mean?

Q.: No. It was a Tuesday morning, wasn't it, early in the morning after midnight?

A.: I can't tell you exactly the time for I was so excited, and our clock was out of the way about three or four hours, so we didn't pay much attention to it.

Q.: What were you doing Monday afternoon, the 15th?

A.: Well, I was trying to finish up the butchering business.

Q.: And where was he working?

A.: He was working at home. He was in town and got things to make sausage in and helped me along the best he could.

Q.: What did you do Monday night?

A.: After I put the children to bed, he ground some meat for me. The first thing I did so far as I remember I made sausage, and he was in here writing; and I was doing some work, and I was out in the kitchen doing that work. And I washed up everything and finished up for the next day, and he was looking at the papers. Then we were sitting here looking at them. I think it was after 11 o'clock, if I am not mistaken. It must have been around that time. I can tell by the work we had done. We was sitting here and I said to him, "I guess it is pretty near time to go to bed;" he thought so too, and he picked up his pipe and went out into the kitchen. He always used to lock the door before we go upstairs to sleep, and I heard him make some kind of a little noise out there. And he always put his shoes back of the stove to warm, and I guess he must have been back to get hold of a pair of shoes because he had a pair of slippers on to go out with. And all at once I heard a terrible noise, and I dropped my paper and went. And when I came out there, he was raising up from the floor and putting both hands on his head. And I had a big bowl with some brine on the back of the stove, and I was going to put it on some headcheese I left there. And the bowl was full and hot, and I thought I couldn't use it until tomorrow morning and thought I might as well leave it there until morning.

Q.: Where was that, on the stove or on the shelf?

A.: On the back part of the stove. I had washed the meat grinder and wiped it off and put it on the shelf of the stove to dry, so that it would not get rusty. I generally put my iron things up there to dry, and at first I didn't notice anything but the water. "Oh, mama," he says, "I burned me so terrible." And I was so scared I didn't know what to do. All his clothes were wet. I said, "You had better take the clothes off." He said, "My head burns terribly." And so I heard baking soda and water was good to put on, so it would not get blistered. And I put that on. I bathed a towel in it and put it over his neck.

Q.: Was all this brine spilt?

A.: Yes, think the bowl was nearly empty.

Q.: How much water was there, a gallon?

A.: Well, it was a common crockery bowl to put milk in.

Q.: Was that brine boiling hot?

A.: Well, it had been boiling, but it had stood for some time back of the stove so it was not so warm. But it was warm enough to burn. I rubbed him with vaseline and liniment.

Q.: When you were rubbing that on, did you find that he cut his head back there?

A.: Yes, I did.

Q.: Was it bleeding?

A.: Not very much. The bleeding seemed all to be stopped.

Q.: Did he have the nose bleed then?

A.: No. I didn't notice anything with the nose at all. I saw the cut in the head, and I asked him two or three times where he had been.
Q.: Then what did he do?
A.: Well, we were sitting around here.
Q.: He came in here and sat down, did he?
A.: Well, I guess we sat in the kitchen awhile. We were rubbing, and he said he was afraid he was going to lose some of his hair on account of that burning. And he was complaining terribly, and I guess pretty near, I can't tell exactly what time, but it was quite awhile we sat there. We were sitting here and he was beginning to get a little better; and I said, "Don't you think you had better lay down. Maybe that burning will go away." And he said, "Probably I will." And I said, "You had better not go up stairs to bed but lay on the lounge and I will fix that up there for it is warmer." He thought so, and I went and fixed the lounge for him and took off his clothes and put on his night shirt and went to bed.
Q.: Did he take his shirt off?
A.: No. I don't think he did. He went in there and went to lay down on the lounge and I told him, "I think I go up and lay down with the girls. And if there is anything you want, call me down." So I went to sleep. I was tired. And all at once I hear him calling. He was over by the door and calling "Mama" so fast as he could. And so the children waked up, and I was trying to think and said they should keep quiet, that I had to go to Papa, that Papa was burned. I tried to put on my clothes because it was so cold. I went down the steps; and when I came down, he was walking around the room and saying, "Oh, mama, my head. I don't know what is the matter with my head." I asked what the matter was. "My head. My head," he says. "It is like something is going on in my head." "Papa," I said, "what are you talking about?" I said, "Let me see what it is. I

suppose you have rubbed off the skin." "Oh, my head, my head." "Well, if you think it is best, I had better send for the doctor," I said. And I went upstairs and got the girl up, and she went over to Nicholson's; and when I came down from upstairs, I found him on the floor and he was holding his head and said, "Oh, mama, I guess I am going to die." I asked what it was that was paining him so terrible and took some water and he said not to touch his head. When Nicholson came to the door, I was rubbing his head. And I opened the door, I think, and they come in and he then thought he was gone, but I did not think he was gone before the doctor came. I think he was only unconscious.

Q.: When you came down first, he was walking around here.

A.: He was walking around this room.

Q.: Then you went upstairs to waken the girl to go for the doctor?

A.: Yes.

Q.: How long were you up there?

A.: I don't know.

Q.: When you came back down, he was laying right there on the floor?

A.: Yes.

Q.: Flat down, was his head on the floor?

A.: I think he was on the back of his head because I tried to turn him.

Q.: When did he turn over on his face?

A.: He must have done that some time inside of that time.

Q.: When Nicholson came, was he laying with his face on the floor or the back of his head on the floor?

A.: Well, I don't know. I guess he was laying with his face on the floor when he came . I remember that the last I was trying to get him a drink, he was turned on his face.

Q.: Did you see his nose was hurt at any time?

A.: I never seen anything about the nose until you spoke about it. I can't tell.

Q.: When you saw him laying on his face with his face on the floor, did you try to turn him over?
A.: Yes, I tried to raise him up so that I could see what it was.
Q.: But he was on his face and the back of his head was up so that you could see it?
A.: Well, I thought that was after that. I can't tell how it was.
Q.: About how long do you think it was from the time that he was hurt out there before he died?
A.: Well, I guess, it must have been after 11 o'clock he was hurt, and I didn't know exactly what time he died. Nicholson said he thought he was gone when he come; and I didn't think he was gone until after you come here, and then he was only unconscious. I tried to feel his pulse but my hands didn't have any feeling in them any more.
Q.: He was hurt at 11 o'clock. Nicholson came up here about three?
A.: It may be. I can't tell the time at all exactly.
Q.: But you sat up with him for two hours after he was hurt?
A.: Yes, of course I wasn't upstairs long. I said goodnight and went upstairs and was there a short time when he called me.
Q.: But he seemed to be easy when you went up there, did he?
A.: Well, the pain seemed to ease over. He never laid down with his head. He always sat up and walked around until he went on the lounge. But he complained terribly of his head, and I thought such a pain that girl must have had and she didn't complain as much as he did at all.
Q.: Did you say that he was burned bad?
A.: He was red on the neck and the skin was blistered by the ear here.
Q.: Did you think it was a bad burn? Was his hair all wet?
A.: Yes, his back hair was.
Q.: Did any skin come off?
A.: I didn't notice that. I rubbed it and I remember it was blistered here and here.

Q.: How do you think he got that hurt on his head?
A.: I don't know, doctor. I picked up the meat grinder from the floor, and I think that must have tumbled on him one way or another. That's what I think, but I didn't see it.
Q.: Did he say anything about it?
A.: He didn't say anything about the hurt on the head.
Q.: When you found that cut, did you tell him his head was cut?
A.: I asked him where he had been with his head because it was sore in the back, but he didn't tell me.
Q.: Was that door locked out there?
A.: No, that door was open.
Q.: I mean the door outdoors?
A.: I don't know about it. He always locked the doors.
Q.: Did you think it was possible that somebody may have come in there while he was out there, and you not hear him.
A.: No. If anybody had come in, I think I must have heard them some way or another.
Q.: Had he ever had a quarrel with anybody around here?
A.: I never think he had a quarrel with anybody. He seemed to get along very nicely with all, so far as I know.
Q.: Did he have a hired man at any time?
A.: No, he hadn't got a hired man. There was a man here to help sometimes. Mr. Smith was here sometimes.
Q.: Who is he?
A.: He used to rent Martin's place.
Q.: What kind of a looking man is Smith, a tall man or short?
A.: He looks like another farmer. He had red hair and fair skin.
Q.: Is he a tall fellow?
A.: Kind of tall.
Q.: Has he a mustache?
A.: I guess he may have some kind. I didn't pay much attention to him.
Q.: What is his first name, this man Smith?

A.: I don't know his first name at all. I don't think I ever heard it, but he hasn't been here very lately.

Q.: He didn't faint away at any time, did he?

A.: No, he didn't faint away.

Q.: Have you suspected or have you been afraid that somebody might have come in there and killed him, hit him with that sausage grinder?

A.: I have never been afraid at all.

Q.: You had always lived happy together, you and him?

A.: As far as I know.

Q.: He was good to your children?

A.: Yes, good to me and he was good to the children.

Q.: He never had a man working for him that he had any dispute with about the wages he was to pay and the man went away mad, or anything like that?

A.: Not so far as I know

Q.: You say Smith owed him some money. How much was that?

A.: Well, that wouldn't amount to much. It couldn't be over three or four dollars.

Q.: Did he tell you how the brine come to tip over on him?

A.: He did not give me any satisfaction on that at all. I said, "How did you happen to do that?" "Well, I don't know," he said. "I must have got against it some way."

Q.: Did he seem to talk out of his head after he got hurt?

A.: Well, he didn't before I come down here. But after I come down, he seemed to be kind of funny. That was the second time. He asked me two or three times if I had sent for the doctor. I said I sent Jennie to Nicholson's because town is too far. And he was asking that over and over again, and I suppose he was getting kind of mixed up. He didn't say very much except that his head was paining him awful.

Q.: Afterward, did he get so he could not say anything?

A.: He got lower and lower so he didn't talk at all.

Q.: How did he break his nose?

A.: I can't say. I didn't notice the nose before they told me.
Q.: Didn't he complain of that? Didn't he bleed from the nose?
A.: He didn't bleed from the nose at all.
Q.: When you were siting out there and after he was scalded, if he had had his nose cut, you would have seen it, would you not?
A.: I guess I would have seen it, but I didn't.
Q.: Did you hear him fall out here in this room when you were upstairs?
A.: I don't know anything about that.

(s) Bella P.S. Gunness

Statement of Coroner on the death of Peter Gunness

This is to certify that on December 16, 1902, I held a postmortem examination on the body of Peter Gunness and beg to submit the following as my report of the same.

There was no evidence of scalds or burns on the entire body or marks of bruises, contusions, or lacerations, only as herein stated.

The nose was lacerated and broken showing evidence of severe blow or the result of falling upon a blunt article such as the edge of a board. There was a laceration through the scalp and external layer of skull about an inch long, situated just above and to left of the occipital protuberance. Upon removing the pericranium, there showed a fracture and depression of the inner plate of the skull at a point corresponding to the external laceration. There was also marked intercranial hemorrhage.

Death was due to shock and pressure caused by fracture and said hemorrhage.

(s) H.H. Martin

Letters from Belle Gunness to Andrew Helgelein

Sept. 2, 1906
Mr. Andrew K. Helgelein:

Dear friend: Many thousand thanks for both your letter and photograph card. I have read the letter many times and studied the picture so much also. I have now so much confidence and interest in our correspondence, especially when I know you are such an understanding and good Norwegian man. I long so to know you better, but I will try to wait with patience until you get ready up there. I think it will be best that you get everything ready before you come, so you will not have to go back, as it is so far and it probably will be so late in the fall. When you once get here, I know I will not like to be alone again; but if you should go to Dakota or any other place you wished to go, we would do the best we could; but how pleasant it will be to sit and talk Norwegian about everything. Don't you think so too?

I would enjoy seeing all your beautiful horses, as I am much interested in horses and other creatures. Could you not bring with you a pretty young driving horse? It would give us so much pleasure. I have only three horses, which is enough for us, but one could always use two more.

In regard to your creatures, you could take them with you to Chicago if you cannot sell them up there, and the same with the horses. If you will hire a car, you can take all of them that you want with you. I am quite sure you can get very good prices for your things in Chicago; and if we wished, we could take some over here too. If you thought it would be too lonesome to stay there alone until you sold out and have no other company, I could come to you and stay with you until you were through. I am well known around there, because we lived there for awhile. Both of us could then look around a little.

When you are all through and come here, then we must have some good cooking; but take everything with you and say goodbye to Dakota, so you can be here with us.

Then you will see how happy we will be, but do not tell a word to anybody up there before you go, but only tell them after you have been here awhile.

You must pardon me for not writing before, but we have been so busy picking apples and pears to send to market. We are well paid for such, as we are so near Chicago.

Yes, I will try and get all the fall work done, just so that when you get ready up there you will not have to return again, as it will be altogether too lonesome. I have now thrown away all the other answers I got and keep all of yours in a secret place by themselves. I will show them all to you when you come here, as I prize them so highly; but I prize the writer more highly; and when I get to know you, I will set the writer above all others, as such a man I have not found among the Norwegians in America.

There is altogether too much cunning and humbug in this land. Honesty, sincerity, and righteousness last the longest. Where they are found on both sides, then everything will be all right.

I have told you of everything as it really is, and this you will find when you come. You can be sure that you are heartily welcome. Well, now I must close for this time and go and milk. Hope soon to hear from you. From your friend. Bella Gunness.

October 27, 1906
Mr. Andrew K. Helgelein:

While I was in town today to mail your letter, I received one from you--many thanks for same. Every time I receive your letters I wish there were more of them. I am sure your pain or worry comes from an honest and sincere feeling and I am sure there is no one else who could feel that way. I never believed there was a person like you in whom a woman could put her trust.

I have passed through much in this life, but I have at any rate taken good care of my womanliness, which has been given to woman by God and therefore it is the best we own. I think that a man with such a heart as yours could be trusted with all.

How light and happy my life would be when I can put everything in such a good and faithful man's hands. But, my dear, you have been sick and all alone. You do not know how badly it makes me feel not to be with you. Make yourself a good hot punch and put on some good warm underclothes and keep good and warm all the time.

Health is the best thing we can have, my dear friend. Now, my dear, you must surely advise me just when you leave and telegraph, if you can, when you come to Minneapolis or St. Paul, and then I may have the permission to be the first one to welcome you to LaPorte, and I will be at the depot with my gray pony. I am a rather stout woman and will have a nice buggy ...

I am a genuine Norwegian, with brown Norwegian hair and blue eyes. You must remember that you will get a meeting that comes from the heart.

Even if the world has been a little hard with me, I have just the same kept my good nature, and I can still take pleasure in my life.

If you come with a servant and a horse, I will have help ready to meet them. Be sure and let me know about this in time, and I will do all I can.

Do not forget to advise me as soon as you can, so you can be sure that I get your letter in time, so I will know whether you come alone or with stock.

But come alone; do not take any one from up there with you here before we have become a little acquainted. It would be rather awkward at first when there are strangers about, just at first, anyway.

Do you not also think that it would be best that we are alone, especially at the beginning? But now I must close because I am getting so sleepy. I will now go to bed and think about you. God take care of us all until we meet. Live well, dear friend, and take good care of yourself until we see each other and hope it will not be long. Heartiest regards from your best friend. Bella Gunness

Nov. 6, 1906
Mr. Andrew K. Helgelein:

Dear friend: When I was to town yesterday to mail the little letter I wrote you, I had the great pleasure of receiving a long and very interesting letter from you, which was very welcome, and for which I send my heartfelt thanks. Yes, you are surely a man who has tried and seen much, that is certain, and I cannot say how lucky I have been to get the chance to know you. There are so many who desire my acquaintance, but I have always kept myself away from them and kept by myself, for I would rather be alone than have anything to do with such who are probably full of humbug and not to be trusted.

It is a mystery to me that I should be fortunate enough to find a real good friend in every way, one whom I can trust myself to.

If you only would soon be through up there and would leave Dakota and come here. I do not think you will leave me after you have first come here; that I am sure of.

My dear friend, do not be afraid to take with you the young horses you talked of, for my sake. It will give me such pleasure to see them, especially as you have raised them yourself, and you will also make money on them by selling those you do not care to keep, as there is hardly any body around here who raises horses. I would like to see your black cat, and you could bring it, too, if it was not too much trouble.

If you are coming with a carload of stock, you could put the cat in a box if you thought it would be too hard to leave it. I shall now tell you if you took with you a carload of your best stock, there would not be a particle of danger. I have an old German man who had done some fixing for me, and he is quite smart and faithful and honest, and he has his family nearby. We could get him to help and take care of them during the winter. He does not need to bother us, as he lives by himself. Everything is now all right, but do what you think is best, my good friend. I think you should do this way as it would be quite interesting to see them, the animals, and I would not in the least mind them or the work they entail--only do not leave anything up there up there, so you will have nothing to worry about when you come.

When one moves away, it is safest and securest to have everything with one, and it will save a lot of worry and you will not have to think about attending to things so far away. Remember the advice I gave you in regard to your money. Do not tell anything even to your nearest. They could soon tell it to some one else, and it seems as if one cannot fully trust any one nowadays, especially when one is going away. Let it be, as I said, a little secret between us two and no one else, not so? We will hold our little private affairs to ourselves.

I am sure that you are a good and faithful friend who never fails. Dear, good friend, I will never cease writing to you, you can be sure of that. I set you higher in my estimation than even the king and I hope soon to hear that you are coming, so I can meet you. Many thousand hearty regards and goodbye for this time. Your best friend. Bella Gunness. Now take good care of yourself.

Nov. 8, 1906
Mr. Andrew K. Helgelein:

Dear Friend:--I received your letter today from Sioux City, Ia., and heartfelt thanks for same. I have thought so much about you and how you got along with traveling with so much cattle and I was so happy when I got your letter and read that you were all right. My dear, it was very sensible of you to go right back and hurry and get through so you could come here. I hope now that it will not take so long.

You will be so heartily welcome and my greatest happiness will, of course, be to meet you at the depot and make your life as happy as possible--only get all through up there so you will have nothing to think about when you come here and stay forever.

You, my dear friend, need a good rest and we shall have good times when we once get settled. I get so happy when I think about this and that I once more can attend to my house properly again and do as I thought best and do a woman's work. Then I would not need to work in the fields and take care of horse, etc., and can see that my house and children get their proper care.

I have always prized an orderly and well-kept house, but when a woman is alone, it is hard to keep things in order--I think you understand this also, as you have been through so much. Hereafter, I think, times will be better for us both. Do you not think so, my dear, good and kindest friend? I hope soon to hear that you are ready to start. Write plenty of time beforehand, so I will be sure to get your letter. I will be so heartily glad when you come. Be very careful on the way and do what I told you in a letter, and you will find that it is good advice and well meant and given to you be a true friend in every respect.

What we two have between us no one else need know. Now, my dear best friend, I must close for this time again. Live well until we meet. Send me at once a few words and you will be so kind. Heartiest regards from your devoted friend. Bella Gunness

Nov. 12, 1906
Mr. Andrew K. Helgelein:

Dear Friend--Today I received a long and interesting letter from you. Hearty thanks for same. I have never received such dear, true letters.

It feels good to be honest, sincere, and natural and then to find a friend who has exactly the same traits! If a woman is ever so honest, good and faithful, what good does it do when one is unfortunate and come in contact with falseness and deceit?

No, it would be much better to be dead. It is too bad that you have had the same experience as I have.

There are so many false people in this world, plenty of them who are low enough to lie and everything else, especially when they see one a little fortunate and can afford to have it a little better.

They cannot do enough harm to us. I have now worked alone for four years and have gotten along pretty well. It is pretty hard for a woman, that you know, but I would rather have done it than to have anything to do with false, mean, and drunken and such kind of people.

There are so many Swedes here, but I do not like them either. Nearly all of them have been so jealous because they see I can manage to get along by myself, and I suppose they will be much worse when you come. Of course, some have been good to me and helped me at times, but there are many who would rather see me not get along.

Now, dear friend, I hope that the worst is over for both of us. It seems that I have known you for a long time, but when I get along so well with such a good friend as you, then I forget the time, and I will now live for the future and you, my good friend, from the first day you come and as long as I can. I really think we will live together always, because a true friend who has exactly the same disposition and heart thoughts as I will surely get along. You can be sure of that. Then I will get my old good nature back again because I then will think that life is worth living and will do the best we can for us both.

We will have some good Norwegian coffee, waffles, and I will always make you a nice "cream pudding" and many other good things. My very best friend, it is just as you say, that if you are going to take a few horses, you might as well take a whole carload of stock. It is going as slowly for me as for you as the stall room is progressing so slowly.

I have already hired the old German man to begin to build the foundation, and that will soon be ready and then we can put up the rest when you come so you can have it to suit yourself, only do not wait until it gets so late so it will not be too cold.

Some winters we do not have any snow. The ground will be bare all winter. Then again, we might have a little snow for two or three months. Seldom is there any snow before Christmas.

I think oats are between 30 and 40 cents a bushel and corn between 40 and 50 cents. I did not raise any oats this year because I did not begin to plant until too late, but I have quite a good bit of corn, and I have a great deal standing in the stocks, which I think will do to feed the horses. I think I will leave I as it stands until you come.

Hurry now and come before the winter sets in and take with you all you have that is good and useful which you can get in a carload and do not stop longer than is necessary. Do not leave anything up there because you cannot leave me afterward and go and get it.

This you will find is true, my dear friend. Rather sell your things a little cheaper for cash, for then you know what you have and then you will not have anything outstanding, especially when you are coming here. I am sure you will find things here just as nice and useful.

Do not even let the banks have anything to do with your money, not even to send it for you, because you do not know what will happen nowadays. One bank closes right after the other, and the cashiers steal. Therefore, follow the advice I gave you in a former letter. You are the first one I have told this secret to but it is practical, and I know you will follow it.

I am very glad to get a friend in whom one can have confidence. It is not so pleasant to think alone. I talked with the man who owns the farm in which I have a $5,000 mortgage, and he begged me to renew the mortgage. It is soon due now.

He has been so prompt in paying the interest, and it is all that he owes, so he is very anxious that I should renew the mortgage. He said that I must not turn it over to the one of whom I borrowed the money, because he was so old now that he might die any time, and then they would not know with whom to deal.

I told him not to worry because I had a good friend who was just as safe as I was, and we would manage that all right. You will have a good investment if you will pay out the $3,000 which I have borrowed, and then you can have my $2,000, and then it will be all right. I will know then that everything is in good hands. I think that when I get everything in your hands, my good friend, that everything will be all right. I am not the least afraid because you are good and faithful, and you know I am the same.

However, do not let anyone know anything of what we write about. This we will keep to ourselves.

Only please hurry and come before it gets so cold, and let me know in your next letter just about when you think you will be ready. Live well until we meet. Hearty regards from your friend. Bella Gunness.

About the Author

The author is a former reporter and editor for The Chicago Tribune. Before leaving the Tribune, she was editor of the Educational Services Department, where she researched and wrote many tabloid-sized textbook supplements on a variety of subjects from crime to American history. Turning to free-lance writing, she continued to do supplements for the Tribune and was associate editor and a researcher and writer for booklets issued by Empak Publishing Company in Chicago. She has been a frequent speaker at seminars and workshops on the editorial aspects of newspaper use in schools. She graduated from Indiana University with a major in journalism and English and also worked as a reporter and feature writer for The Indianapolis Star. Her hometown is LaPorte, Indiana.

Printed in the United States
150945LV00001B/37/A

9 780759 606654